英国诗歌选译（下册）

郝翠屏 译著

燕山大学出版社
·秦皇岛·

内容简介

《英国诗歌选译》以汉英对照的形式出版，既可作为英语专业英国文学、英国诗歌课程的补充，也可成为英国诗歌爱好者读物，还可为诗歌翻译爱好者提供参考。读者在使用过程中各取所需，可以选读为重点，译文为参考；也可以翻译为重点。建议翻译研究者注意译文与原文的对比，还要注意本书译文与其他译文的比较。

《英国诗歌选译》分五章。第一章“文艺复兴及新古典主义诗歌”，主要选译这个时期英国著名诗人的作品，诗歌样式主要有斯宾塞体、伊丽莎白歌行、十四行诗、莎士比亚戏剧歌词、双韵体等。第二章“浪漫主义诗歌”，主要选译浪漫主义五大诗人，以及其他重要诗人作品，其中有些是经典诗歌重译。第三章“维多利亚诗歌”，除这个时期的重要诗人的作品外，重点选译了维多利亚时期著名小说家的诗歌。第四章“二十世纪诗歌”，选译既有现代派主要代表作家的诗作，又有转向传统、古典，并以各种方式反拨现代派创作的诗歌，还有世纪之交的新诗及新一代诗人的创作。除此之外，也重点选译了两次世界大战期间的诗歌。第五章“其他重要诗人作品”，主要包含了对英国诗歌产生重要影响的爱尔兰诗人和英美两栖诗人的作品。

《英国诗歌选译》每章所选篇目不等，每位入选诗人的篇目也不等，或者就某一作家选译多篇作品，或者就某一主题选译多位作家的作品，以方便读者体会作者基调、熟悉某类诗歌的样式、拓展对某一主题的体验。

前　言

《英国诗歌选译》主要基于笔者英国文学教学需要和个人爱好。从教学需要出发，重点翻译了伊丽莎白歌行、莎士比亚十四行诗、新古典主义诗歌、浪漫主义诗歌、维多利亚小说家的诗歌、两战诗歌、现代派诗歌等不同专题方向的诗作。依个人爱好，选译威廉·莎士比亚（William Shakespeare）、珀西·比西·雪莱（Percy Bysshe Shelley）、约翰·济慈（John Keats）、克里斯蒂娜·吉奥尔吉娜·罗塞蒂（Christina Georgina Rossetti）、威廉·巴特勒·叶芝（William Butler Yeats）、托马斯·哈代（Thomas Hardy）、狄兰·托马斯（Dylan Thomas）、菲利普·拉金（Philip Larkin）等诗人的作品相对多一些。在整理这些译作时，就编排体例犹豫了很长时间，最后决定按英国文学史线索分为文艺复兴及新古典主义诗歌、浪漫主义诗歌、维多利亚诗歌、二十世纪诗歌等四章，此外增加第五章，以便收译其他重要诗人的诗作，主要包括著名爱尔兰诗人和英美两栖诗人的作品。各章均按所选诗人的生卒年月编次并形成目录，目录中注明了每位作家的英文姓名及生卒年月。为方便初学者阅读，译文还对诗作中重点专有名词加了脚注。编排体例确定之后，又根据各章应覆盖的主要诗人进行了补译。除个别诗歌为节选翻译之外，绝大多数都是完整作品。这些作家及作品主要依据《不列颠百科全书》（网络版）、《新天地》、《新诗行》、《新诗》、《英国诗史》等专业介绍及诗歌选集选译，所有参考书目列于书后“参考文献”。有些作品未能查到一手资料来源，主要从诗歌协会等各大知名网站摘录，网址也列于“参考文献”。

第一章“文艺复兴及新古典主义诗歌”：文艺复兴时期主要选译托马斯·怀亚特爵士（Sir Thomas Wyatt）、埃德蒙·斯宾塞（Edmund Spenser）、沃尔特·罗里爵士（Sir Walter Raleigh）、菲利普·西德尼爵士（Sir Philip Sidney）、乔治·查普曼（George Chapman）、安东尼·蒙迪（Anthony Munday）、塞缪尔·丹尼尔（Samuel Daniel）、迈克尔·德雷顿（Michael Drayton）、约翰·邓恩（John Donne）、安德鲁·马韦尔（Andrew Marvell）、本·琼生（Ben Jonson）、罗伯特·赫里克（Robert Herrick）、约翰·弥尔顿（John Milton）等著名诗人，尤其选译了以托马斯·坎皮恩（Thomas Campion）、托马斯·纳什（Thomas Nashe）、罗伯特·索思韦尔（Robert Southwell）为代表的伊丽莎白歌行。

文艺复兴诗歌选译，重点在莎士比亚戏剧歌词、莎士比亚抒情诗及十四行诗。莎士比亚是中国读者接触英国文学的必读作家，作品用早期现代英语写成，普通读者借助工具书一般能读懂原文。一提莎士比亚，读者自然联想到他的戏剧。莎士比亚戏剧以诗体写成，其中不乏节律韵式工整的歌曲，往往提示作品的情节线索，烘托作品主题，是理解整个作品的关键。对于没有精力阅读完整剧作的读者来说，选读其中歌曲，可以对莎士比亚戏剧略知一二。莎士比亚也不乏抒情诗，更有一百五十四首之多的十四行诗。十四行诗是在文艺复兴时期，由托马斯·怀亚特爵士（Sir Thomas Wyatt）从意大利译介到英国的。亨利·霍华德（Henry Howard）对彼特拉克十四行诗的形式进行改造，经莎士比亚创作实践，形成莎士比亚体十四行诗的韵式。莎士比亚体十四行诗是了解体会英诗格律的门径。

新古典主义诗歌主要选译埃德蒙·沃勒（Edmund Waller）、塞缪尔·巴特勒（Samuel Butler）、约翰·德莱顿（John Dryden）、亚历山大·蒲伯（Alexander Pope）、约翰·威尔莫特（John Wilmot）、乔纳森·斯威夫特（Jonathan Swift）、塞缪尔·约翰逊（Samuel Johnson）等诗人的作品，也特别选译了安妮·金斯米尔·芬奇（温彻尔西伯爵夫人）（Anne Kingsmill Finch，Countess of Winchilsea）、玛丽·沃特利·蒙塔古夫人（Lady Mary Wortley Montagu）等两位

女诗人的作品。新古典主义诗歌一般韵律整齐，篇幅较长，翻译很有挑战。目前，国内已有吕千飞、王佐良等前辈对其作出非常出色的翻译。然而，凡笔者读之感慨较深的地方，或者译文处理稍有不同的地方，也尝试节选翻译，或对一些篇幅相对较短且有代表性的诗作进行完整翻译。

第二章“浪漫主义诗歌”：英国浪漫主义“五大诗人”，即威廉·华尔华兹（William Wordsworth）、塞缪尔·泰勒·柯勒律治（Samuel Taylor Coleridge）、拜伦勋爵（Lord Byron）、珀西·比西·雪莱（Percy Bysshe Shelley）、约翰·济慈（John Keats）等，无论在题旨理解还是形式掌控上，查良铮、屠岸等名家的翻译，已经到了炉火纯青的地步。然而，在个别地方偶有不同理解或不同处理的，译者也斗胆重译。本章选译的其他诗人主要包括乔治·格拉布（George Grabbe）、威廉·布莱克（William Blake）、罗伯特·彭斯（Robert Burns）等浪漫主义先驱，以小说著名的夏洛特·史密斯（Charlotte Smith）、沃尔特·斯格特爵士（Sir Walter Scott），以戏剧诗著称的托马斯·洛威尔·贝多斯（Thomas Lovell Beddoes），被称为农民诗人的约翰·克莱尔（John Clare），拒绝桂冠头衔的塞缪尔·罗杰斯（Samuel Rogers），散文诗歌成就等身的罗伯特·索西（Robert Southey），既浪漫又古典的沃尔特·萨维奇·兰多（Walter Savage Landor），轻松谐趣的托马斯·胡德（Thomas Hood）等。

本章浪漫主义诗歌选篇较少。一是浪漫主义诗歌在中国译介相对较多，有较好的译本；二是浪漫主义诗歌语言较为简单，意象及表达比较合乎中国读者的审美习惯，因此，很多读者不借助翻译也能欣赏。然而，也不乏有难度的作品，尤其是那些貌似都懂，却有关节处不好掌控的作品，笔者也进行了选译。

第三章“维多利亚诗歌”：主要选译维多利亚时期著名诗人，包括布朗宁夫妇（The Brownings）、亚瑟·休·克劳夫（Arthur Hugh Clough）、阿尔弗雷德·丁尼生（Alfred Tennyson）、科文特里·帕特莫尔（Coventry Patmore）、但丁·加百利·罗塞蒂（Dante Gabriel Rossetti）、克里斯蒂娜·吉奥尔吉娜·罗塞蒂（Christina Georgina Rossetti）、威廉·莫里斯（William Morris）、杰拉德·曼利·霍普金斯（Gerard Manley Hopkins）、阿尔加侬·查尔斯·斯温伯恩（Algernon Charles Swinburne）、法兰西斯·汤普生（Francis Thompson）、阿尔弗雷德·爱德华·豪斯曼（Alfred Edward Housman）、欧内斯特·道森（Ernest Dowson）等的作品。

英国文学史上，维多利亚时期小说成就突出，但很多小说家也有诗歌作品，成为观察其思想境界及其创作才华的窗口，没有时间读鸿篇巨制的读者，不妨从诗歌开始，了解这一时期小说家的创作思想与主题。本章选译涉及的小说家主要有威廉·梅克皮斯·萨克雷（William Makepeace Thackeray）、查尔斯·狄更斯（Charles Dickens）、夏洛特·勃朗特（Charlotte Brontë）、艾米丽·勃朗特（Emily Brontë）、查尔斯·金斯利（Charles Kingsley）、乔治·艾略特（George Eliot）、乔治·梅瑞狄斯（George Meredith）、罗伯特·路易斯·史蒂文森（Robert Louis Stevenson）、鲁德亚德·吉卜林（Rudyard Kipling）、亚瑟·西蒙斯（Arthure Symons）、赫伯特·乔治·威尔斯（Herbert George Wells）等。

第四章“二十世纪诗歌”：二十世纪及二十一世纪初的英国诗歌非常丰富，有支系纷呈的现代派诗歌，有对现代派形成反拨的诗歌，有新诗及新一代诗人，当然也有处于世纪之交，与埃兹拉·庞德（Ezra Pound）进行诗歌对话，并对后期诗人产生深刻影响的托马斯·哈代（Thomas Hardy），以及颇具早期浪漫风格的拉尔夫·霍奇森（Ralph Hodgson）等。除却纷杂的各种流派，二十世纪最不能忘怀的还有战争慨叹、乡土之吟。所以，本章选择的诗人最多，选译的篇目也最多。

现代派诗歌 现代派诗歌对初学者来说很难分析和理解。一方面，十九世纪末和二十世纪初发生巨大变革，新技术、新文化和新思想变革了诗歌的表现手法，尤其是交通技术的发展，使各地交流日益频繁，进而使诗歌流派的相互影响及促发成为可能；另一方面，不断增长的人口导致失序，大众市场意识使个人不知所措，尤其经过第一次世界大战的折磨，人们的世界观支离破碎，很多诗人自己不能确定本体方位，缺乏清晰连贯的自我意识，所以现代主义诗歌让读者感到困惑和迷惘。本章选译诗人包括早期发轫者到尝试诗歌各种可能性的现代派作家，如象征主义诗人亚瑟·西蒙斯（Arthur Symons）；意象派诗人托马斯·厄内斯特·休姆（Thomas Ernest Hulme）等。有的诗人，如杰拉德·曼利·霍普金斯（Gerard Manley Hopkins），虽然收录在维多利亚时代，但因其对诗歌声音效果的推崇，拓展了诗歌创作空间，实为现代主义的先行者。还有些著名的现代派诗人，考虑其出生背景，收录于第五章的其他重要诗人中，如威廉·巴特勒·叶芝（William Butler Yeats）；托马斯·斯特尔那斯·艾略特（Thomas Stearns Eliot）等。

反拨现代派的诗歌　二十世纪三十年代，英国诗歌史上出现四位诗人，即威斯坦·休·奥登（Wystan Hugh Auden）、斯蒂芬·斯彭德（Stephen Spender）、塞西尔·戴·刘易斯（Cecil Day Lewis）和路易斯·麦克尼斯（Louis MacNeice），他们虽然都崇拜艾略特，但背离了现代主义先行者在诗歌技艺方面的创新，在诗歌形式上更接近传统，可以称为回归古典的代表。迈克尔·罗伯茨（Michael Roberts）在名为《新天地》的诗歌选集中，将这四位诗人及其他相似创作风格的诗人推介给读者，所以有些评论也将这一派称为"《新天地》诗人"。后来，以狄兰·托马斯（Dylan Thomas）、乔治·巴克（George Barker）、威廉·悉尼·格雷厄姆（William Sydney Graham）、凯瑟琳·雷恩（Kathleen Raine），亨利·特里斯（Henry Treece）和詹姆斯·芬德利·亨德利（James Findley Hendry）为代表的"新浪漫主义"诗人，再次形成对"《新天地》诗人"的古典主义的反拨，转而以杰拉德·曼利·霍普金斯（Gerard Manley Hopkins）以及詹姆斯·乔伊斯（James Joyce）的文字游戏为榜样。二十世纪五十年代，罗伯特·康奎斯特（Robert Conquest）的诗歌选集《新诗行》出版，使"运动派"诗人菲利普·拉金（Philip Larkin）、伊丽莎白·詹宁斯（Elizabeth Jennings）、丹尼斯·约瑟夫·恩莱特（Dennis Joseph Enright）、金斯利·艾米斯（Kingsley Amis）、汤姆·冈恩（Thom Gunn）和唐纳德·戴维（Donald Davie）等面世，他们对现代主义及国际主义心存芥蒂，转向以哈代为典范的诗歌创作。作为"运动派"的追随者，"诗人小组"（the Groups）成员，如菲利普·霍布斯鲍姆（Philip Hobsbaum）、亨利·特里斯（Henry

Treece)、詹姆斯·芬德利·亨德利（James Findley Hendry）、马丁·贝尔（Martin Bell）、彼得·雷德格罗夫（Peter Redgrove）、大卫·韦维尔（David Wevill）等在剑桥、伦敦等地讨论诗歌创作，也形成对现代派创作的反拨。

两战诗歌 两战诗歌，以“一战”作品居多。“一战”中有奔赴战场的诗人，有战争中成长的诗人，也有殒命沙场的诗人。他们身处堑壕，生存环境的彻底改变，不仅激发他们对人生与社会的深刻思考，也促成诗歌表达方式上的变革。相对于“一战”来说，“二战”在作战方式和战争宣传上，都有很大不同，诗人对战争的反思也有不同的角度，丰富了读者对战争的想象、对社会的认识以及对人性的思考。局部战争不断的今天，读一些战争诗歌，了解战争对人性的考验，大有裨益。因此，本章也特别选译了理查德·阿尔丁顿（Richard Aldington）、罗伯特·劳伦斯·宾雍（Robert Laurence Binyon）、阿兰·刘易斯（Alun Lewis）、基思·道格拉斯（Keith Douglas）等二十多位诗人的战地诗歌。

乡土之吟 乡土诗歌主要指英国二十世纪四十年代，以诺曼·尼科尔森（Norman Nicholson）、维农·瓦特金斯（Vernon Watkins）、罗纳德·斯图亚特·托马斯（Ronald Stuart Thomas）和诺曼·亚历山大·麦凯格（Norman Alexander MacCaig) 为代表的诗歌创作，他们体现出诗歌创作趋向地方区域书写的特点，分别代表了对坎伯兰、威尔士、苏格兰等地域的书写，是读者了解地域文化及情感的渠道之一。

新诗及新一代诗人的诗歌 新诗主要选自阿尔·阿尔瓦雷斯（Al Alvarez）的《新诗》，该书 1962 年出版，辑录了 1950 年后成名的英国诗人作品，因此可以作为“二战”后英国诗歌读本，也是本章所选新诗的主要来源。“新一代诗人”指在 1994 年英国诗歌节上崭露头角的诗人，其中很多人在诗歌创作上受到广泛认可。鉴于现有教科书英国文学选篇多止于“二战”，且新近作品偏少的现状，本章选译了西蒙·阿米特吉（Simon Armitage）、格伦·麦氏威尔（Glyn Maxwell）、安德鲁·莫申（Andrew Motion）、温迪·柯普（Wendy Cope）等新一代诗人的作品。

第五章“其他重要诗人作品”：由于历史的原因，英国诗歌很难隔断与爱尔兰诗歌及美国诗歌的联系，本章主要选译爱尔兰作家托马斯·莫尔（Thomas Moore）、奥斯卡·王尔德（Oscar Wilde）、威廉·巴特勒·叶芝（William Butler Yeats）、詹姆斯·斯蒂芬斯（James Stephens）、谢默斯·希尼（Seamus Heaney）等的诗作，此外还选译后来转为英籍的英美两栖诗人托马斯·斯特尔那斯·艾略特（Thomas Stearns Eliot）的诗作。最后选择的是北爱尔兰诗人保罗·穆顿（Paul Muldoon），人称“二战”后出生的最杰出的英语诗人。

《英国诗歌选译》每章所选篇目不等，每位入选诗人的篇目也不等，或者就某一作家选译多篇作品，或者就某一主题选译多位作家的作品，以方便读者体会作者基调、熟悉某类诗歌的样式、拓展对某一主题的体验。当然，英国诗歌流派繁多，体量巨大，本书选译不及沧海一粟。如果说所选诗人大致有比较可靠的依据，针对每位诗人所选作品，则非常受限。其中有译者学术功底和阅读量限制，有材料可获得性限制，有教学需要对选材难度的限制，有前人已有杰出译本的限制，有个人偏好限制……所以，本书所选远不能囊括各章应有的覆盖面和专业深度，望读者多提宝贵意见！

目　录

第四章

二十世纪诗歌

托马斯·哈代（Thomas Hardy，1840—1928）

城中骤雨

她穿着褐色的裙子
与我停留，因这雨没缓，
车厢里安全幽隐，
马儿驻足，不动。
我们一直坐着，舒服且温暖。
车窗刚刚还映出俩人，
这会儿大开，她起来冲向家门；
我本该吻上她的唇，
这雨只要多下一分。

A Thunderstorm in Town

Thomas Hardy

She wore a “terra-cotta” dress,
And we stayed, because of the pelting storm,
Within the hansom’s dry recess,
Though the horse had stopped; yea, motionless
We sat on, snug and warm.
Then the downpour ceased, to my sharp sad pain,
And the glass that had screened our forms before
Flew up, and out she sprang to her door:
I should have kissed her if the rain
Had lasted a minute more.

生之前后

曾经——如你可猜，

当然，大地也可证见——
意识还没生出来，
一切安然。

无病痛、爱情、失落，
不知悔恨、绝望、心焦，
不担心飞来横祸弄得
筋断形销。

故去了，没有哀叹，
缺失了，也不动心弦，
光明淡去生黑暗，
不触感官。

然而知觉酿痼疾，
无上的正确染上谬误；
重归无知无识，
需多久？多久？

Before Life and Death

Thomas Hardy

A time there was—as one may guess
And as, indeed, earth's testimonies tell—
Before the birth of consciousness,
When all went well.

None suffered sickness, love, or loss,
None knew regret, starved hope, or heart-burnings;
None cared whatever crash or cross
Brought wrack to things.

If something ceased, no tongue bewailed,
If something winced and waned, no heart was wrung;
If brightness dimmed, and dark prevailed,
No sense was stung.

But the disease of feeling germed,
And primal rightness took the tinct of wrong;
Ere nescience shall be reaffirmed
How long, how long?

林中

苍榉青松，
同生黄土。
枝条交映，
时日共度？
雨来如洗，
津脉欲滴。
甘露沥沥？
互为荼毒！

市井欺压，
我心困扰。
当来树下，
如鸟还巢。
自然呈祥，
慰我创伤，
实我梦想，
远离尘嚣。

树木无异，
来此方知。
无论高低，
一样僵持。
榕欺橡小，
蔓缠弱苗，
藤索如绞，
是榆不支。

楞触山榆，
叮咬如刺。
冬青无畏，
荆旁战栗。
白杨无争，
祸起丛生，
污黑溃脓，
自弃生机。

来此方知，
树无可贵。
回心转意，
归我同类。
笑语欢声，
其乐可从，
生之赤诚，
勿与相违。

In a Wood

Thomas Hardy

Pale beech and pine so blue,

Set in one clay,
Bough to bough cannot you
Live out your day?
When the rains skim and skip,
Why mar sweet comradeship,
Blighting with poison-drip
Neighbourly spray?

Heart-halt and spirit-lame,
City-opprest,
Unto this wood I came
As to a nest;
Dreaming that sylvan peace
Offered the harrowed ease—
Nature a soft release
From men's unrest.

But, having entered in,
Great growths and small
Show them to men akin—
Combatants all!
Sycamore shoulders oak,
Bines the slim sapling yoke,
Ivy-spun halters choke
Elms stout and tall.

Touches from ash, O wych,
Sting you like scorn!
You, too, brave hollies, twitch
Sidelong from thorn.
Even the rank poplars bear

Lothly a rival's air,
Cankering in black despair
If overborne.

Since, then, no grace I find
Taught me of trees,
Turn I back to my kind,
Worthy as these.
There at least smiles abound,
There discourse trills around,
There, now and then, are found
Life-loyalties.

黄昏画眉

我倚在柴门边，
　　霜如惨白的幽灵。
逐渐虚弱的天眼
　　落魄于残冬。
缠绕的藤条划破天空，
　　像折断的琴弦。
出没的人们，找到家中
　　炉火的温暖。

大地身形突兀，
　　像世纪倾出的尸体，
云翳的穹庐是它坟墓，
　　风为它哀歌悲戚。
古老的萌生的冲动，
　　萎缩得又干又硬。
大地上每一个生灵，

　　好像我一样了无激情。

突然一个声音响起，
　　从头顶荒凉的枝条，
传来至诚的歌曲，
　　那欢乐无边的晚祷。
老画眉，虚弱、瘦小、憔悴，
　　在风中皱起细羽，
把它的灵魂，抛给
　　不断膨胀的阴郁。

世间种种俗物，
　　远远近近，
似无欢歌的理由，
　　却烙印如此欢欣。
我想晚祷的空气中，
　　震颤着某种希望，
那种福佑他能懂
　　而我却迷茫。

The Darkling Thrush

Thomas Hardy

I leant upon a coppice gate
　　When Frost was spectre-gray,
And Winter's dregs made desolate
　　The weakening eye of day.
The tangled bine-stems scored the sky
　　Like strings of broken lyres,
And all mankind that haunted nigh
　　Had sought their household fires.

The land's sharp features seemed to be
　　The Century's corpse outleant,
His crypt the cloudy canopy,
　　The wind his death-lament.
The ancient pulse of germ and birth
　　Was shrunken hard and dry,
And every spirit upon earth
　　Seemed fevourless as I.

At once a voice arose among
　　The bleak twigs overhead
In a full-hearted evensong
　　Of joy illimited;
An aged thrush, frail, gaunt, and small,
　　In blast-beruffled plume,
Had chosen thus to fling his soul
　　Upon the growing gloom.

So little cause for carolings
　　Of such ecstatic sound
Was written on terrestrial things
　　Afar or nigh around,
That I could think there trembled through
　　His happy good-night air
Some blessed Hope, whereof he knew
　　And I was unaware.

啊，你在我坟上挖土?

"啊，你在我坟上挖土，

爱人？——种忘忧草？”
“不，昨天他去迎亲，
娶了一位贵夫人。
‘伤不着她了，’他沉吟，
‘我娶个新相好。’”

“那谁在我坟上挖土，
是我的子女？”
——“不，他们坐下想‘什么用！
种些花草有什么用？
上坟也难以使亡灵
脱离它的冥府。’”

“却有人在我坟上挖土，
情敌？——狐疑窥探？”
——“不，她听说你进鬼门关，
血肉之躯早晚都难免，
便提不起对你的宿怨，
不管你躺哪边。”

“那谁在我坟上挖土，
说吧——我猜不对。”
——“啊，是我，亲爱的主人，
你的小狗住在附近，
但愿我在这儿逡巡，
没打扰您安息。”

“啊，你在我坟上挖土……
怎么我没想起
一颗真心在我身后！
什么情感啥人能够

比得上我这小狗儿
始终不离不弃！”

“主人，我在您坟上挖土，
埋根骨头，以防万一
这附近没吃食，
因我常从这儿来去。
对不起，我全忘记，
有主人在安息。”

Ah, Are You Digging on My Grave?

Thomas Hardy

“Ah, are you digging on my grave,
My loved one?—planting rue?”
— “No: yesterday he went to wed
One of the brightest wealth has bred.
‘It cannot hurt her now,’ he said,
‘That I should not be true.’”

“Then who is digging on my grave,
My nearest dearest kin?”
— “Ah, no: they sit and think, ‘What use!
What good will planting flowers produce?
No tendance of her mound can loose
Her spirit from Death’s gin.’”

“But someone digs upon my grave?
My enemy?—prodding sly?”
— “Nay: when she heard you had passed the Gate
That shuts on all flesh soon or late,

She thought you no more worth her hate,
And cares not where you lie."

"Then, who is digging on my grave?
Say—since I have not guessed!"
— "O it is I, my mistress dear,
Your little dog , who still lives near,
And much I hope my movements here
Have not disturbed your rest?"

"Ah yes! You dig upon my grave...
Why flashed it not to me
That one true heart was left behind!
What feeling do we ever find
To equal among human kind
A dog's fidelity!"

"Mistress, I dug upon your grave
To bury a bone, in case
I should be hungry near this spot
When passing on my daily trot.
I am sorry, but I quite forgot
It was your resting place."

针线盒

"瞧，针线盒，小娘子，
我刨的橡木！"
他是乡下木匠，
她是城里媳妇。

他将礼物递给她，
她笑着向前，
对奉礼的人回答：
“够我一辈子针线！”

“约翰的棺材板，
够你两辈子针线。
不知可怜的约翰，
怎么归了西天。

“针线盒用橡木一端，
主料做棺材装约翰；
这针线盒的边缘，
连着地下棺材板。

“我边干活边琢磨
这木头的命运；
一头看人吃喝，
另一头陪着死人。

“亲，为啥脸色难看，
把头扭向一旁？
怕你不认识约翰，
即便你们是同乡。”

“虽然乡里乡亲，
我怎知他啥样？
他很早就进城去，
那时我是小姑娘。”

“噢，我知道为什么，

你竟如此惊愕，
是我给的针线盒
连着坟里棺椁？”

“不，我虽无知，
纯属巧合的事，
即便巧合如此，
也无碍我心志。”

她却嘴唇麻木，
脸向一边扭着，
她应与约翰相熟，
知他为啥进坟墓。

The Workbox

Thomas Hardy

“See, here’s the workbox, little wife,
That I made of polished oak.”
He was a joiner, of village life;
She came of borough folk.

He holds the present up to her
As with a smile she nears
And answers to the profferer,
“Twill last all my sewing years!”

“I warrant it will. And longer too.
‘Tis a scantling that I got
Off poor John Wayward’s coffin, who
Died of they knew not what.

The shingled pattern that seems to cease
Against your box's rim
Continues right on in the piece
That's underground with him.

And while I worked it made me think
Of timber's varied doom;
One inch where people eat and drink,
The next inch in a tomb.

But why do you look so white, my dear,
And turn aside your face?
You knew not that good lad, I fear,
Though he came from your native place?"

"How could I know that good young man,
Though he came from my native town,
When he must have left there earlier than
I was a woman grown?"

"Ah, no. I should have understood!
It shocked you that I gave
To you one end of a piece of wood
Whose other is in a grave?"

"Don't, dear, despise my intellect,
Mere accidental things
Of that sort never have effect
On my imaginings."

Yet still her lips were limp and wan,
Her face still held aside,
As if she had known not only John,
But known of what he died.

罗伯特·劳伦斯·宾雍

（Robert Laurence Binyon，1869—1943）

悼阵亡者

以母亲之于子女的骄傲与感恩，
英格兰向阵亡海外的将士致哀，
生为母亲的骨肉母亲的灵魂，
他们为自由的事业奋不顾身。

鼓声肃穆：死得威严与忠诚
直把悲歌传入不朽的苍穹，
让哀乐在寂寞凄凉中回荡，
让我们的泪花闪耀荣光。

他们伴着歌声走向战场，他们
身强力壮、目光坚定、神采飞扬，
他们所向披靡前赴后继，
倒下直面敌人视死如归。

生者老去，他们却永远年轻：
不疲于岁月，不辱于时光，
每当日落，每当清晨，
我们就会想起他们。

他们不再与欢笑的战友们相聚；
他们不再坐在家里熟悉的餐桌旁；
他们不再参与我们的工作日常；
他们已然长眠，远隔英格兰海疆。

然而，我们的愿望深深，
犹如涌泉暗自流淌，
愿他们在自己的家乡，
一如群星在夜空闪亮；

一如群星在朗朗的天空列阵；
在我们化作尘土时依旧明亮，
在我们置身冥界后依旧耀眼，
直至永远，永远，永远。

For the Fallen

Robert Laurence Binyon

With proud thanksgiving, a mother for her children,
England mourns for her dead across the sea.
Flesh of her flesh they were, spirit of her spirit,
Fallen in the cause of the free.

Solemn the drums thrill: Death august and royal
Sings sorrow up into immortal spheres.
There is music in the midst of desolation
And a glory that shines upon our tears.

They went with songs to the battle, they were young,
Straight of limb, true of eye, steady and aglow.
They were staunch to the end against odds uncounted,

They fell with their faces to the foe.

They shall grow not old, as we that are left grow old:
Age shall not weary them, nor the years condemn.
At the going down of the sun and in the morning
We will remember them.

They mingle not with their laughing comrades again;
They sit no more at familiar tables of home;
They have no lot in our labour of the day-time;
They sleep beyond England's foam.

But where our desires are and our hopes profound,
Felt as a well-spring that is hidden from sight,
To the innermost heart of their own land they are known
As the stars are known to the Night;

As the stars that shall be bright when we are dust,
Moving in marches upon the heavenly plain,
As the stars that are starry in the time of our darkness,
To the end, to the end, they remain.

拉尔夫·霍奇森（Ralph Hodgson，1871—1962）

夏娃

夏娃提着竹篮，
穿行花盏草间，
花盏与草高得
没过膝盖。

在树下的花盏
草间，她正采摘，
采一盘甜蜜的
浆果树莓。

角落有一条蛇，
安静得像老鼠，
盘绕着高高的
樟树枝条……
正是拉下摆平
天堂骄傲之时，
这大好的机会
失不再来。

“娃儿！”每个音节
就像花瓣轻落，
“娃儿！”他向女子
低声私语。
声音柔美，好像
赤胸朱顶雀在
口吐玉珠歌唱，
轻唤“娃儿！”

好个园中精灵：
夏娃身体白皙，
柔软顺滑直到
纤纤指尖。
她好奇地听着，
听得那样好奇，
一枚浆果就要
触到唇齿。

啊，天真的夏娃
若能看穿假象！
要是她能知道
他的乔装！
他从枝间过来，
轻唤她的名字，
他二十个翻滚，
来到草间。

世界不管哪里，
都奇怪成双。
花盏草间，夏娃
跪下来，他
轻诉他的故事……
鸟儿啁啾，他们
沿幽径走向
亵渎的果树。

黄雀巧妇鸟儿
又躁动又嘈杂，
看见他得了手，
看他离开。
它们多瞧不起，
它们多么恨他！
它们多可怜
丧母的夏娃！

外边巷子里，
怎样的哭喊！
夏娃没有吃到

甜浆果和树莓，
徒劳地游荡在
果园门口……
今夜，就在山下，
怎样的欢情快感！
“娃儿！”推杯换盏，
“娃儿！”再来。

Eve

Ralph Hodgson

Eve, with her basket, was
Deep in the bells and grass,
Wading in bells and grass
Up to her knees,
Picking a dish of sweet
Berries and plum to eat,
Down in the bells and grass
Under the trees.

Mute as a mouse in a
Corner the cobra lay,
Curled round a bough of the
Cinnamon tall...
Now to get even and
Humble proud heaven and
Now was the moment or
Never at all.

“Eva!” Each syllable
Light as a flower fell,

"Eva!" he whispered the
Wondering maid,
Soft as a bubble sung
Out of a linnet's lung,
Soft and most silverly
"Eva!" he said.

Picture that orchard sprite,
Eve, with her body white,
Supple and smooth to her
Slim finger tips,
Wondering, listening,
Listening, wondering,
Eve with a berry
Half-way to her lips.

Oh had our simple Eve
Seen through the make-believe!
Had she but known the
Pretender he was!
Out of the boughs he came,
Whispering still her name.
Tumbling in twenty rings
Into the grass.

Here was the strangest pair
In the world anywhere,
Eve in the bells and grass
Kneeling, and he
Telling his story low...
Singing birds saw them go

Down the dark path to
The Blasphemous Tree.

Oh, what a clatter when
Titmouse and Jenny Wren
Saw him successful and
Taking his leave!
How the birds rated him,
How they all hated them!
How they all pitied
Poor motherless Eve!

Picture her crying
Outside in the lane,
Eve, with no dish of sweet
Berries and plums to eat,
Haunting the gate of the
Orchard in vain…
Picture the lewd delight
Under the hill tonight—
"Eva!" the toast goes round,
"Eva!" again.

福特·马多克斯·福特（Ford Madox Ford，1873—1939）

椋鸟

人怎么就奇怪地变了……
广阔的平原上，

我沿高处牧场走起，
正值雨季，
渐干的乡路白杨行道，
突然，
羽翼急扇
飞来前后呼哨的
椋鸟，
翅膀生风不断吹响如管弦缭绕，
婉转回旋像海水翻波
扑向路边的草坡。

长路上，一里又半里，
一群又一群，
穿过寂森森
铁白的日子，
它们呼哨回旋于路边，
白杨云影下，不近不远。

人怎么就奇怪地变了……
此时最让我惊叹的
是群鸟展翅
掠过平原消失，
却有一只停留，
它孑立枝条
仰喙高叫，
鼓着歌喉，
独唱，
孤栖。

稍息半晌，
它学汩汩泉水，

学清脆的铃铛，
学婉转的画眉，
又模仿鸦叫……
而我，
在椋鸟学唱的时刻，
在它鼓喉振翅之时，
若有所思，
我向前走过牧场，
这就是奇怪费解的地方。

穿行烟草谷物之间，
我走下星罗棋布的平原，
走过苹果林玉米地，
来到围墙的村口，
栅栏门旁，
山羊咔哒咔哒地踏着石板，
牧草散落成精美的图案，
年迈的牧羊人步履蹒跚，
它毛绒短袜，身着披风，
鼻梁上架着牛角眼睛，
三角帽盖着秃头，
他手持长棒，
捎来口信——
邀人，
无论平民将相，
无论君子畜生，
都参加婚礼宴请；
牧羊人的摇铃声起，
圣徒望出尖塔，
村姑穿着蕾丝婚纱，
王后一样从门口望去，

身边的妹妹，古怪精灵，
像椋鸟叫个不停。
古老的一隅，
如此奇特，
如此欢乐，
时钟与教堂的钟声响起，
婚礼仪仗走向我，
牛车，提琴，礼品，
而我
走向树林，
若有所思。

若是多年前，我会停下来，
看椋鸟五彩的脖颈，
惊叹于它的各种叫声，
我会跟那孩子说：“亲爱的，
给你银币，给我一个吻！”我会留下……
坐在伴娘的桌旁，
我会有机会
跳一支舞曲，
蕾丝婚纱的新娘，
温柔的金发伴娘，
丝带花环偎在我的臂膀……

教堂的钟声还在响起，
而我已远远地踏上平原，
迷蒙的天气里走在烟草谷物之间，
村庄，围墙，大门，
连同教堂化为地平线。
椋鸟在高空飞旋而过，
一里又一里的旋涡，

掠过远处的牧场。
琴弦拉起，
震颤中日子苍白，
我……我若有所思，
呀，人怎么就奇怪地变了。

The Starling

Ford Madox Ford

It's an odd thing how one changes…
Walking along the upper ranges
Of this land of plains,
In this month of rains,
On a drying road where the poplars march along,
Suddenly,
With a rush of wings flew down a company,
A multitude, throng upon throng,
Of starlings,
Successive orchestras of song,
Flung, like the babble of surf,
On to the roadside turf—

And so, for a mile, for a mile and a half—a long way,
Flight follows flight
Thro' the still grey light
Of the steel-grey day,
Whirling beside the road in clamorous crowds,
Never near, never far, in the shade of the poplars and clouds.

It's an odd thing how one changes…
And what strikes me now as most strange is:

After the starlings had flown
Over the plain and were gone,
There was one of them stayed on alone
In the trees; it chattered on high,
Lifting its bill to the sky,
Distending its throat,
Crooning harsh note after note,
In soliloquy,
Sitting alone.

And after a hush
It gurgled as gurgled a well,
Warbled as warbles a thrush,
Had a try at the sound of a bell
And mimicked a jay…
But I,
Whilst the starling mimicked on high
Pulsing its throat and its wings,
I went on my way
Thinking of things,
Onwards and over the range
And that's what is strange.

I went down 'twixt tobacco and grain,
Descending the chequer board plain
Where the apples and maize are;
Under the loopholed gate
In the village wall
Where the goats clatter over the cobbles
And the intricate, straw-littered ways are…
The ancient watchman hobbles

Cloaked, with his glasses of horn at the end of his nose,
Wearing velvet short hose
And a three-cornered hat on his pate,
And his pike-staff and all.
And he carries a proclamation,
An invitation,
To great and small,
Man and beast
To a wedding feast,
And he carries a bell and rings…
From the steeple looks down a saint,
From a doorway a queenly peasant
Looks out, in her bride-gown of lace
And her sister, a quaint little darling
Who twitters and chirps like a starling,
And this little old place,
It's so quaint,
It's so pleasant;
And the watch bell rings, and the church bell rings
And the wedding procession draws nigh,
Bullock carts, fiddlers and goods.
But I
Pass on my way to the woods
Thinking of things.

Years ago I'd have stayed by the starling,
Marking the iridescence of his throat,
Marvelling at the change of his note;
I'd have said to the peasant child: "Darling
Here's a groschen and give me a kiss" … I'd have stayed
To sit with the bridesmaids at table,

And have taken my chance
Of a dance
With the bride in her laces
Or the maids with the blonde, placid faces
And ribbons and crants in the stable…

But the church bell still rings
And I'm far away out on the plain,
In the grey weather amongst the tobacco and grain,
And village and gate and wall
Are a long grey line with the church over all
And miles and miles away in the sky
The starlings go wheeling round on high
Over the distant ranges.
The violin strings
Thrill away and the day grows more grey.
And I … I stand thinking of things.
Yes, it's strange how one changes.

屋里的猫

我眯眼对着壁炉深思，直等
最后一块炭火熄灭。
每个老鼠出没的洞穴，
我闻到，
感觉到
霉烂的屋檐悄悄移动，
听到
灌木丛中的每一只小鸟。
看清
你

栖于树上的夜莺！
我，生自异类，
困于沙漠、庙堂、权威，
灼热的沙子里莺歌难为！

The Cat of the House

Ford Madox Ford

Over the hearth with my 'minishing eyes I muse; until after
The last coal dies.
Every tunnel of the mouse,
Every channel of the cricket,
I have smelt,
I have felt
The secret shifting of the mouldered rafter,
And heard
Every bird in the thicket.
I see
You
Nightingale up in the tree!
I, born of a race of strange things,
Of deserts, great temples, great kings,
In the hot sands where the nightingale never sings!

爱德华·托马斯（Edward Thomas，1878—1917）

融雪

译一

点点斑斑雪已残

柔柔软软似花团
鸦巢枝上啼不住
树下不知冬已远

译二
鸦巢榆枝望雪原
斑斑点点雪已残
惊啼残雪宛如花
树下不知冬已远

Thaw

Edward Thomas

Over the land freckled with snow half-thawed
The speculating rooks at their nests cawed
And saw from elm-tops, delicate as flowers of grass,
What we below could not see, Winter pass.

夜行

夜行雪原，
母鹿蹒跚，
小鹿渐远，
疾风吹，
星斗慢转。

灯火悄然熄，
黑暗偷袭，
赛狼匹，
瞬间至，
万物迷失。

星风鹿与，
黑暗威逼，
恐怖相随；
鼓声起，
都令心悸。

光明微渺，
视界小，
欢爱逍遥
暗笼罩，
尚觉夜好？

Out in the Dark

Edward Thomas

Out in the dark over the snow
The fallow fawns invisible go
With the fallow doe;
And the wind blows
Fast as the stars are slow.

Stealthily the dark haunts around
And, when the lamp goes, without a sound
At a swifter bound
Than the swiftest hound,
Arrives, and all else is drowned;

And star and I and wind and deer,
Are in the dark together, —near,
Yet far, —and fear

Drums on my ear
In that sage company drear.

How weak and little is the light,
All the universe of sight,
Love and delight,
Before the might,
If you love it not, of night.

鹰

下山饥饿尚可忍
寒气袭来未透心
身心疲惫得休憩
檐下算是幸福人

馆内饱食火烘人
饥寒交迫忆犹新
黑夜幽幽关门外
鹰啼忧郁动人心

鹰啼声声久回荡
只有悲情无欢畅
今夜逃亡入馆中
他人却在荒山上

我食我息不知味
鹰啼警我其中苦
可怜将士卧星辰
人间欢娱隔黄土

The Owl

Edward Thomas

Downhill I came, hungry, and yet not starved,
Cold, yet had heat within me that was proof
Against the north wind; tired, yet so that rest
Had seemed the sweetest thing under a roof.

Then at the inn I had food, fire, and rest,
Knowing how hungry, cold, and tired was I.
All of the night was quite barred out except
An owl's cry, a most melancholy cry.

Shaken out long and clear upon the hill
No merry note, nor cause of merriment,
But one telling me plain what I escaped
And others could not, that night, as in I went.

And salted was my food, and my repose,
Salted and sobered too, by the bird's voice
Speaking for all who lay under the stars,
Soldiers and poor, unable to rejoice.
I have a rendezvous with Death.

七月

湖水无声一镜平
小舟倒影杂云影
寂寥困顿停舟楫
浮游水上云相随
隔空忽见一斑点

小舟惊起欲分辨
尘埃鸟影难断定
绕岸树林醒未醒

破晓多时天光散
日头爬高上三杆
此时再看湖水里
芦苇低垂接天际
影影生凉好将息
是是非非不足虑
卧听斑鸠叫深林
咕咕声里最安心

July

Edward Thomas

Naught moves but clouds, and in the glassy lake
Their doubles and the shadow of my boat.
The boat stirs only when I break
This drowse of heat and solitude afloat
To prove if what I see be bird or mote.
Or learn if yet the shore woods be awake.

Long hours since dawn grew, —spread, —and passed on high
And deep below, —I have watched the cool reeds hung
Over images more cool in imaged sky:
Nothing there was worth thinking of so long;
All that the ring-doves say, far leaves among,
Brims my mind with content thus still to lie.

威尔弗里德·威尔森·吉布森（Wilfried Wilson Gibson，1878—1962）

早餐

我们仰面躺着吃早餐，
因为炮弹在头顶呼啸。
我赌上腊肉换面包：
比利吉米两后卫互换，
舰队定会将码头端掉。
金哥抬头，骂咧咧，接招，
猛然倒下，他就死翘翘。
我们仰面躺着吃早餐，
因为炮弹在头顶呼啸。

Breakfast

Wilfred Wilson Gibson

We ate our breakfast lying on our backs
Because the shells were screeching overhead.
I bet a rasher to a loaf of bread
That Hull United would beat Halifax
When Jimmy Stainthorpe played full-back instead
Of Billy Bradford. Ginger raised his head
And cursed, and took the bet, and dropt back dead.
We ate our breakfast lying on our backs
Because the shells were stretching overhead.

米娜·洛伊（Mina Loy，1882—1966）

情歌（节选）

一

幻想的种子
淤在猪比特[①]
诱人的玫瑰色的嘴巴
长出色性的垃圾
“淤一次长一次”
从种在黏液上的野麦里
拔出来是根顶着白星儿的草。

我渴求蓝光灯下的一只眼，
高潮中的永恒，
海洋中的星团儿，
那河流得
不比哈喇子新鲜。

这些都是禁区。

我必须活在自己的灯里，
潜在的一星处女之光
修剪成嘈杂的
经验世界的

万花筒。

① 猪比特（Pig Cupid）：对丘比特的调侃。

Love Songs (Excerpt)

Mina Loy

I

Spawn of Fantasies
Silting the appraisable
Pig Cupid his rosy snout
Rooting erotic garbage
"Once upon a time"
Pulls a weed white star-topped
Among wild oats sown in mucous-membrane

I would an eye in a Bengal light
Eternity in a sky-rocket
Constellations in an ocean
Whose rivers run no fresher
Than a trickle of saliva

These are suspect places

I must live in my lantern
Trimming subliminal flicker
Virginal to the bellows
Of Experience

Coloured glass

托马斯·厄内斯特·休姆（Thomas Ernest Hulme，1883—1917）

秋夜一点凉

我在外徜徉，
看见红色的月亮靠在篱笆墙上，
像个红脸儿的农民。
我没说话，只是点点头，
周围是渴望的星星，
白皙得像镇子里儿童的脸庞。

A Touch of Cold in the Autumn Night —

Thomas Ernest Hulme

I walked abroad,
And saw the ruddy moon lean over a hedge
Like a red-faced farmer.
I did not stop to speak, but nodded,
And round about were the wistful stars
With white faces like town children.

堤防

（刺骨的寒夜里，落魄绅士的幻想。）

曾经，欺名盗世给我以狂喜，
铁骑在坚硬的人行道上踢出火花。
此时我理解，
诗的真谛在于温度。
上帝啊，把那吞噬星星的

古老天幕，弄小些，
让我裹在身上舒舒服服躺下。

The Embankment

Thomas Ernest Hulme

(The fantasia of a fallen gentleman on a cold, bitter night.)

Once, in finesse of fiddles found I ecstasy,
In the flash of gold heels on the hard pavement.
Now see I
That warmth's the very stuff of poesy.
Oh, God, make small
The old star-eaten blanket of the sky,
That I may fold it round me and in comfort lie.

大卫·赫伯特·劳伦斯（David Herbert Lawrence，1885—1930）

赤脚宝宝

小脚丫踩过草地，
像风中点头的白花，
一起一落像水上溅起涟漪；
草上嬉戏，
欢快得像小鸟的歌，
像两只白蝴蝶驻足花盏，
瞬间，又振翅飞去。

多想宝宝向我跑来，

像风影拂过水面，
我双手托着小脚丫，
让她立在我的膝上，
清爽得像丁香的花骨朵，
粉红柔韧一如初开的牡丹。

A Baby Running Barefoot

David Herbert Lawrence

When the bare feet of the baby beat across the grass
The little white feet nod like white flowers in the wind,
They poise and run like ripples lapping across the water;
And the sight of their white play among the grass
Is like a little robin's song, winsome,
Or as two white butterflies settle in the cup of one flower
For a moment, then away with a flutter of wings.

I long for the baby to wander hither to me
Like a wind-shadow wandering over the water,
So that she can stand on my knee
With her little bare feet in my hands,
Cool like syringa buds,
Firm and silken like pink young peony flowers.

人心

还有一个宇宙，驻于人心，
我们对此无知而却步。

一片奇怪的灰色地带，
隔开苍白的头脑与脉动的心底。

几乎没有登临彼岸的先驱，
善男信女，谁也不能洞悉
那内心的奥秘，
它幽深莫测，堪比刚果和亚马孙河，
流淌着完美、欲望与焦虑。

The Heart of Man

David Herbert Lawrence

There is the other universe, of the heart of man
That we know nothing of, that we dare not explore.

A strange grey distance separates
Our pale mind still from the pulsing continent
Of the heart of man.

Fore-runners have barely landed on the shore
And no man knows, no woman knows
The mystery of the interior
When darker still than Congo or Amazon
Flow the heart's rivers of fulness, desire and distress.

琴思

暮色中，一位女子对我轻唱；
将我带回金色的童年时光：
一个小孩儿坐在琴下，听着叮叮咚咚的和弦，
按着妈妈纤细有力的脚趾，望着她歌唱的笑脸。

魅惑的歌声令我童真复归，

我的心儿哭泣，皈依远去的礼拜日：
屋外严寒，屋里炉火温暖，
角落里琴声引领我，吟唱那首圣赞。

此刻女子徒然高唱，
黑色钢琴只是空响。
我投身记忆的洪流，凝神于过往，
为着孩童时代，我哭得泪人一样。

Piano

David Herbert Lawrence

Softly, in the dusk, a woman is singing to me;
Taking me back down the vista of years, till I see
A child sitting under the piano, in the boom of the tingling strings
And pressing the small, poised feet of a mother who smiles as she sings.

In spite of myself, the insidious mastery of song
Betrays me back, till the heart of me weeps to belong
To the old Sunday evenings at home, with winter outside
And hymns in the cosy parlour, the tinkling piano our guide.

So now it is vain for the singer to burst into clamour
With the great black piano appassionato. The glamour
Of childish days is upon me, my manhood is cast
Down in the flood of remembrance, I weep like a child for the past.

倾听

我倾听你的静默，
亲爱的，在寂寂无言中；

一开口，就觉着你的沉默触到我的话语，
将它们俘获。

锤炼过的语言，
飞逝的火星儿；
夜空轻易将它
吞没于黑暗。

云雀欢快地高歌，
然而，我愿
沉默将歌声和鸟儿捉走，
双双失落。

火车呼啸向南，
车头旗子飘扬；
寂寞的影子静悄悄
一路相伴。

溅出熔炉的世界，
旋转于人生的气流中，
芸芸众生的火星儿，
熙熙攘攘填着黑夜。

然而，他们从未改变黑暗，
喧嚣也无法将它驱散；
攻不可破的寂寥之上，
唯有作浮标的星辰。

Listening

David Herbert Lawrence

I listen to the stillness of you,
My dear, among it all;
I feel your silence touch my words as I talk,
And take them in thrall.

My words fly off a forge
The length of a spark;
I see the night-sky easily sip them
Up in the dark.

The lark sings loud and glad,
Yet I am not loth
That silence should take the song and the bird
And lose them both.

A train goes roaring south,
The steam-flag flying;
I see the stealthy shadow of silence
Alongside going.

And off the forge of the world,
Whirling in the draught of life,
Go sparks of myriad people, filling
The night with strife.

Yet they never change the darkness
Or blench it with noise;
Alone on the perfect silence

The stars are buoys.

弗兰克·斯图尔·特弗林特（Frank Stuart Flint，1885—1960）

战士

老兄。
在法国，
泥泞的路上，
我见你经过，
斜挎长枪，左右摆臂，
全速前进；
我抱着枪，
与我的部队
稍息。
你走过我时，我们目光相遇。
自从我们一起爬过德文[①]山，
就再也没见过；
我们目光相遇，惊诧；
因命令肃静，
我们没敢说话。

老兄的那张脸颊，
在队列里那么与众不同，
你走啊，走啊，
走进黑夜；
我与她相对而坐，

① 德文（Devon hills）：英格兰西南部，布里斯托尔海峡和英吉利海峡之间的山丘。

牙关紧咬，
忍住泪水，
知道你就在身旁，
比梦中还近。

Soldiers

Frank Stuart Flint

Brother.
I saw you on a muddy road
In France
Pass by with your battalion,
Rifle at the slope, full marching order,
Arm swinging;
And I stood at ease,
Folding my hands over my rifle,
With my battalion.
You passed me by, and our eyes met.
We had not seen each other since the days
We climbed the Devon hills together;
Our eyes met, startled;
And, because the order was Silence,
We dared not speak.

O face of my friend,
Alone distinct of all that company,
You went on, you went on,
Into the darkness;
And i sit her at my table,
Holding back my tears,
With my jaw set and my teeth clenched,

Knowing i shall not be
Even so near you as i saw you
In my dream.

哀悼

世上年轻人
被处死刑。
他们为父辈的罪行
召去送死。

世上年轻人，
成长，成熟的果子，
被从枝条上扯下，
花季的记忆
在女子心中依旧甜美；
他们为着残酷的目的
被抛进压榨机和熔炉。

世上年轻人
彼此凝视，
从目光中读出
还没到时候！还没到时候！
但也许会，肯定会。

世上年轻人
不再占领道路，
道路占领他们。
他们不再继承土地，
土地继承他们。
他们不再掌管火焰，

火焰掌管他们。
他们服务他，他毁了他们。
他们不再统治海域，
海的天才
发明了新的怪物，
他们从它口里逃生。

他们不再自由呼吸：
空中的天才
发明新的恐怖，
将他们撕成碎片。

世上年轻人
被死亡包围，
刺刀包围中，
死神无处不在。

老太太哭啊哭，
老爷子心欲碎。

Lament

Frank Stuart Flint

The young men of the world
Are condemned to death.
They have been called up to die
For the crime of their fathers.

The young men of the world,
The growing, the ripening fruit,
Have been torn from their branches,

While the memory of the blossom
Is sweet in women's hearts;
They have been cast for a cruel purpose
Into the mashing-press and furnace.

The young men of the world
Look into each other's eyes,
And read there the same words:
Not yet! Not yet!
But soon perhaps, and perhaps certain.

The young men of the world
No longer possess the road:
The road possesses them.
They no longer inherit the earth:
The earth inherits them.
They are no longer the masters of fire:
Fire is their master;
They serve him, he destroys them.
They no longer rule the waters:
The genius of the seas
Has invented a new monster,
And they fly from its teeth.

They no longer breathe freely:
The genius of the air
Has contrived a new terror
That rends them into pieces.

The young men of the world
Are encompassed with death

He is all about them
In a circle of fore and bayonets.

Weep, weep, O women,
And old men break your hearts.

西格夫里·萨松（Siegfried Sassoon，1886—1967）

战壕里自杀

我认识一个单纯的士兵，
总能对着生活傻笑相迎，
总能安然睡过黑暗寂寞，
一大早起来与云雀对歌。

冬天的壕沟里阴郁恐怖，
炮火虱子横行，却没有酒。
他被一发子弹射穿脑瓜，
此后再没人提起过他。

自鸣得意的群氓，不用
激情似火地欢迎士兵；
溜回家去祈祷吧，祷祈
青春欢笑永不识地狱。

Suicide in the Trenches

Siegfried Sassoon

I knew a simple soldier boy
Who grinned at life in empty joy,

Slept soundly through the lonesome dark,
And whistled early with the lark.

In winter trenches, cowed and glum,
With crumps and lice and lack of rum,
He put a bullet through his brain.
No one spoke of him again.

You smug-faced crowds with kindling eye
Who cheer when soldier lads march by,
Sneak home and pray you'll never know
The hell where youth and laughter go.

鲁伯特·布鲁克（Rupert Brooke，1887—1915）

《1914》第1首：安宁

感谢我主在上随时检点，
捉我青春，唤醒我美梦，
你力强、眼准、有铁腕，
推着我们跃入清水游泳，
洗脱老朽冷漠乏味的世界，
洗脱麻木不仁的心病，
洗脱不人不鬼的疲竭，
洗脱卿卿我我的虚空。

噢，自惭的我们，找到解脱，
罪恶悲伤在长眠中修补，
毁灭的是身体，是呼吸；
除了痛苦，没什么能打破

笑心永宁，痛苦终有尽处；
只有死亡是最坏的友敌。

1914 I: Peace

Rupert Brooke

Now, God be thanked Who has watched us with His hour,
And caught our youth, and wakened us from sleeping,
With hand made sure, clear eye, and sharpened power,
To turn, as swimmers into cleanness leaping,
Glad from a world grown old and cold and weary,
Leave the sick hearts that honour could not move,
And half-men, and their dirty songs and dreary,
And all the little emptiness of love!

Oh! we, who have known shame, we have found release there,
Where there's no ill, no grief, but sleep has mending,
Naught broken save this body, lost but breath;
Nothing to shake the laughing heart's long peace there
But only agony, and that has ending;
And the worst friend and enemy is but Death.

《1914》第 5 首：战士

如果我死了，只需记着：
异国他乡的某个去处
永远是英国。那里的
沃野掩埋富贵的尘土——
英国生长、英国意识，
爱国之花，爱国之游，
英国之躯，英国呼吸，

故乡的河流阳光沐浴。

想想此心洗尽了罪恶，
某时某地，以永恒脉动，
归还英国赋予的思想：
所见、所闻、所梦、所乐；
朋友那学来温存、笑声；
英国苍穹下，此心安详。

1914 V: The Soldier

Rupert Brooke

If I should die, think only this of me:
That there's some corner of a foreign field
That is for ever England. There shall be
In that rich earth a richer dust concealed;
A dust whom England bore, shaped, made aware,
Gave, once, her flowers to love, her ways to roam,
A body of England's, breathing English air,
Washed by the rivers, blest by suns of home.

And think, this heart, all evil shed away,
A pulse in the eternal mind, no less
Gives somewhere back the thoughts by England given;
Her sights and sounds; dreams happy as her day;
And laughter, learnt of friends; and gentleness,
In hearts at peace, under an English heaven.

朱立恩·格伦费尔（Julian Grenfell，1888—1915）

参战

赤裸的大地在春天变暖，
草木勃发，绿意葱茏，
太阳瞩目下倾心鼓舞，
在和煦的微风中抖动。
生命的色彩、温度、光明，
为之永恒的渴望与抗争。
怯战者难逃一死，
战死者虽死犹生。
战斗者接受太阳的温暖，
大地的微明中获得生机；
战斗者御轻风而疾行，
他们与树木共呼吸。
天空朗朗相伴，
星辰熠熠生辉，
看猎户①束腰挎剑，
天狼②在望，七姐妹③列队。
林地树木并肩挺立，
每一株都是朋友，
它们在微风中私语，
引导战士走向山梁沟谷
白天鹰隼盘桓，
夜里猫头鹰召唤，
让战士像它们一样——
耳朵般敏锐，目光般躲闪。

---

① 猎户（Orion）：星空中的猎户座。
② 天狼（Dog star）：天狼星。
③ 七姐妹（Sisters Seven）：北斗七星。

乌鸦向他们唱“哥哥，弟弟，
如果这是你们最后一首歌，
好好唱吧，因为不会再来，
弟兄们，唱起！”
在沉闷难料的等待时刻，
冲锋陷阵即将开始，
战马向他展示高贵的力量；
哦，耐心的眼神，勇敢的心！
当战火点燃的时候，
所有一切都置之度外，
只有战斗的快乐擎在咽喉，
其他一切都不予理睬。
虽然不想那么多，
但快乐与盲目让他懂得，
果真还是刀枪不入，
就无注定一说。
枪林弹雨的战线上，
空气中死神在吟吟歌唱，
但白天有力的双手握住他，
夜晚柔软的羽翼护他无恙。

Into Battle

Julian Grenfell

The naked earth is warm with Spring,
And with green grass and bursting trees
Leans to the sun's gaze glorying,
And quivers in the sunny breeze;
And life is Colour and Warmth and Light,
And a striving evermore for these;
And he is dead who will not fight,

And who dies fighting has increase.
The fighting man shall from the sun
Take warmth, and life from glowing earth;
Speed with the light-foot winds to run
And with the trees to newer birth;
And find, when fighting shall be done,
Great rest, and fullness after dearth.
All the bright company of Heaven
Hold him in their bright comradeship,
The Dog star, and the Sisters Seven,
Orion's belt and sworded hip:
The woodland trees that stand together,
They stand to him each one a friend;
They gently speak in the windy weather;
They guide to valley and ridges end.
The kestrel hovering by day,
And the little owls that call by night,
Bid him be swift and keen as they,
As keen of ear, as swift of sight.
The blackbird sings to him: "Brother, brother,
If this be the last song you shall sing,
Sing well, for you may not sing another;
Brother, sing."
In dreary doubtful waiting hours,
Before the brazen frenzy starts,
The horses show him nobler powers; -
O patient eyes, courageous hearts!
And when the burning moment breaks,
And all things else are out of mind,
And only joy of battle takes
Him by the throat and makes him blind,

Through joy and blindness he shall know,
Not caring much to know, that still
Nor lead nor steel shall reach him, so
That it be not the Destined Will.
The thundering line of battle stands,
And in the air Death moans and sings;
But Day shall clasp him with strong hands,
And Night shall fold him in soft wings.

艾萨克·罗森伯格（Isaac Rosenberg，1890—1918）

穿越苍凉的日子

穿越苍凉的日子，
三千年焦灼渴望，
一张张脸，一双双眼，
多么阴暗，多么疯狂！

眉眼之下的灵魂，
流浪者一样摸索，
摸索希伯伦[1]的池塘，
黎巴嫩夏日的山坡。

他们的脚步扬起烟尘，
留下寂静发黄的日子，
他们以生者的眼光打量，
究竟有多少时光已死。

① 希伯伦（Hebron）：约旦河西岸的一个城市，位于耶路撒冷西南偏南，是亚伯拉罕的出生和埋葬地，也是大卫王的首都。

Through These Pale Cold Days

Isaac Rosenberg

Through these pale cold days
What dark faces burn
Out of three thousand years,
And their wild eyes yearn,

While underneath their brows
Like waifs their spirits grope
For the pools of Hebron again—
For Lebanon's summer slope.

They leave these blond still days
In dust behind their tread
They see with living eyes
How long they have been dead.

艾娃·格尔尼（Ivor Gurney，1890—1937）

靶子

我射中他，“没办法”，
我们俩，非我既他。
不得已，谁都怨不得，
换作你也会这么做。

我的母亲睡不着，
她害怕我被射中。
或许最好是我死，

好让她解脱恐惧。

解脱，坏莫过如此，
或许他是个独生子……
可上帝麻木，奈何
一个字不肯说。

若他们瞄准我，首先
我会找那小子谈谈。
看谁最敏感枪子儿，
别介意我有种一试。

都是结，要我来解。
真是一团淌血的结！
或笑，或叫，或哭；
上帝取舍从不在乎。

The Target

Ivor Gurney

I shot him, and it had to be
One of us 'Twas him or me.
"Couln't be helped" and none can blame
Me, for you would do the same

My mother, she cant sleep for fear
Of what might be a-happening here
To me. Perhaps it might be best
To die, and set her fears at rest

For worst is worst, and worry's done.

Perhaps he was the only son…
Yet God keeps still, and does not say
A word of guidance anyway.

Well, if they get me, first I'll find
That boy, and tell him all my mind,
And see who felt the bullet worst,
And ask his pardon,if I durst.

All's a tangle. Here's my job.
A man might rave, or shout, or sob;
And God He takes takes no sort of heed.
This is a bloody mess indeed.

理查德·阿尔丁顿（Richard Aldington，1892—1962）

轰炸

四天里，大地被撕裂，
爆炸的钢铁，
摧毁周围的房屋；
三个晚上我们都不敢睡，
捏着汗，听着轰隆声
将死亡逼近。

第四个晚上，
紧张的神经一根根绷断，
睡意中，人们咕哝着，抽搐着，
弹片在头上崩裂。

第五天静下来，
我们钻出掩体，
透过废墟向上张望，
只见白云鳞次栉比，
默默地掠过平静的蓝天。

Bombardment

Richard Aldington

Four days the earth was rent and torn
By bursting steel,
The houses fell about us;
Three nights we dared not sleep,
Sweating, and listening for the imminent crash
Which meant our death.

The fourth night every man,
Nerve-tortured, racked to exhaustion,
Slept, muttering and twitching,
While the shells crashed overhead.

The fifth day there came a hush;
We left our holes
And looked above the wreckage of the earth
To where the white clouds moved in silent lines
Across the untroubled blue.

休·麦克迪儿米德（Hugh MacDiarmid，1892—1978）

苏格兰

要有深深的大爱，
才能读懂国家的配置；
逐渐意识到对小符号的伟大解读
有着细微的含义；
最终听到柔弱言辞中的宏大之音；
看到全大不列颠这块大理石上的雕塑，
其侧面的膨胀、坍塌。
像春天，像窗口的一双手，
小心地把新旧来回挪动，
这儿留一瓣花，
那儿留一道缝，
不打碎任何东西。
我收集起
苏格兰所有没着落的部件，
给他们命名，接纳他们，
爱他们，认同他们，
试着拼出个完整。

Scotland

Hugh MacDiarmid

It requires great love of it deeply to read
The configuration of a land,
Gradually grow conscious of fine shadings,
Of great meanings in slight symbols,
Hear at last the great voice that speaks softly,
See the swell and fall upon the flank

Of a statue carved out in a whole country's marble,
Be like Spring, like a hand in a window
Moving New and Old things carefully to and fro,
Moving a fraction of flower here,
Placing an inch of air there,
And without breaking anything.
So I have gathered unto myself
All the loose ends of Scotland,
And by naming them and accepting them,
Loving them and identifying myself with them,
Attempt to express the whole.

一小朵白玫瑰

致约翰·高斯沃思

不是世上玫瑰都归我。
我只要我应得的，
只要苏格兰那洁白的一小朵。
馨香袭人——动人魂魄。

The Little White Rose

Hugh MacDiarmid

To John Gawsworth

The rose of all the world is not for me.
I want for my part
Only the little white rose of Scotland
That smells sharp and sweet—and breaks the heart.

威尔弗雷德·欧文（Wilfred Owen，1893—1918）

悼青年阵亡者的圣歌

死如牲畜，敲丧钟做啥？
只要惊魂的枪声怒嚎。
只要长枪，结结巴巴
咔嗒出匆匆的祈祷。
别用祷词丧钟嘲笑，
别发出哀悼的声响，
只要子弹哀号和号角，
要疯狂刺耳地合唱。
拿什么来引领亡灵？
不要双手捧着蜡烛，
要男童眼亮来送行，
要女童额白盖灵柩。
要温柔耐心作鲜花，
要黄昏悄降作帷幕。

Anthem for Doomed Youth

Wilfred Owen

What passing-bells for these who die as cattle?
Only the monstrous anger of the guns.
Only the stuttering rifles' rapid rattle
Can patter out their hasty orisons.
No mockeries now for them; no prayers nor bells;
Nor any voice of mourning save the choirs,
The shrill, demented choirs of wailing shells;
And bugles calling for them from sad shires.
What candles may be held to speed them all?

Not in the hands of boys, but in their eyes
Shall shine the holy glimmers of good-byes.
The pallor of girls' brows shall be their pall;
Their flowers the tenderness of patient minds,
And each slow dusk a drawing-down of blinds.

睡着

钢盔盖脸，背包垫腰，
多日的鏖战与警醒后，
困意爬额头将他放倒。

酣睡甜美没一秒钟，
死神突袭，他一挺胸口，
便没了心脏的跳动，
胸脯胳膊再次瘫倒。

少顷，血迹从弹孔慢涌，
像蚂蚁成群爬出一道。

是否长眠有鹏翼把守？
是否悬于星斗的思想
安卧上帝赐予的枕头？
是否枪林弹雨均无扰，
没有乌云风刀于顶上？
或者瘦削呆滞的大脑
逐渐模糊，从底处霉变，
头发缠于收割的枯草，
绞上锈迹斑斑的电线，
谁知？谁关心？一了百了！
睡着，少些冷，少些寒战，

比我们醒着苦熬好！

Asleep

Wilfred Owen

Under his helmet, up against his pack,
After so many days of work and waking,
Sleep took him by the brow and laid him back.

There, in the happy no-time of his sleeping,
Death took him by the heart. There heaved a quaking
Of the aborted life within him leaping,
Then chest and sleepy arms once more fell slack.

And soon the slow, stray blood came creeping
From the intruding lead, like ants on track.

Whether his deeper sleep lie shaded by the shaking
Of great wings, and the thoughts that hung the stars,
High-pillowed on calm pillows of God's making,
Above these clouds, these rains, these sleets of lead,
And these winds' scimitars,
—Or whether yet his thin and sodden head
Confuses more and more with the low mould,
His hair being one with the grey grass
Of finished fields, and wire-scrags rusty-old,
Who knows? Who hopes? Who troubles? Let it pass!
He sleeps. He sleeps less tremulous, less cold,
Than we who wake, and waking say Alas!

罗伯特·尼科斯（Robert Nichols，1893—1944）

战斗（节选）

正午
正午，明晃的战壕里……
嗡蝇火舌一般……
热风吹起目眩的空气……
烈日犁上九天。

污泥寂静的壕沟里，
站四十条硬汉，
一身恶臭一身沙砾，
就像公牛困圈。

时而狙击子弹呼啸
或像离弦之箭，
时而地狱之火煎熬，
战士扭身哀叹。

战壕外，凉爽的云端，
传来飞机呻吟；
太阳俯冲，薄云溃散，
好像黑点逡巡。

高天之下，战壕闷热，
汗渍，眩晕，孤寂，
我们盼命运快点裁夺，
不管生还是死。

Battle (Excerpt)

Robert Nichols

Noon
It is midday; the deep trench glares…
A buzz and blaze of flies…
The hot wind puffs the giddy airs…
The great sun rakes the skies.

No sound in all the stagnant trench
Where forty standing men
Endure the sweat and grit and stench,
Like cattle in a pen.

Sometimes a sniper's bullet whirs
Or twangs the whining wire,
Sometimes a soldier sighs and stirs
As in hell's frying fire.

From out a high, cool cloud descends
An aeroplane's far moan,
The sun strikes down, the thin cloud rends…
The black speck travels on.

And sweating, dazed, isolate
In the hot trench beneath,
We bide the next shrewd move of fate
Be it of life or death.

赫伯特·瑞德（Herbert Read，1893—1968）

为1940年征兵而作

新下的雪里，一个士兵擦身而过，
他脚步轻轻，一脸惨白。
我的心突然一窒，
如同打量二十五年前的魂魄。

我喊：站住！声音还是那么灵，
他收了脚步，就像过去的我，
在朦胧的过去被喝令

站在未知的路上。见他转身我说：
“我先你二十五年参编，
我们中很多都没回还。
很多回来了，却徒有躯壳。

我们在雨里泥里挺进，
我们与死亡黑暗绝望作战，
我们抛头颅洒热血，
你也将和我们一样拼。

我们付出化为乌有，世界依旧，
家园里有希望，大街上有愤怒；
世界复原，我们又回到
工厂田间，回到贫富世仇。

我们胜而犹败，
弄权者依旧专权，
只剩年轻人打扫脚下

过火后四散的灰烬尘埃。

但我们懂了：直到战士戴旧徽章，
死者毫无荣耀而言。
多少英雄听到集结的号角，
多少英雄看到花环闪光。

他们胜得虚无。他们被欺瞒。
但你是我兄弟，如果你入伍时，
知道没有回报，没有牺牲的必要，
这样，荣誉方能有缓。

无希望而战，战的是体面，
重构自我，找回迷失的心。”
说完我转身笑了，士兵回应我时，
活像白鞋带，靠烂篱而站。

To a Conscript of 1940

Herbert Read

A soldier passed me in the freshly fallen snow,
His footsteps muffled, his face unearthly grey:
And my heart gave a sudden leap
As I gazed on a ghost of five-and-twenty years ago.

I shouted Halt! and my voice had the old accustom’d ring
And he obeyed it as it was obeyed
In the shrouded days when I too was one

Into the unknown. He turned towards me and I said:
“I am one of those who went before you

Five-and-twenty years ago: one of the many who never returned,
Of the many who returned and yet were dead.

We went where you are going, into the rain and the mud:
We fought as you will fight
With death and darkness and despair;
We gave what you will give-our brains and our blood.

We think we gave in vain. The world was not renewed.
There was hope in the homestead and anger in the streets,
But the old world was restored and we returned
To the dreary field and workshop, and the immemorial feud

Of rich and poor. Our victory was our defeat.
Power was retained where power had been misused
And youth was left to sweep away
The ashes that the fires had strewn beneath our feet.

But one thing we learned: there is no glory in the dead
Until the soldier wears a badge of tarnish'd braid;
There are heroes who have heard the rally and have seen
The glitter of garland round their head.

Theirs is the hollow victory. They are deceived.
But you my brother and my ghost, if you can go
Knowing that there is no reward, no certain use
In all your sacrifice, then honour is reprieved.

To fight without hope is to fight with grace,
The self reconstructed, the false heart repaired."
Then I turned with a smile, and he answered my salute

As he stood against the fretted hedge, which was like white lace.

维拉·玛丽·布里顿（Vera Mary Brittain，1893—1970）

一九一四年八月

上帝说："我已被忘记，
沉睡的灵魂应该苏醒，
　　眼睛失明须恢复视力。"

既然救赎需经历苦痛，
他便向大地挥杖驱使，
　　让那恐怖的毁灭当政。

他令荒芜驻足之地，
人们痛苦绝望煎熬，
　　高声呼喊"上帝已死。"

August, 1914

Vera Mary Brittain

God said, "Men have forgotten Me:
The souls that sleep shall wake again,
　　And blinded eyes must learn to see."

So since redemption comes through pain
He smote the earth with chastening rod,
　　And brought destruction's lurid reign;

But where His desolation trod
The people in their agony
Despairing cried, "There is no God."

梅·韦德伯恩·卡南（May Wedderburn Cannan，1893—1973）

灯光

我们曾想一起震撼世界，你和我，
我们年轻，也很聪明；
如今在树荫掩映的灯光下，
我几乎看到你的眼睛
含着过去的微笑，你和我
在那个年代梦想着伟大的帝国。
我们长途跋涉，
你追求的荣誉，
亲爱的，是部队名册里
你名字前的"剑十字"[①]。

我们曾想一起震撼世界，你和我，
我们系于一海；
如今在寒风刺骨的寂寂黑夜，
你的声音悄悄向我袭来，
满载忘却的记忆：你和我，
在那个年代梦想着伟大的未来。
我们踏足未知，
我追求的荣誉
是胸前血红的十字，亲爱的，

① 剑十字（crossed swords）：两剑交叉，代表牺牲的战士。

纪念你名字前的“剑十字”。

我们从来撼不动世界，你和我，
你牺牲了自己，
我的心被战争打碎；
那年夏天，
你走上了我们没提过的路，你和我，
在那个年代有着帝国的梦想；
你迈步走向了西方，
无求于荣誉——
我的胸前有个血红的十字，亲爱的，
一个磨坏了的，写着你名字的十字。

Lamplight

May Wedderburn Cannan

We planned to shake the world together, you and I.
Being young, and very wise;
Now in the light of the green shaded lamp
Almost I see your eyes
Light with the old gay laughter; you and I
Dreamed greatly of an Empire in those days,
Setting our feet upon laborious ways,
And all you asked of fame
Was crossed swords in the Army List;
My Dear, against your name.

We planned a great Empire together, you and I,
Bound only by the sea;
Now in the quiet of a chill Winter's night
Your voice comes hushed to me

Full of forgotten memories: you and I
Dreamed great dreams of our future in those days,
Setting our feet on undiscovered ways,
And all I asked of fame
A scarlet cross on my breast, my Dear,
For the swords by your name.

We shall never shake the world together, you and I,
For you gave your life away;
And I think my heart was broken by war,
Since on a summer day
You took the road we never spoke of; you and I
Dreamed greatly of an Empire in those days;
You set your feet upon the Western ways
And have no need of fame—
There's a scarlet cross on my breast, my Dear,
And a torn cross with your name.

玛格丽特·波特盖特·科尔（Margaret Postgate Cole，1893—1980）

老兵

我们碰见他正在晒太阳，
战争致盲，他得以残生；
年轻士兵晃出“手余香[①]”
询问他所经历的战争。

他说这说那，一阵白话，

① 手余香（Hand&Flower）：花店名。

每个空脑壳里的噩梦
都飘散。他听我们在侧——
“可怜的孩子，怎知战争？”

我们站在那儿，看着他
不停地拽松垮的袜子，
一个人便忍不住问他，
“你多大？”
“五月三日十九岁。”

The Veteran

Margaret Postgate Cole

We came upon him sitting in the sun—
Blinded by war, and left. And past the fence
Wandered young soldiers from the Hand & Flower,
Asking advice of his experience.

And he said this and that, and told them tales;
And all the nightmares of each empty head
Blew into air. Then, hearing us beside—
“Poor kids, how do they know what it’s like?” he said.

And we stood there, and watched him as he sat
Turning his sockets where they went away;
Until it came to one of us to ask
“And you’re—how old?”
“Nineteen the thire of May.”

查尔斯·汉密尔顿·索利（Charles Hamilton Sorley，1895—1915）

致德国

没有谁想成心害人，
没有谁把疆土掠夺，
你我一样都是盲人，
有限的疆域中摸索。
我说我的曲径通幽，
你见你的前程远大，
彼此截了对方通途，
义愤填膺瞎子盲打。

等到和平，我们再看，
新视野互为欣赏称奇。
双手紧握笑对旧疾，
我们变得友好温暖。
然而，和平未到之际，
暴风骤雨雷鸣电闪。

To Germany

Charles Hamilton Sorley

You are blind like us. Your hurt no man designed,
And no man claimed the conquest of your land.
But gropers both through fields of thought confined
We stumble and we do not understand.
You only saw your future bigly planned,
And we, the tapering paths of our own mind,
And in each other's dearest ways we stand,

And hiss and hate. And the blind fight the blind.

When it is peace, then we may view again
With new-won eyes each other's truer form
And wonder. Grown more loving-kind and warm
We'll grasp firm hands and laugh at the old pain,
When it is peace. But until peace, the storm
The darkness and the thunder and the rain.

死神造就了他不朽的模样

当你梦见成千上万没嘴巴的
阵亡者在惨白的军营边走过，
你不必像他人那样说些软话，
会不会缅怀他们，都不必说。
不必赞美，因为他们已聋聩，
怎知那不是对爆头的诅咒？
你不必哭，瞎眼看不到流泪。
你不必嘉奖，人很难不朽。
只需说：“他们死了。”“可是，
从前也死过很多更好的人。”
然后，你将拥挤的人群扫视，
认一认其中哪个是你的至亲。
都是幽灵，一张脸都不熟悉；
死神造就的模样总是难辨认。

Great Death Has Made All His for Evermore

Charles Hamilton Sorley

When you see millions of the mouthless dead
Across your dreams in pale battalions go,

Say not soft things as other men have said,
That you'll remember. For you need not so.
Give them not praise. For, deaf, how should they know
It is not curses heaped on each gashed head?
Nor tears. Their blind eyes see not your tears flow.
Nor honour. It is easy to be dead.
Say only this, "They are dead." Then add thereto,
"Yet many a better one has died before."
Then, scanning all the o'ercrowded mass, should you
Perceive one face that you loved heretofore,
It is a spook. None wears the face you knew.
Great death has made all his for evermore.

大卫·斯图尔特·琼斯（David Stuart Jones，1895—1974）

枪子儿和炮弹

枪子儿炮弹化学武器与我何干。
来喝一杯，我们谈谈。
我与枪子儿炮弹何干。
枪子儿炮弹，现又有核弹，
你们与我何干。
屠杀人家子女，
他们与你何干。
现在你按下按钮，
一切与我无关，
咱俩就此免谈。

Bullets and Bombs

David Stuart Jones

Bullets and bombs and chemicals to what have I done to you.
Please can we talk, and have a pint or two.
Bullets and bombs what have i done to you.
Bullets and bombs, now nuclear weapons to,
What have i done to you.
Slaughter sons and daughters
What have they done to you.
You've now pressed the button
And i've done nothing to you
Thats the end of me and you.

罗伯特 · 格瑞夫（Robert Graves，1895—1985）

死去的德国鬼子

曾经读我战歌的人们，
只听说过鲜血和荣誉，
我要说（你从前已熟稔）
“战争就是地狱！”如果你
还不信，我今天就在丛林[①]，
找一个治愈嗜血的人。

死去的德国佬坐靠断桩，
周围一片污浊、杂乱、腐朽，

---

① 丛林：原文为默迈特丛林（Mametz Wood），法国北部的一个村庄，附近林子是第一次世界大战战场。1916 年 7 月，英国和德国军队在此展开了五天恶战，约 4000 英军牺牲。

他湿绿衣服湿绿脸庞，
瞪着双眼，全身恶臭，
他大肚子，戴眼镜，短发，
鼻子和胡须黑血滴答。

A Dead Boche

Robert Graves

To you who'd read my songs of War
And only hear of blood and fame,
I'll say (you've heard it said before)
"War's Hell!" and if you doubt the same,
Today I found in Mametz Wood
A certain cure for lust of blood:

Where, propped against a shattered trunk,
In a great mess of things unclean,
Sat a dead Boche; he scowled and stunk
With clothes and face a sodden green,
Big-bellied, spectacled, crop-haired,
Dribbling black blood from nose and beard.

埃德蒙·布兰敦（Edmund Blunden，1896—1974）

五年后回首一九一六

我未老先衰，痛苦麻木，
独自一人坐着，只听得
长长的窃笑，沮丧的低语，
不再强烈的希望与惊愕；

长枪依旧躺在原来的湿地，
单薄的掩体里碎片颤动，
我读过的书也在那里，
我与亲朋，死寂中苦等。

伤痕从悲情的巷战展开，
直铺向为我专有的绿野；
然而曾属于我的已经不再，
我到处寻找却一无所得。
怀着轻柔与坚忍的意志，
心中燃烧着摧毁的房屋，
我疯狂地搜寻寂寞的楼宇，
只见焦黑的木桩喑哑大树。

一只鸟儿鸣唱令我起身，
我悄悄地沿着巷子逃脱；
处处人家，家却无人。
我谁都不敢见啥也不敢说。
玫瑰深红在碉堡里燃烧，
野生的麦子洪水般围拢，
炽热的小路上蜥蜴垂吊，
打碎的圣龛血一样鲜明。

玛丽之龛在梧桐树间，
幽暗的树荫让光明突显；
我和战友一起奔赴那里，
可恶的战火中寻得心安。
狡黠刺透晨雾，报怨枪响
混合着传来嘈杂的报务：
然后，阳光悄静，树荫凉爽，
我们匍匐进草丛直睡到正午。

1916 Seen from 1921

Edmund Blunden

Tired with dull grief, grown old before my day,
I sit in solitude and only hear
Long silent laughters, murmurings of dismay,
The lost intensities of hope and fear;
In those old marshes yet the rifles lie,
On the thin breastwork flutter the grey rags,
The very books I read are there—and I
Dead as the men I loved, wait while life drags.

Its wounded length from those sad streets of war
Into green places here, that were my own;
But now what once was mine is mine no more,
I seek such neighbours here and I find none.
With such strong gentleness and tireless will
Those ruined houses seared themselves in me,
Passionate I look for their dumb story still,
And the charred stub outspeaks the living tree.

I rise up at the singing of a bird
And scarcely knowing slink along the lane,
I dare not give a soul a look or word
Where all have homes and none's at home in vain:
Deep red the rose burned in the grim redoubt,
The self-sown wheat around was like a flood,
In the hot path the lizard lolled time out,
The saints in broken shrines were bright as blood.

Sweet Mary's shrine between the sycamores!

There we would go, my friend of friends and I,
And snatch long moments from the grudging wars,
Whose dark made light intense to see them by.
Shrewd bit the morning fog, the whining shots
Spun from the wrangling wire: then in warm swoon
The sun hushed all but the cool orchard plots,
We crept in the tall grass and slept till noon.

遗产

今天的房子铺明天的路；
我知道一堆堆石头
曾经是优雅、雄伟的高墙，
举国的声誉，艺术的迷狂；
曾经无尽的庄严与肃穆
彰显对荣耀的捍卫。
如今继承有了新的工作：
统一带来分崩离析；
强悍就是美的，毫无差别，
有如洪水与寒霜的气节。
如今血性男儿不会逃脱
新的人生颐指。
带着好奇与高昂的热忱，
奥雷里[①]与颂诗并举；
那废墟上有光芒照人的
塔楼和绝无仅有的石头！
因为梦想纵使芜杂混沌，
也能勾勒未来征途。

① 奥雷里（orrery）：一种太阳系仪器，由著名的钟表法师洛蒂（Lottie）创造，以联系星轨，占卜并引导星星的力量。

The Survival

Edmund Blunden

To-day's house makes to-morrow's road;
I knew these heaps of stone
When they were walls of grace and might,
The country's honour, art's delight
That over fountain'd silence show'd
Fame's final bastion.
Inheritance has found fresh work,
Disunion union breeds;
Beauty the strong, its difference lost,
Has matter fit for flood and frost.
Here's the true blood that will not shirk
Life's new-commanding needs.
With curious costly zeal, O man,
Raise orrery and ode;
How shines your tower, the only one
Of that especial site and stone!
And even the dream's confusion can
Sustain to-morrow's road.

埃杰尔·里克沃德（Edgell Rickword，1898—1982）

战壕诗人

我认识一个老兄，
他一天比一天灰暗，
他不赶身上的苍蝇，
也不怕横飞的炮弹。

为唤醒他的心神，
我给他读邓恩[1]的诗，
“让孩子拔曼陀罗根[2]”，
他心不在焉的样子，
张嘴躺那，翻着鱼眼，
像根木头，知觉全消，
任凭邓恩复活高喊，
“我想和我那先鬼[3]聊聊。”

一天我试着念挽歌，
他似乎听到我说：
“不过是人，有啥好遮掩[4]？”
他下流地一笑，我知道
他定是精虫上了脑。
我能做的是饿死精虫；
我绞尽脑汁想些健康的，
就引了一句“莫德”[5]。
我发现他更加下流地
嘲笑纯真的激情。
他一身恶臭，虽是好友，
我也得离开；任老鼠吃他指头。

---

① 邓恩（Donne）：17 世纪英国玄学派诗人，以奇喻（conceit）著称。

② 让孩子拔曼陀罗根（Get with child a mandrake-root）：喻指不可能的事。传说人的手不能与该植物接触，只有在月光下，经过适当的祈祷和仪式，用绳子将黑狗拴在曼陀罗上，才能安全地将根拔起。参见邓恩的《歌谣：去抓流星来》（*Song: Go and Catch a Falling Star*）。

③ 先鬼（some old lover's ghost）：指在爱神产生前就死掉的爱之鬼（Who died before the god of love was born）。参见邓恩的《爱的神性》（*Love's Deity*）。

④ 不过是人，有啥好遮掩（What needst thou have no more covering than a man?）：参见邓恩的《致上床的情人》（*To His Mistress Going to Bed*）。

⑤ 莫德（Maud）：1855 年发表的丁尼生的一首诗，讲述了演讲者父亲的自杀，演讲者与邻居女儿莫德的关系，以及随后发生的一系列令人不安的事件。

Trench Poets

Edgell Rickword

I knew a man, he was my chum,
But he grew blacker every day,
And would not brush the flies away,
Nor blanch however fierce the hum
Of passing shells; i used to read,
To rouse him, random things from donne—
Like "get with child a mandrake-root."
But you can tell he was far gone,
For he lay gaping, mackerel-eyed,
And stiff, and senseless as a post
Even when that old poet cried
"I long to talk with some old lover's ghost."

I tried the Elegies one day,
But he, because he heard me say:
"What needst thou have no more covering than a man?"
Grinned nastily, and so I knew
The worms had got his brains at last.
There was one thing that I might do
To starve the worms; I racked my head
For healthy things and quoted Maud.
His grin got worse and I could see
He sneered at passion's purity.
He stank so badly, though we were great chums
I had to leave him; then rats ate his thumbs.

巴兹尔·班廷（Basil Bunting，1900—1985）

在布瑞格弗莱特礼拜堂[①]

时间吹嘘，大罗马蔑视。
瑞恩[②]建起自己的丰碑。
他人视线模糊，以为
太阳之火沉落。

石头确会碎成沙土，橡树
也会融进圣徒的尸骨。
然而，这里的石头和橡树
尚可稍作庇护。

此地宁静——除此之外
我们别无所求。看啊，
风翼之下，白云起舞，
叶子瞬间欣喜。

At Briggflatts Meetinghouse

Basil Bunting

Boasts time mocks cumber Rome. Wren
Set up his own monument.
Others watch fells dwindle, think
The sun's fires sink.

---

① 布瑞格弗莱特礼拜堂（Briggflatts Meetinghouse）：位于坎布里亚郡（Cumbria），著名的贵格会教堂。

② 瑞恩（Wren）：克里斯托弗·雷恩（Christopher Wren），英国建筑师，伦敦大火后，他设计了圣保罗大教堂和其他几十座伦敦教堂及世俗建筑。

Stones indeed sift to sand, oak
Blends with saint's bones.
Yet for a little longer here
Stone and oak shelter

Silence while we ask nothing
But silence. Look how clouds dance
Under the wind's wing, and leaves
Delight in transience.

主任对汤姆说

诗？就是个爱好。
我玩儿模型火车，
肖先生养鸽子。

不是工作，不用出汗，
也没人付工资，
不如写肥皂广告。

艺术，就是歌唱；剧目只一个：
《沙漠之歌》，
南希在合唱队待过。

要一周付十二镑——
结婚了，是吧？
你倒有胆子提。

给你十二镑，
我怎么面对售票员的
一张脸？

再说了，谁说那是诗？
我十岁的孩子，
也会写会押韵。

我有三千开销，
车子，账单，
但我也得算计。

我圈子里的，
都听我忠告。
至于你干啥？

烂词烂句，
有碍身体，
见诗人我就想一通洗。

写出来的破烂，
竟是些红魔，瘾君子，
全都是混混儿。

海因斯先生就这么说，他是中学老师，
应该说不错。
找份工作吧。

What the Chairman Told Tom

Basil Bunting

Poetry? It's a hobby.
I run model trains.
Mr Shaw there breeds pigeons.

It's not work. You dont sweat.
Nobody pays for it.
You could advertise soap.

Art, that's opera; or repertory—
The Desert Song.
Nancy was in the chorus.

But to ask for twelve pounds a week—
Married, aren't you?—
You've got a nerve.

How could I look a bus conductor
In the face
If i paid you twelve pounds?

Who says it's poetry, anyhow?
My ten year old
Can do it and rhyme.

I get three thousand and expenses,
A car, vouchers,
But i'm an accountant.

They do what i tell them,
My company.
What do you do?

Nasty little words, nasty long words,
It's unhealthy.

I want to wash when I meet a poet.

They're Reds, addicts,
All delinquents.
What you write is rot.

Mr Hines says so, and he's a schoolteacher,
He ought to know.
Go and find work.

致庞德诗章之扉页

那是阿尔卑斯山。有什么可说？
都不靠谱。致命的冰川，峭壁迂回，
乱石杂草，牧场孤石，冰砾；
细看，或许是，轻盈快乐的合唱。
谁知道打磨岩石的冰会刮落什么？

山在那儿，你得绕道很远，
才可以避开。
想习惯也得费点周折。那是阿尔卑斯山，
笨蛋！坐下来等它碎掉！

On the Fly-Leaf of Pound's Cantos

Basil Bunting

There are the Alps. What is there to say about them?
They don't make sense. Fatal glaciers, crags cranks climb,
Jumbled boulder and weed, pasture and boulder, scree,
Et l'on entend, maybe, le refrain joyeux et leger.
Who knows what the ice will have scraped on the rock it is

smoothing?

There they are, you will have to go a long way round
If you want to avoid them.
It takes some getting used to. There are the Alps,
Fools! Sit down and wait for them to crumble!

史蒂维·史密斯（Stevie Smith，1902—1971）

不是挥手而是被淹

没人听见那疲惫的男人，
但他还在躺着呻吟：
你们想不到我游得太远，
我不是挥手而是被淹。

可怜的家伙，他总贪玩，
如今动弹不得，
人们说肯定是天太冷，
他的心脏打不着火。

唉，不是，不是，哪天都冷，
（垂死的男子躺着呻吟）
我一生总是游得太远，
我不是挥手而是被淹。

Not Waving But Drowning

Stevie Smith

Nobody heard him, the dead man,

But still he lay moaning:
I was much further out than you thought
And not waving but drowning.

Poor chap, he always loved larking
And now he's dead
It must have been too cold for him his heart gave way,
They said.

Oh, no no no, it was too cold always
(Still the dead one lay moaning)
I was much too far out all my life
And not waving but drowning.

塞西尔·戴·刘易斯（Cecil Day Lewis，1904—1972）

欣喜

冲天的云雀，把圆润如玉的声音
投到天空静谧的湖心，
激起涟漪填满正午，
太阳之侧渺小谁见？

狂热的翱翔，凌空的气势！
歌如弦动，震颤不已！
盘旋处声音与翅膀合一，
是歌星，是光明的音符！

飞翔着泊进正午的港湾，
很快光潮即转——噢，留下来，

直到日光西流，
冲着河口落入宁静。

The Ecstatic

Cecil Day Lewis

Lark, skylark, spilling your rubbed and round
Pebbles of sounds in air's still lake,
Whose widening circles fill the noon; yet none
Is known so small beside the sun:

Be strong your fervent soaring, your skyward air!
Tremble there, a nerve of song!
Float up there where voice and wing are one,
A singing star, a note of light!

Buoyed, embayed in heaven's noon—wide reaches—
For soon Light's tide will turn—Oh Stay!
Cease not till day streams to the west, then down
That estuary drop down to peace.

维农·瓦特金斯（Vernon Watkins，1906—1967）

钟声不振

从前石头闪光鸽子灰亮，
娶亲生子钟声敲响明媚，
我歌颂高天，那里夜以继日
周而复始。然而，好像东方
日出渐缓，报导着潮汐。

我留意随手翻开的历史，
看了两遍，就搁在一旁。

疾病来袭，盗贼四起，
与生俱来的伊甸余荫
远远地挂在松针上打战。
叶枯前我没看到天堂的设计？
圆圆的太阳向地面下沉，
着地的瞬间，低如落叶，随之，
所有姿势生计都重重地沉下去。

垂露像漂洗工染白苍天，
多么寂静！我听，尖塔的钟声
没有敲响。夜里钟点守望
隐隐约约的群星轮转。
新被单打发孤魂陷于空城，
时间宝贵，我像花瓶守影一样，
更替的声音中，为你默然。

A Bell Unrung

Vernon Watkins

In those days stone became bright and the dove bright-grey.
Bells in sunlight fell upon births and weddings.
My tongue clove to heaven's roof, where might and morning
Moved as before. Yet it seemed from the East each day
The sun rose more slowly, announcing tidings.
I noticed the page of history my hand was turning,
And looked at it twice before I laid it away.

Sickness struck. Thieves overheard, or Shades,

In the garden of Eden known to me from my birth
Held distance hung on a sensitive needle's trembling.
Had I not seen in a leaf before it fades
The symmetry of the heavens? And touching earth,
The round sun dropped, as low as a leaf, assembling
In a heavy drop all places, postures and trades.

A fuller's whiteness filled heaven from the fall of dew.
How still the world! I listened, the bell in the steeple
Did not move. All night the loom of the stars
Was winding, watched by the counting clocks, a new
Sheet for one soul in a city emptied of people.
Precious time! I kept my shade, like a vase,
From the voices of substitution, silent for you.

约翰·贝杰曼（John Betjeman，1906—1984）

泥沼

炸弹友好，落泥沼！
不要往人群里掉，
如今已无放牧草，
死亡成帮！

炸弹投来都粉碎，
空调餐厅也摧毁，
豆奶果肉罐头飞，
人烟消亡。

废墟之城再席卷，

九十七人房子坍，
每周只花半分钱，
一过二十载。

捉那男子重下巴，
事事恒通靠瞎话，
恶贯满盈怎洗刷，
女人泪满腮。

炸毁刨光橡木桌，
炸毁他的手乱摸，
止住他的嘴乱说，
让他嚎叫。

饶了秃头的公差，
虽则为恶棍敛财，
不怪他们胡来，
地狱有报。

不怪他们无知，
分不清鸟语收音机，
不怪他们常去
约会处女。

王朝酒吧冒牌货，
谈论体育与造车，
不敢望灿烂星河，
只管阨逆。

节省劳力的人家，
家庭主妇烫了发，

混凤机吹出干花，
美甲涂油。

炸弹友好落沼泥，
炸开的土地好犁，
卷心菜正值旺季，
地气伏流。

Slough

John Betjeman

Come friendly bombs and fall on Slough!
It isn't fit for humans now,
There isn't grass to graze a cow.
Swarm over, Death!

Come, bombs and blow to smithereens
Those air -conditioned, bright canteens,
Tinned fruit, tinned meat, tinned milk, tinned beans,
Tinned minds, tinned breath.

Mess up the mess they call a town-
A house for ninety-seven down
And once a week a half a crown
For twenty years.

And get that man with double chin
Who'll always cheat and always win,
Who washes his repulsive skin
In women's tears:

And smash his desk of polished oak
And smash his hands so used to stroke
And stop his boring dirty joke
And make him yell.

But spare the bald young clerks who add
The profits of the stinking cad;
It's not their fault that they are mad,
They've tasted Hell.

It's not their fault they do not know
The birdsong from the radio,
It's not their fault they often go
To Maidenhead

And talk of sport and makes of cars
In various bogus-Tudor bars
And daren't look up and see the stars
But belch instead.

In labour-saving homes, with care
Their wives frizz out peroxide hair
And dry it in synthetic air
And paint their nails.

Come, friendly bombs and fall on Slough
To get it ready for the plough.
The cabbages are coming now;
The earth exhales.

威廉·燕卜荪（William Empson，1906—1984）

仿奥登（节选）

等末日来临，哥们儿，等末日来临。
有什么，什么能做？
我成什么你成什么？
我们善吗，我们真吗？
两两相坐，哥们儿，等末日来临。

我要筑塔，哥们儿，知道它分分
秒秒就崩塌，哥们儿，等末日来临？
我要掐花，哥们儿，留着，送人？
全都腐化，哥们儿，等末日来临。

我要发报，哥们儿，哪儿有通讯？
都火烧火燎，哥们儿，等末日来临。
我要传宗，哥们儿，我要挑好人？
油脂火烤，哥们儿，等末日来临。

我要澄清，哥们儿，要都挑明，
他们不听，哥们儿，等末日来临。
知道很近，哥们儿，假惺惺
脊骨冒凉风，哥们儿，等末日来临。

我们要通讯，哥们儿，字字写真，
觉着我们通音，哥们儿，等末日来临。
用巴别塔[①]，哥们儿？基督不会攀岩，

① 巴别塔（Tower of Babel）：根据《创世纪》，巴比伦人想通过建造一座强大的城市和一座“尖顶直达天堂”的塔扬名。上帝使工人的语言无法相互理解，从而打断施工。

他藏在牛栏，哥们儿，等末日来临。

我们要吹泡，哥们儿，膨胀得耀人，
与麻烦藏猫，哥们儿，等末日来临？
瓦砾上码高，哥们儿，自然要详审，
错上错难逃，哥们儿，等末日来临。

我们编故事，哥们儿，诸事定修新，
牛皮吹破时，哥们儿，等末日来临？
生于腐朽地，哥们儿，臭气直熏人，
僵而不死，哥们儿，等末日来临。

我们全疯狂，哥们儿，糟尽再当债务人，
向孩儿打谜诳，哥们儿，等末日来临？
一切都存档，哥们儿，历史潮流不认人，
孤岛陷汪洋，哥们儿，等末日来临。

等末日来临，哥们儿，等末日来临。
不可能含混，哥们儿，事总有人问。
想想那些小贩，哥们儿，想想前进，
等末日来临，哥们儿，等末日来临。

Just a Smack at Auden (Excerpt)

William Empson

Waiting for the end, boys, waiting for the end.
What is there to be or to do?
What's become of me or you?
Are we kind or are we true?
Sitting two and two, boys, waiting for the end.

Shall I build a tower, boys, knowing it will rend
Crack upon the hour, boys, waiting for the end?
Shall I pluck a flower, boys, shall I save or spend?
All turns sour, boys, waiting for the end.

Shall I send a wire, boys? Where is there to send?
All are under fire, boys, waiting for the end.
Shall I turn a sire, boys? Shall I choose a friend?
The fat is in the pyre, boys, waiting for the end.

Shall I make it clear, boys, for all to apprehend,
Those that will not hear, boys, waiting for the end,
Knowing it is near, boys, trying to pretend,
Sitting in cold fear, boys, waiting for the end?

Shall we send a cable, boys, accurately penned,
Knowing we are able, boys, waiting for the end,
Via the Tower of Babel, boys? Christ will not ascend,
He's hiding in his stable, boys, waiting for the end.

Shall we blow a bubble, boys, glittering to distend,
Hiding from our trouble, boys, waiting for the end?
When you build on rubble, boys, Nature will append
Double and re-double, boys, waiting for the end.

Shall we make a tale, boys, that things are sure to mend,
Playing bluff and hale, boys, waiting or the end?
It will be born stale, boys, stinking to offend,
Dying ere it fail, boys, waiting for the end.

Shall we go all wild, boys, waste and make them lend,

Playing at the child, boys, waiting for the end?
It has all been filed, boys, history has a trend,
Each of us enisled, boys, waiting for the end.

Waiting for the end, boys, waiting for the end.
Not a chance of blend, boys, things have got to tend.
Think of those who vend, boys, think of how we wend,
Waiting for the end, boys, waiting for the end.

路易斯·麦克尼斯（Louis MacNeice，1907—1963）

雪

弧窗飘雪，
与静静的玫瑰粉白相映，
房间顿时充盈，
世界突变，超出想象。

世界奇妙有加，永远多元，
我剥橘子分瓣，
就在吐籽的瞬间，
迷醉于万物的多彩。

火烧水冒泡儿，人间烟火
可鄙可乐，非你所想——
舌尖，眼帘，耳边，掌上——
雪与玫瑰间远不只玻璃。

Snow

Louis MacNeice

The room was suddenly rich and the great bay-window was
Spawning snow and pink roses against it
Soundlessly collateral and incompatible:
World is suddener than we fancy it.

World is crazier and more of it than we think,
Incorrigibly plural. I peel and portion
A tangerine and spit the pips and feel
The drunkenness of things being various.

And the fire flames with a bubbling sound for world
Is more spiteful and gay than one supposes—
On the tongue on the eyes on the ears in the palms of one's hands—
There is more than glass between the snow and the huge roses.

威斯坦·休·奥登（Wystan Hugh Auden，1907—1993）

街头向晚

译一

晚上我出门散步。
布里斯托大街两旁，
熙熙攘攘人头攒动，
像麦穗簇拥甬道上。

往前走是盈盈河水，
我听见有人在歌唱。

歌声来自拱桥下边，
唱着“此爱悠长。

爱你，亲爱的，我爱你，
直到非洲连接中国，
直到海水跃上高山，
直到鱼在街上放歌。

我爱你，亲爱的，直到
大海能折挂能晒干，
北斗星可以嘎嘎叫，
就像鸭子漫天游浣。

时光会像兔子奔跑，
因为我自己的臂弯
抱有这岁月的花朵，
抱有这世上的初恋。”

可是啊，城里的时钟
都叮当叮当地作响：
“唉，可别让时间骗了，
你永远无法战胜时光。

正义与公道裸露
在梦魇的千沟万壑，
时间在暗地里观瞧，
你接吻时它便干咳。

在头疼与焦虑中
生命暗暗崩漏衰减，
时间则心想事成，

不管今天还是明天。

暴雪阴森，飘荡进
一道道青山绿谷；
时间打断那舞步，
打断潜水者划弧。

噢，伸出你的手，
将手腕在水中淹没，
然后，盯着水盆，
想想错过了什么。

冰川在橱柜中敲打，
沙漠在床上叹息，
茶杯张开一条裂缝，
通往死者亡灵之地。

那里乞丐抽中钞票，
杰克则对巨人着迷，
白人男孩儿得哮喘，
吉尔仰面朝天倒地。

看啊，照着镜子看，
看看你的不幸；
生活的福佑依旧，
尽管你啥也不灵。

噢，请你站在窗前，
此时你已潸然泪下；
你要用你扭曲的心，
去爱你扭曲的邻家。”

天渐晚，夜色沉沉，
恋人们都已经离去；
钟声也已经停止，
只有河水深流不息。

译二

街头向晚（节译，用桂枝香词牌）

街头向晚。似麦簇田间，路边人满。桥下盈盈河水，恋歌流转。爱结秦晋何时散，水飞山，街鱼搁浅。海堪折挂，嘎嘎北斗，漫天游浣。

念往惜，奇葩阆苑，却兔走流年，吻香咳断。梦魇还昭公理，日窥幽遣。愁肠暗度成迷幻，绿葱茏，雪花飞卷。冻川橱内，床嗟沙漠，裂壶冥返。

As I Walked out One Evening

Wystan Hugh Auden

As I walked out one evening
Walking down Bristol Street,
The crowds upon the pavement
Were fields of harvest wheat.

And down by the brimming river
I heard a lover sing
Under an arch of the railway:
"Love has no ending.

I'll love you, dear, I'll love you
Till China and Africa meet,

And the river jumps over the mountain
And the salmon sing in the street,

I'll love you till the ocean
Is folded and hung up to dry
And the seven stars go squawking
Like geese about the sky.

The years shall run like rabbits,
For in my arms I hold
The Flower of the Ages,
And the first love of the world."

But all the clocks in the city
Began to whirr and chime:
"O let not Time deceive you,
You cannot conquer Time.

In the burrows of the Nightmare
Where Justice naked is,
Time watches from the shadow
And coughs when you would kiss.

In headaches and in worry
Vaguely life leaks away,
And Time will have his fancy
To-morrow or to-day.

Into many a green valley
Drifts the appalling snow;
Time breaks the threaded dances

And the diver's brilliant bow.

O plunge your hands in water,
Plunge them in up to the wrist;
Stare, stare in the basin
And wonder what you've missed.

The glacier knocks in the cupboard,
The desert sighs in the bed,
And the crack in the tea-cup opens
A lane to the land of the dead.

Where the beggars raffle the banknotes
And the Giant is enchanting to Jack,
And the Lily-white Boy is a Roarer,
And Jill goes down on her back.

O look, look in the mirror,
O look in your distress;
Life remains a blessing
Although you cannot bless.

O stand, stand at the window
As the tears scald and start;
You shall love your crooked neighbour
With your crooked heart."

It was late, late in the evening,
The lovers they were gone;
The clocks had ceased their chiming,
And the deep river ran on.

月亮美人

月亮美人，
史无写真，
初始混沌。
如果后来
备美华彩，
许是因了爱
才另有投胎。

另一时空，
像一场梦；
白天一到，
它就遁逃。
光阴移步，
心不如初。
鬼使神差
难寻去来。

然而，从不是
鬼神驱使，
即便鬼神安歇，
也不会完结，
直至成为过去。
这旦的爱意
不近甜蜜，
这旦的愁容
却有始终。

英国

诗歌选译

This Lunar Beauty

Wystan Hugh Auden

This lunar beauty
Has no history
Is complete and early,
If beauty later
Bear any feature
It had a lover
And is another.

This like a dream
Keeps other time
And daytime is
The loss of this,
For time is inches
And the heart's changes
Where ghost has haunted
Lost and wanted.

But this was never
A ghost's endeavor
Nor finished this,
Was ghost at ease,
And till it pass
Love shall not near
The sweetness here
Nor sorrow take
His endless look.

特工

他发现，扼住咽喉要道，
是通向此地的关键，可谁去？
他，老练的特务，都掉陷阱，
被假向导的惯用伎俩算计。

格林壑[①]是建路障的好地方，
也容易开火，要是火车站
更近些就好了。但他们忽视了
他的发报，说桥断了，麻烦。

荒漠里守了几个星期，
此时街曲都显得温雅。
黑暗中流水把他唤醒，
他常常责骂梦中的伙伴。
当然，他们会一起射击，
也会轻易地不合而离。

The Secret Agent

Wystan Hugh Auden

Control of the passes was, he saw, the key
To this new district, but who would get it?
He, the trained spy, had walked into the trap
For a bogus guide, seduced by the old tricks.
At Greenhearth was a fine site for a dam
And easy power, had they pushed the rail
Some stations nearer. They ignored his wires:

① 格林壑（Greenhearth）：音译。

The bridges were unbuilt and trouble coming.
The street music seemed gracious now to one
For weeks up in the desert. Woken by water
Running away in the dark, he often had
Reproached the night for a companion
Dreamed of already. They would shoot, of course,
Parting easily two that were never joined.

船长与水手长之歌

乔家邋遢，迪克脏，
我们照样灌黄汤，
酒后大家楼上走，
马格丽凯特配成双。
一双双像猫与鼠，
流浪汉也有房子宿。
米格阔，亲水手，
马力安眼睛像牛犊，
张开双臂拉上楼，
我偏不往里边走。
我才不要进牢笼，
不要里边度残生。
我们母亲的园子，
有夜莺正在哭泣，
我们伤透的心，
早就在伤别人。
泪珠圆，大海深。
珠子滚落好安寝。

Song of the Master and Boatswain

Wystan Hugh Auden

At Dirty Dick's and Sloppy Joe's
We drank our liquor straight,
Some went upstairs with Margery,
And some, alas, with Kate;
And two by two like cat and mouse
The homeless played at keeping house.
There Wealthy Meg, the Sailor's Friend,
And Marion, cow-eyed,
Opened their arms to me but I
Refused to step inside;
I was not looking for a cage
In which to mope my old age.
The nightingales are sobbing in
The orchards of our mothers,
And hearts that we broke long ago
Have long been breaking others;
Tears are round, the sea is deep:
Roll them overboard and sleep.

多爱一点

译一[1]

举目繁星，我深知，
它们才不管我活我死。
但究竟冷漠最不值得惊恐，
无论是人还是畜生。

① 题意 星星无情，还要去爱，爱得无以言表，爱得清高凄凉，直到地老天荒。

万一星星激情燃火，
我无以回报又当奈何？
如果情感无平等而言，
就让我多爱一点。

我自以为爱慕星星，
莫我肯顾的星星。
此时，它们就在眼前，
我道不出整日的思念。

倘若星星泯灭无踪，
我会学着仰望天空，
体会它的幽暗庄严，
纵使这需要些时间。

译二[①]
举目繁星，我深知，
我死了它们都无所谓，
但究竟冷漠最不值吃惊，
无论是人还是畜生。

万一星星激情似火，
无以回报又当如何？
如果感情无平等而言，
就让我多爱一点。

自以为爱慕星星，
星星却无动于衷。

① 题意：不怕人无情，只怕己不爱。爱不只在逻辑，不只在嘴皮，更来不得半点儿虚诳与犹豫。否则，只能学着面对失去后的虚无黑暗。

此时，它们都在眼前，
总不能说白天有多眷恋。

倘若星星全部泯灭，
我只合学着仰望空空如也，
感悟它的幽暗庄严，
纵使这也需要些时间。

译三[①]
举目繁星，我深知，
博它们眷顾我愿赴死，
却最不怕世间无情，
不管是人还是畜生。

万一星星激情燃烧，
无以回报怎么得了？
如果情感无平等而言，
就让我多爱一点。

我自以为爱慕星星，
莫我肯顾的星星。
此时，与它们相见，
道不出整日的思念。

倘若星星泯灭无踪，
我会学着仰望天空，
体味它的幽暗庄严，
纵使这需要些时间。

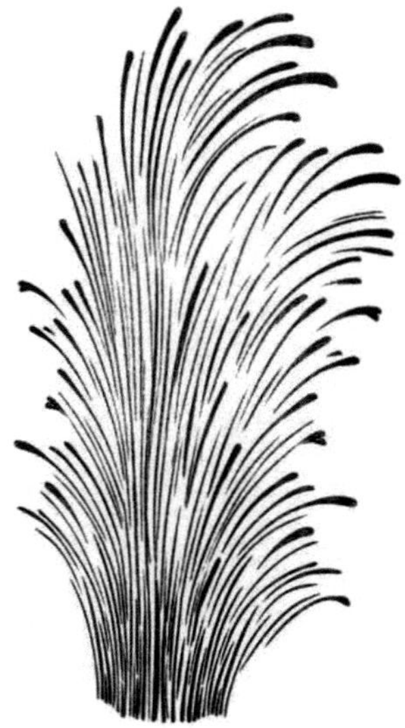

① 题意：生为凡俗，枉求于天。天不眷顾，爱也孤独。莫说崇高，苍凉凄苦。

The More Loving One

Wystan Hugh Auden

Looking up at the stars, I know quite well
That, for all they care, I can go to hell,
But on earth indifference is the least
We have to dread from man or beast.

How should we like it were stars to burn
With a passion for us we could not return?
If equal affection cannot be,
Let the more loving one be me.

Admirer as I think I am
Of stars that do not give a damn,
I cannot, now I see them, say
I missed one terribly all day.

Were all stars to disappear or die,
I should learn to look at an empty sky
And feel its total dark sublime,
Though this might take me a little time.

凯瑟琳·雷恩（Kathleen Raine，1908—2003）

世界的尽头

什么都没改变，
河流、机车、电车，都没改道，
房顶、烟囱，依旧，

但世界已结束。

街灯从树林里发出绿光，
湿漉漉的人行道上一汪黄，
一片绿，一汪黄，悄无声息，

因时间凝固。

浓雨中的一片叶子，
笼罩着自然的各种交织，
小径幽幽，明晰，

探索结束。

群星中的一颗，
在尘世栖爱的屋顶，
坚定地站到黎明，

距离已无。

微尘中的一粒，
在街灯光线下进入视野，
被看到，感知到，称为
独特的一个。

因聚众结束。

梦想之屋曾经迷失，
如今，大门向街道打开，
我们回家了，

伟大的世界结束。

The End of the World

Kathleen Raine

Nothing is changed,
Not the river's course, the dynamos' or the trams',
The chimneys and the housetops are as always

But the world is ended.

Green radiance of a streetlamp in the trees
And pool of yellow light on the wet pavement
Shines quietly upon here and now

For time is ended.

The single leaf among the myriad leaves
Veiled with all nature's intersecting ways,
The little labyrinth, is traced, is plain

The quest is ended.

The single star among the myriad stars
Stands steadfast at the end of night
Over love's earthly house

Distance is ended.

The single grain of infinitesimal dust,
The mote in the lamplight enters the field of vision,

Is seen, is recognized, is known
As the unique one

For multitude is ended,

And the door into the lost home of our dreams
Opens from the street,
We have come home,
And the great world is ended.

约翰·普德尼（John Pudney，1909—1977）

继承人

我们轮流
在二厂汽笛的间歇小睡；
或者利用这段时间
打量并记录
悲伤、恐惧、罪行，
咧嘴笑那遗留，
传统老套
统统死在村子里。

继承
威风扫地的国家，
我们斜着嘴巴，
侧着身子跟人说话，
好像怕训练有素的枪弹
从远处飞来；
说不好谁是靶子，

不敢冒险。

Heirs

John Pudney

Allotted hours
We slept between factory hooters;
Or used our time
Admiring, making notes
Of scores and scares and crimes,
Grinning at vestiges
Of customs and old tunes
That died in villages.

Inheritors
Of that dishonored country,
We sloped our mouths,
Spoke slantwise man to man,
As if we feared guns trained
Across great distances;
Uncertain where they aimed,
Taking no chances.

休·赛克斯·戴维斯（Hugh Sykes Davies，1909—1984）

空房里的音乐

房子是空的
　　房子里的人

离开了好几个月

将房子留给象鼻虫
慢吞吞的虫子
木鼹鼠轻轻打洞
耗子聚群开会

脚步溜过
潮湿的墙根
顺着
长长的
走廊

慢慢地
警觉地拖着脚步
走在光秃的木板上
咬破的
挂毯
爬着
很多
蛾子

在一个挂窗帘的房间
停下脚步
躲避盖着白单的椅子

晃动包裹大钢琴的
布单
阵阵窸窣
磨尖腐败变黄的
牙齿

咬碎的
　　挂毯
　　爬着
　　很多
　　蛾子

在老鼠的齿缘
　　举指
　　犹豫

落下
　随着房客
　　锈琴弦的
　　　模糊和音
奏出死寂的曲子

最强音撕碎
　　不成样的挂毯
　　撼动附近
　　粘着的许多
　　蛛网蛾子

Music in an Empty House

Hugh Sykes Davies

The house was empty and
　　The people of the house
　　Gone many months

Months for the weevil

For the patient worm
Timber-mole softly tunnelling
For the parliament of rats

Footsteps slink past
Damp walls
Down
Long
Corridors

Slow feet
Warily scuff
Bare boards
The much-bitten
Tapestry
Holds
Many
Moths

In a certain curtain'd room
The halting steps evade
Chairs white shrouded

To twitch the winding-sheet
Around a grand piano
Thin phalanx of sound
Sharp rat's teeth edge yellow
With decay

The much-bitten
Tapestry

Holds
Many
Moths

On rat's teeth-edge
Fingers preparate
Hesitate

Then falling send
As tenantry
Darnp-muffied chords
Rusting strings
A still-born song

Their fortissimoThe tattered
Scarcetapestry
Stirsholds
Nearmany
Cobwebsmoths

斯蒂芬·斯彭德（Stephen Spender，1909—1995）

一只秒表和一张军用地图

一只秒表和一张军用地图。
凌晨五点一人倒地，
秒表飞出手腕，
像月亮射出地球，
划出空洞的时间，
盯着下边潮起潮落。

就在橄榄树下，
一只秒表和一张军用地图。
他把守的阵地，
一个战友中弹，
弹片炸裂身体，
与他划出一段
遥远孤独的距离。

就在橄榄树下，
一只秒表和一张军用地图。
凌晨五点的尸骨，
定格在无垠月色中；
犹有幸存者，
心中永远抹不去
被子弹炸裂的空间，
就在橄榄树下。

A Stopwatch and an Ordnance Map

Stephen Spender

A stopwatch and an ordnance map.
At five a man fell to the ground
And the watch flew off his wrist
Like a moon struck from the earth
Marking a blank time that stares
On the tides of change beneath.
All under the olive trees.
A stopwatch and an ordnance map.
He stayed faithfully in that place
From his living comrade split
By dividers of the bullet

Opening wide the distances
Of his final loneliness.

All under the olive trees.
A stopwatch and an ordnance map.
And the bones are fixed at five
Under the moon's timelessness;
But another who lives on
Wears within his heart forever
Space split open by the bullet.
All under the olive trees.

诺曼·亚历山大·麦凯格（Norman Alexander MacCaig，1910—1996）

好日子

阳光炫目的海面，树木止息，
凤尾草的气味深达五六尺
一动不动。我感觉颧骨上
有石楠粉在爬……寂寂然而无睡意。

一只白鹭收敛羽毛，
立在退潮的水里，我也如此，
感觉我的世界在退潮的水里搁置，
等待更幽暗更苦涩的卤水。

突然，崖面上飞出
鸽子和猎鹰——他们腾空，
消失在气流中。日子站着不动，

好像搏击蓝天的事从没发生。

伤到什么？不过虚假的
意象。没有什么可以违逆
聪明的鹭，璀璨的光，无声的桤木，
或者悄悄滑走的海水。

A Good Day

Norman Alexander MacCaig

Sun-stunned the water; trees hold their breath.
The bracken smell is six foot deep
And never stirs. I feel green crumbs of heather
Crawling on cheekbones … Stillness but not sleep.

A heron, folded round himself,
Stands in the ebb, as I in mine.
I feel my world beneath me, like his, shelving
To darker depths of dark and bitter brine.

Suddenly round the cliff face bolt
Pigeon and falcon–they tear the air
And are gone in it. And the day stands, without motion,
As though nothing had drawn that savage blue stroke there.

What has been wounded? Only false
Images. Nothing can betray
Wise heron, shattering light or breathless alder
Or water slipping soundlessly away.

约翰·贾曼（John Jarmain，1911—1944）

阿拉曼[1]

人们说，阿拉曼长花了；
没错，过去的雷区现在长花了。
大漠的空旷引来游客，
在曾经充满死亡与伤痛的地方，
会看到百合花开放——
花朵，与我们无缘。
它们为我们也为阿拉曼敲钟，
我们无法听到的钟声：
听到钟声的人又做何想？
牺牲、骄傲、凡此种种？
——不是战争的黑暗与伤害，
而是他们的希望，他们热诚的祈祷。
它会变成干巴巴的历史名胜，
那疯狂的沙漠之海！
就像特洛伊[2]或阿金科特[3]，它的声名
将化作我们额上的花环，我们所获，
最终不过光荣历史的一个斑点：
而牺牲的人将长眠神圣的战地。
我们不愿回忆，
沙漠翻波吞没拥挤的人群，
建筑斑驳，断壁颓垣，

---

① 阿拉曼（El Alamein）：埃及北部一城镇，位于地中海沿岸。在第二次世界大战的决定性战役中，伯纳德·蒙哥马利领导的英国军队于 1942 年 11 月在这里击败了埃尔温·隆美尔的德国军队。

② 特洛伊（Troy）：传说中的特洛伊战争遗址，约公元前 1200 年被希腊军队占领并摧毁。

③ 阿金科特（Agincourt）：法国北部一村庄。1415 年英格兰的亨利五世指挥长弓部队，在这里击败了规模更大的法国重甲骑士部队。

苍白的人们，满脸沙尘；
坦克、枪支、车辆，
黢黑冒烟的废墟，
是的，唯有我们懂得这片土地：
阿拉曼只属于我们，
属于混战沙场的十天。
来此的观光客不会懂得，
他们在生锈的地雷线旁
发现——花朵。

El Alamein

John Jarmain

There are flowers now, they say, at Alamein;
Yes, flowers in the minefields now.
So those that come to view that vacant scene,
Where death remains and agony has been
Will find the lilies grow—
Flowers, and nothing that we know.
So they rang the bells for us and Alamein,
Bells which we could not hear:
And to those that heard the bells what could it mean,
That name of loss and pride, El Alamein?
—Not the murk and harm of war,
But their hope, their own warm prayer.
It will become a staid historic name,
That crazy sea of sand!
Like Troy or Agincourt its single fame
Will be the garland for our brow, our claim,
On us a fleck of glory to the end:
And there our dead will keep their holy ground.

But this is not the place that we recall,
The crowded desert crossed with foaming tracks,
The one blotched building, lacking half a wall,
The grey-faced men, sand powdered over all;
The tanks, the guns, the trucks,
The black, dark-smoking wrecks.
So be it: none but us has known that land:
El Alamein will still be only ours
And those ten days of chaos in the sand.
Others will come who cannot understand,
Will halt beside the rusty minefield wires
And find there—flowers.

亨利·特里斯（Henry Treece，1911—1966）

林肯郡军用机场[①]

思乡的罗马人跨过道路，
地上的霜像乳白的尸衣；
潮湿的旷野上羊叫着死者，
不时的叫声，说不出的悲戚，
林肯郡为全世界煎熬。

罗马人若在这里感觉如何？
旷野，阴晨，泥泞，潮湿，
总是雨点嘀答，打湿万物，
锈了刀剑铠甲，湿透鞋子，

① 林肯郡军用机场（Lincolnshire Bomber Station）：1916 年英国战斗机攻击德国齐柏林飞艇的紧急降落机场，后于 1919 年关闭。1939 年至 1942 年间作为英国皇家空军迪格比（RAF Digby）的诱饵机场重新启用。

直湿到骨髓，湿到心里……

Lincolnshire Bomber Station

Henry Treece

Across the road the homesick Romans made
The ground-mist thickens to a milky shroud;
Through flat, damp fields call sheep, mourning their dead
In cracked and timeless voices, unutterably sad,
Suffering for all the world, in Lincolnshire.

And I wonder how the Romans liked it here;
Flat fields, no sun, the muddy misty dawn,
And always, above all, the mad rain dripping down,
Rusting sword and helmet, wetting the feet
And soaking to the bone, down to the very heart…

詹姆斯·芬德利·亨德利（James Findley Hendry，1912—1986）

拯救派

曾经款待公牛 英雄们身着缁衣
处死奢望绸缎的矿工
因为他们眼里黑炭掌控着动力
还是武装唱诗班更安全

曾经乞丐部队 禁忌与流亡的部队
以狗和孩童的耐心
饱受贫困的鞭笞与屠戮

给借来的望远镜和火药桶披上伪装

饲养员硬币射苍鹭
饥饿者画饼充饥
所谓自由就是吐沫
荣耀不过漂浮的羽毛一瞥即逝

功劳簿上论胜负
令墙上匕首哭泣怨愤
号角勋章战于泼墨的漆黑夜色
供狼添光骸骨

谁能锯断流水
谁能将卡车装满梦想
月亮是他们心爱好的面庞
他们因她嘴唇苍白走向战场

这场悲剧坚如磐石
难以切割移动
我不过用指甲盖儿撕扯
为那深埋的黎明

Rescue-Party

James Findley Henry

Once the bulls were feted and the heroes dressed in black
Lynched the miners in illusions of silk
For the coal in their eyes harnessed cycles of power
And it was safer to arm the choirs

Once the beggared armies armies in taboo and exile

Suffering the slow whip and butchery of poverty
With the patience of the dog and the child
Dying borrowed binoculars and powder-horns for eyes

Liberty they said is saliva in the mouth
Since the heron was shot by a keeper with a sixpence
And the hungry fed on a narcotic landscape
Where glory is the glimpse of drifting feathers

So assessment of defeat or victory in ledgers
Embitters the daggers of weeping on the wall
And the picking clean of their bones by wolves involves
Trumpet and star in war against an ignorant night of ink

Who can cut the river with a hacksaw
Who can load a lorry with their dreams
The moon was the face of the woman they loved
They went to war because of her drawn mouth

This tragedy is a block of stone
The cutters will never remove
I tear at it with only my fingernails
For dawn buried underground

罗伊·富勒（Roy Fuller，1912—1991）

中年

哈代，用他平易直白且老套的笔墨，
或可将我这平生的瞬间入诗。

头发落在理发围裙上，我随口一句，
　　头上有了白丝。
理发师说，如果不是金发，
　　　　白的更显多。

金发？我没对自己的金发用过心，
我过世的父亲是黑发，我妈妈
年轻时棕发，临死时头发灰白。
　　发色遗传应有其他。
不等深究过往，
　　　　我就发现传自何人。

——原来是我姥爷，他传来的
幽默、古怪、肤色。
我的内向则另有来由。
　　这样，人到中年的我，
在死者中挖掘
　　　　无心的安排。

哈代式的，我从理发师的明镜中，
看到的不是自己熟悉的脸，而是幽暗躯壳，
白发苍苍，汇聚了我所有祖先的元素特点；
　　觉得自己好像魂魄，
懊悔地，讽刺地，检阅
　　　　自己的一生。

The Middle Years

Roy Fuller

Hardy, with his plain, speaking style, old fashioned air,
Might have made verse of a moment of my life today:

Hair falling on the barber's sheet, my idle remark

    That I was turning grey

And the barber saying that the grey would show much more

        Were I not fair.

Fair: the word seemed incongruous; I had never thought

My brown fair, my late father being dark, my mother

Chestnut when young, although before she died quite grey.

    My hair came from some other.

It was a time before I reached the further past

        And found whom I sought.

—My mother's father, that dead civic humorous man

Whose eccentricity and color I inherit:

My introversion flows along another stem.

    Thus does the human ferret

Among the dead in his sad middle years to find

        The unmeaning plan.

And, Hardyesque, I saw in the barber's candid glass,

Instead of the face I know so well, a dim dead host,

Its composite ancestral features topped with grey;

    And felt myself a ghost

That watches regretfully, ironically, the living

        Procession pass.

乔治·巴克（George Barker，1913—1991）

一月蹦跳

一月蹦跳
在锅底，
温暖
冻僵的脚，
就像加拿大佬。

二月小跑
在盘盖下，
觉得藏得很好，
应该干燥，
可是仍旧下雨，
一个月没完没了。

三月坐浴缸，
拧开水龙头，
冷热不匀。
冬天走了么？
来如猛虎去如羊，
走啊，走啊，在路上。

四月到处溜，
有时屋里，
有时屋外头，
有时像躲避细雨
霏霏，藏在
空奶瓶里，
然后又冲出来。

五月无处藏，
藏不住；
像骄傲的孔雀
顺墙根走，
五月啊五月，
遍地花叶；
五月啊五月，
可爱的时节。

六月丢衬衫，
裤子脱河边，
年来初冷饮，
舔碗冰淇淋。
六月欢娱，
少男少女，
载歌载舞，
欢乐无咎。

七月海边，
坐玩沙滩，
满把沙子
滑指尖，慵懒
有时哀叹：
“我坐这里
年光已过半，
日子苦短！”

八月尊崇，
帝王御赐，
紫气金光，

如同名誉。
（我觉得又湿又凉
没什么出奇。）

九月影子里，
夏荫正消逝，
听，远处传来
冬的银号子，
还有秋鼓
近在咫尺。

十月，十月，
苹果树上摘，
山鹑在林里，
大风海上来。
街巷泥泞，
莓果鲜红，
树冠摇晃，
依旧曾经。

十一月天干物燥。
叶子飞落，
掠地悬空；
老树吟哦，
十一月，十一月，
名字像星座，
曾照万物
此刻已无多。

十二月最后，
不几周就临终。

我们听得到
鹿拉雪橇的银铃
从冻土传来，
跨过遥远的路途
给我们带来
圣诞节的礼物。

January Jumps About

George Barker

January jumps about
In the frying pan
Trying to heat
His frozen feet
Like a canadian.

February scuttles under
Any dish's lid
And she thinks she's dry because she's
Thoroughly well hid
But it still rains all month long
And it always did.

March sits in the bath tub
With the taps turned on.
Hot and cold, cold or not,
Has the Winter gone?
In like a lion, out like a lamb
March on, march on, march on.

April slips about

Sometimes indoors
And sometimes out
Sometimes sheltering from a little
Shower of bright rain
In an empty milk bottle
Then dashing out again.

May, she hides nowhere,
Nowhere at all,
Proud as a peacock
Walking by a wall.
The Maytime O the Maytime,
Full of leaf and flower.
The Maytime O the Maytime
Is the loveliest of all.

June discards his shirt and
Trousers by the stream
And takes the first dip of the year
Into a jug of cream.
June is the gay time
Of every girl and boy
Who run about and sing and shout
In pardonable joy.

July by the sea
Sits dabbling with sand
Letting it run out of
Her rather lazy hand,
And sometimes she sadly
Thinks: "as i sit here

Ah, more than half the year is gone,
The evanescent year."

August by an emperor
Was given his great name.
It is gold and purple
Like a Hall of Fame.
(I have known it rather cold
And wettish, all the same.)

September lies in shadows
Of the fading summer
Hearing, in the distance,
The silver horns of winter
And not very far off
The coming autumn drummer.

October, October
Apples on the tree,
The Partridge in the Wood and
The big winds at sea,
The mud beginning in the lane
The berries bright and red
And the big tree wildly
Tossing its old head.

November, when the fires
Love to burn, and leaves
Flit about and fill the air
Where the old tree grieves.
November, november

Its name is like a star
Glittering on many things that were
But few things that are.

Twelfth and last December.
A few weeks away
We hear the silver bells
Of the stag and the sleigh
Flying from the tundras
Far far away
Bringing to us all the gift
Of our Christmas Day.

罗纳德·斯图亚特·托马斯（Ronald Stuart Thomas，1913—2000）

姻缘

相遇时，
一阵燕语呢喃，
一晃五十载，
仿佛一瞬间：
坠红尘，
转流年。
正豆蔻年华，
我闭上眼吻她，
睁眼时已皱纹满脸。
死神说“来，”
他选她
做伴，

跳最后一支舞。
她的一生，
如鸟儿一样优雅，
此时她张开嘴，
跌落
一声叹息，
轻轻的像一片儿鸟羽。

A Marriage

Ronald Stuart Thomas

We met
Under a shower of bird-notes.
Fifty years passed,
Love's moment
In a world in
Servitude to time.
She was young;
I kissed with my eyes
Closed and opened
Them on her wrinkles.
"Come, " said death,
Choosing her as his
Partner for
The last dance. And she,
Who in life
Had done everything
With a bird's grace,
Opened her bill now
For the shedding
Of one sigh

No heavier than a feather.

秋日

并不总是这样，
没有风，最后几片
叶子，点缀着树的
肩膀，为枝条织上
金袖口；草坪汪水，

鸟儿梳理羽毛。日常
琐碎停一停，抬眼
观瞧，让大脑摄入
明亮的风景，存一张
严寒里暖心的照片。

A Day in Autumn

Ronald Stuart Thomas

It will not always be like this,
The air windless, a few last
Leaves adding their decoration
To the trees' shoulders, braiding the cuffs
Of the boughs with gold; a bird preening

In the lawn's mirror. Having looked up
From the day's chores, pause a minute,
Let the mind take its photograph
Of the bright scene, something to wear
Against the heart in the long cold.

狄兰·托马斯（Dylan Thomas，1914—1953）

不肯温顺地走进那夜幕

不肯温顺地走进那夜幕，
日之尽头暮年如此狂躁；
渴望，渴望把光明挽留。

智者临终自知黑暗无误，
只恨妙语未发惊雷之啸，
不肯温顺地走进那夜幕。

最后一浪退去，仁者悲愁，
脆弱的善行未在绿湾起舞，
渴望，渴望把光明挽留。

光阴飞跑狂人追日吟讴，
终究苦于他不如流光早，
不肯温顺地走进那夜幕。

庄严者死到临头都追求，
一双瞎眼像流星般闪亮，
不肯温顺地走进那夜幕。

父啊，在高高的悲伤之处，
请用热泪诅咒我，祝福我。
不肯温顺地走进那夜幕。
渴望，渴望把光明挽留。

Do Not Go Gentle into That Good Night

Dylan Thomas

Do not go gentle into that good night,
Old age should burn and rave at close of day;
Rage, rage against the dying of the light.

Though wise men at their end know dark is right,
Because their words had forked no lightning they
Do not go gentle into that good night.

Good men, the last wave by, crying how bright
Their frail deeds might have danced in a green bay,
Rage, rage against the dying of the light.

Wild men who caught and sang the sun in flight,
And learn, too late, they grieved it on its way,
Do not go gentle into that good night.

Grave men, near death, who see with blinding sight
Blind eyes could blaze like meteors and be gay,
Rage, rage against the dying of the light.

And you, my father,there on the sad height,
Curse, bless, me now with your fierce tears, I pray.
Do not go gentle into that good night.
Rage, rage against the dying of the light.

我欠墓穴中的同胞

墓穴中所有的同胞，

为区区遗产赴死的人，
我对你们所有的亏欠，
是幸存的骨头和一腔血，
像豆叶在残梗上颤抖；
我对你们所有的亏欠，
是这肉皮囊的承受，
父亲的慈爱令我揪心，
姐妹的泪水滴我额头，
兄弟的热血腌我伤口。

继承爱得灼热的血脉，
亡者灌以死的信息，
继承知无不言的感官，
唯它熟悉难忘的麻痒，
我像阳光围绕这遗产，
它的一天酒红和月亮
烛照我的艰辛。我是
卖笑的女人生的孩子，
是饱受瘟疫者的子嗣，
是垂死吻别之恋的孩子，
我从血液中诊出些疾病，
所有的爱都如鲠在喉。

我的目光在倒霉蛋身上，
扫视一个个死去的模样；
我日夜从坟地往外潜望，
打量着衣衫褴褛的地球；
我日日夜夜地游荡，穿戴
与入殓的尸衣一模一样，
我的遗产在殓单里挺尸，
看啊，我的心脏紧贴宝藏，

看啊，谷粒在倒伏的麦秸上，
我的遗产在殓单里挺尸。

All That I Owe the Fellows of the Grave

Dylan Thomas

All that I owe the fellows of the grave
And all the dead bequeathed from pale estates
Lies in the fortuned bone, the flask of blood,
Like senna stirs along the ravaged roots.
O all I owe is all the flesh inherits,
My fathers' loves that pull upon my nerves,
My sisters tears that sing upon my head
My brothers' blood that salts my open wounds

Heir to the scalding veins that hold love's drop,
My fallen filled, that had the hint of death,
Heir to the telling senses that alone
Acquaint the flesh with a remembered itch,
I round this heritage as rounds the sun
His winy sky, and , as the candles moon,
Cast light upon my weather. I am heir
To women who have twisted their last smile,
To children who were suckled on a plague,
To young adorers dying on a kiss.
All such disease I doctor in my blood,
And all such love's a shrub sown in the breath.

Then look, my eyes, upon this bonehead fortune
And browse upon the postures of the dead;
All night and day I eye the ragged globe

Through periscopes rightsighted from the grave;
All night and day I wander in these same
Wax clothes that wax upon the ageing ribs;
All night my fortune slumbers in its sheet.
Then look, my heart, upon the scarlet trove,
And look, my grain, upon the falling wheat;
All night my fortune slumbers in its sheet.

我的沉郁之术

我的沉郁之术
施展在寂静的夜里，
此时只有月光滔滔，
恋人们躺在床上，
怀抱所有的悲哀。
我在唱响的灯光里
匠心独运，不为理想
面包，不为象牙舞台
趾高气扬卖弄风骚；
我只图寻常的酬劳，
——那最隐秘的心声。

在那月光滔滔中，
我不会为高傲之辈
一页页泼我墨宝；
我不会为幽幽魍魉，
将圣诗或夜莺写来；
我只写恋人心怀
经年累月的煎熬，
他们不知赞美酬劳，
不懂我的沉郁之术。

In My Craft or Sullen Art

Dylan Thomas

In my craft or sullen art
Exercised in the still night
When only the moon rages
And the lovers lie abed
With all their griefs in their arms,
I labour by singing light
Not for ambition or bread
Or the strut and trade of charms
On the ivory stages
But for the common wages
Of their most secret heart.

Not for the proud man apart
From the raging moon I write
On these spindrift pages
Nor for the towering dead
With their nightingales and psalms
But for the lovers, their arms
Round the griefs of the ages,
Who pay no praise or wages
Nor heed my craft or art.

二十四年

二十四年使我眼含泪水。
（埋葬死者以免他们难入坟茔。）
我蹲在天然拱道里像个裁缝，
我借着食肉的阳光，

缝制一件上路的寿衣。
好好装裹，盛装赴死。
我的血脉里金钱流淌，
沿着最终通往小镇的方向，
朝永恒走去。

Twenty-Four Years

Dylan Thomas

Twenty-four years remind the tears of my eyes.
(Bury the dead for fear that they walk to the grave ln labour.)
In the groin of the natural doorway I crouched like a tailor
Sewing a shroud for a journey
By the light of the meat-eating sun.
Dressed to die, the sensual strut begun,
With my red veins full of money,
In the final direction of the elementary town
I advance for as long as forever is.

掰开的面包

掰开的面包原是燕麦，
这酒原是异乡藤条上
摘光的葡萄；
人在白天酒在晚，
放倒禾苗，搅了葡萄欢。

此时酒里有夏天的血，
混有青藤上葡萄的肉；
这面包里
有燕麦曾在风中娱悦；

人敲碎太阳，拉下风。

肉体掰开，鲜血流淌，
使得血脉里灌注荒凉。
燕麦和葡萄，
原是有根有脉的生灵；
你喝了我酒，掰了我面包。

This Bread I Break

Dylan Thomas

This bread I break was once the oat,
This wine upon a foreign tree
Plunged in its fruit;
Man in the day or wine at night
Laid the crops low, broke the grape's joy.

Once in this time wine the summer blood
Knocked in the flesh that decked the vine,
Once in this bread
The oat was merry in the wind;
Man broke the sun, pulled the wind down.

This flesh you break, this blood you let
Make desolation in the vein,
Were oat and grape
Born of the sensual root and sap;
My wine you drink, my bread you snap.

你的痛将是音乐

你的痛将是弦上音乐，
是舌头堵天堂之口。
你的痛将是
我一脉搏，
噢，因难产，
而被加快。

你的琴弦紧勒拇指，
灼热的血搓上弦头。
你的痛将是
血脉散乱，
噢，你我间
还未铺开。

你的痛将是嘴角示意，
是吃奶时的吸吮声。
你的痛将是
我奶水涨多，
噢，无人见，
自己吮不来。

你的痛将是断不了的奶，
是奶滴成血流的音乐。
你的痛将是
血肉包裹，
噢，已离散，
筋断骨开。

Your Pain Shall Be a Music

Dylan Thomas

Your pain shall be a music in your strings
And fill the mouths of heaven with your tongue
Your pain shall be
O my unborn
A vein of mine
Made fast by me.

Your string shall stretch a gully twixt the thumbs
Whose flaming blood shall rub it at the rims
Your pain shall be
O my unsown
A ragged vein
Twixt you and me

Your pain shall be a meaning in your lips
As milk shall be a music in the paps
Your pain shall be
O my unknown
A stream of mine
Not milked by me

Your pain shall not unmilk you of the food
That drops to make a music in your blood
Your pain shall be
O my undone
Flesh blood and bone
Surrounding me

月亮里的小丑

我的泪流无声，
像魔术玫瑰落英；
我的悲哀无凭，
像天开雪崩。

我想，只要我一碰，
地球就会破；
它如此凄美，
像梦的脆弱。

Clown in the Moon

Dylan Thomas

My tears are like the quiet drift
Of petals from some magic rose;
And all my grief flows from the rift
Of unremembered skies and snows.

I think, that if I touched the earth,
It would crumble;
It is so sad and beautiful,
So tremulously like a dream.

亨利·瑞德（Henry Reed，1914—1986）

战争课（节选）

献给阿兰·米歇尔

活着就是为了战斗，
我的战斗并非没有荣耀[1]。

一、认识部件

今天我们认部件。昨天
我们搞了日常卫生，明天早上
布置打靶后做什么。今天
今天我们认部件。山茶
像珊瑚一样闪耀在附近花园。
今天我们认部件。

这是下带环，这是
上带环，具体什么用，
给你们背带就知道。这是架枪环，
现在你们没有。枝条
在花园里宁静、优雅的姿态，
我们看不到。

这是保险，动拇指就开，
这会儿你们可别动手指；
不用试，很简单，
只要拇指稍稍用力。花朵

① 活着就是为了战斗，我的战斗并非没有荣耀（Vixi duellis nuper idoneus，Et militavi non sine gloria）：贺拉斯名言。

娇嫩无声，从没看见
谁动过手指。

看，这是枪栓，它的用途是
打开枪膛，看，
可以前后快速推动；
这动作叫拉栓。蜜蜂
来来回回骚扰花朵，
那叫散春。

这叫拉栓，非常容易，
只要拇指有一点点力气。
枪栓、枪膛、扳机、准星，都容易。
我们这儿还没有。蟠桃花儿
静静开放，蜜蜂来回地飞，
今天我们只认部件。

Lessons of the War (Excerpt)

Henry Reed

To Alan Mitchell

Vixi duellis nuper idoneus
Et militavi non sine gloria

I. Naming of Parts

Today we have naming of parts. Yesterday
We had daily cleaning. And tomorrow morning,
We shall have what to do after firing. But today,
Today we have naming of parts. Japonica

Glistens like coral in all of the neighbouring gardens,
And today we have naming of parts.

This is the lower sling swivel. And this
Is the upper sling swivel, whose use you will see,
When you are given your slings. And this is the piling swivel,
Which in your case you have not got. The branches
Hold in the gardens their silent, eloquent gestures,
Which in our case we have not got.

This is the safety-catch, which is always released
With an easy flick of the thumb. And please do not let me
See anyone using his finger. You can do it quite easy
If you have any strength in your thumb. The blossoms
Are fragile and motionless, never letting anyone see
Any of them using their finger.

And this you can see is the bolt. The purpose of this
Is to open the breech, as you see. We can slide it
Rapidly backwards and forwards; we call this
Easing the spring. And rapidly backwards and forwards
The early bees are assaulting and fumbling the flowers:
They call it easing the Spring.

They call it easing the Spring. It is perfectly easy
If you have any strength in your thumb; like the bolt,
And the breech, and the cocking piece, and the point of balance,
Which in our case we have not got; and the almond-blossom
Silent in all of the gardens and the bees going backwards and forwards,
For today we have naming of parts.

诺曼·尼科尔森（Norman Nicholson，1914—1987）

城墙

城墙走塌——
灰白的千足虫慢慢地
在石头上的马蹄印里
拱起松软的后背，
在沟槽里打洞，
或者把肩膀挤进
经年的鹅卵石——
大到滚不动的石头。
一些碎块儿
跌下高高的崖壁，
与城墙一起爬行。

一道干打垒的城墙，
两面墙靠在一起，
（坎伯兰和威斯特摩兰[①]的
摔跤冠军）
两侧生绿，凋敝，
中间填充瓦砾——
像两墙夹成的
石坝：
石板伸出两侧，
形成梯形台阶。

城墙缓慢行走，
一点点侵吞土地，

① 坎伯兰和威斯特摩兰（Cumberland-and-Westmorland）：英国相互接壤的两个郡。

一点点碎裂岩石，
它步履谨慎，
拱券隆起，
让石头与凹槽
咬合在一起。
当滑落的一边
侵蚀移动时，
城墙也在移动，
它总在移动。

人们慢慢筑起城墙，
一天挨一天
竖起的城墙，
却站不稳。
人们建了道会走的墙。

Wall

Norman Nicholson

The wall walks the fell—
Grey millipede on slow
Stone hooves;
Its slack back hollowed
At gulleys and grooves,
Or shouldering over
Old boulders
Too big to be rolled away.
Fallen fragments
Of the high crags
Crawl in the walk of the wall.

A dry-stone wall Is a wall and a wall,
Leaning together
(Cumberland-and-Westmorland
Champion wrestlers),
Greening and weathering,
Flank by flank,
With filling of rubble
Between the two—
A double-rank
Stone dyke:
Flags and through-
stones jutting out sideways,
Like the steps of a stile.

A wall walks slowly,
At each give of the ground,
Each creak of the rock's ribs,
It puts its foot gingerly,
Arches its hog-holes,
Lets cobble and knee-joint
Settle and grip.
As the slipping fellside
Erodes and drifts,
The wall shifts with it,
Is always on the move.

They built a wall slowly,
A day a week;
Built it to stand,
But not stand still.
They built a wall to walk.

阿兰·刘易斯（Alun Lewis，1915—1944）

整天下雨

整天下雨，沼泽边上的钟形帐篷里，
我们四脚朝天，像乡巴佬，无聊阴郁；
防潮布和毯子下面满地泥泞，
我们第一次从灰蒙蒙中苏醒：
原来逃不脱细雨的侵袭，
逃不脱呼啦啦吹着篷布的风，
湿漉漉的帐篷——拉绳一紧一松。
雨落一整天，水波雾气和梦幻
浸透荆豆石楠；橡子被西南
吹来的狂风抖出它的杯盏，
砸着帐篷，砸着仰天做梦的脸；
细流如蛛丝，轻得推不动橡子。
我们伸伸腰，解开绑腿，
抽支忍冬，补补脏袜子，
看看周报——我还看见只狐狸，
把它写进潦草的书信寄回家；
大家议论女孩儿议论炸罗马。

议论默默无闻的死者和鼓动杀人的
高调政客，还有成群结队的难民。

我们也谈论自己，或者至亲，
我们爱他们，爱了很多年，
或许明天还爱。但眼前
深陷黄昏，深陷细雨绵绵。

唯记忆最珍贵最意味深长：

看着一群儿童在周末钻进树林里，
摇落咋嘴儿的栗子带到校园游戏，
或者温顺的毛毛狗跟在我身旁，
深一脚浅一脚翻过乱石岗，
来到酒馆，那里，托马斯深思良久，
所谓生死美丑——直至子弹穿喉。

All Day It Has Rained

Alun Lewis

All day it has rained, and we on the edge of the moors
Have sprawled in our bell-tents, moody and dull as boors,
Groundsheets and blankets spread on the muddy ground
And from the first grey wakening we have found
No refuge from the skirmishing fine rain
And the wind that made the canvas heave and flap
And the taut wet guy-ropes ravel out and snap.
All day the rain has glided, wave and mist and dream,
Drenching the gorse and heather, a gossamer stream
Too light to stir the acorns that suddenly
Snatched from their cups by the wild south-westerly
Pattered against the tent and our upturned dreaming faces.
And we stretched out, unbuttoning our braces,
Smoking a Woodbine, darning dirty socks,
Reading the Sunday papers - I saw a fox
And mentioned it in the note I scribbled home; -
And we talked of girls and dropping bombs on Rome,

And thought of the quiet dead and the loud celebrities
Exhorting us to slaughter, and the herded refugees;

As of ourselves or those whom we
For years have loved, and will again
Tomorrow maybe love; but now it is the rain
Possesses us entirely, the twilight and the rain.

And I can remember nothing dearer or more to my heart
Than the children I watched in the woods on Saturday
Shaking down burning chestnuts for the schoolyard's merry play,
Or the shaggy patient dog who followed me
By Sheet and Steep and up the wooded scree
To the Shoulder o' Mutton where Edward Thomas brooded long
On death and beauty - till a bullet stopped his song.

附言：给格维诺

如果我走了，
亲爱的，不要说
“他已把我忘记”。
因为你留在
我梦侧的肋骨里欢歌，
从未离开过。
在虐人发狂的山谷，
饥饿与血腥同流合污，
死亡这猛兽抓不着，驯不服，
我们忍着内心的惊恐，
在你歌唱的群星闪烁中，
浪得镇定之名。

Postscript: for Gweno

Alun Lewis

If I should go away,
Beloved, do not say
"He has forgotten me".
For you abide,
A singing rib within my dreaming side;
You always stay.
And in the mad tormented valley
Where blood and hunger rally
And Death the wild beast is uncaught, untamed,
Our soul withstands the terror
And has its quiet honour
Among the glittering stars your voices named.

大卫·盖斯科因（David Gascoyne，1916—2001）

笼子

不眠之夜
森林停止生长
贝壳倾听
池塘中的阴影暗淡
珍珠隐没影子里
我回到你的怀中

你的脸映在钟面
我的手在你头发下边
如果你说该放鸟儿了

如果鸟儿飞向森林
时间便离我们而去

留下做摆设的鸟笼
满满一杯水
书的序言
时钟嘀答作响
黑暗的屋子都在移动
空气的神经裸露

一旦放飞
插翅的时间便不会折返
我也就已经离开

The Cage

David Gascoyne

In the waking night
The forests have stopped growing
The shells are listening
The shadows in the pools turn grey
The pearls dissolve in the shadow
And I return to you

Your face is marked upon the clockface,
My hands are beneath your hair
And if the time you mark sets free the birds
And if they fly away towards the forest
The hour will no longer be ours

Ours is the ornate birdcage

The brimming cup of water
The preface to the book
And all the clocks are ticking
All the dark rooms are moving
All the air's nerves are bare.

Once flown
The feathered hour will not return
And I shall have gone away.

雪落欧洲

欧洲人从沉睡中醒来，
编织梦想：绥靖，奇迹，闪光的
金色时代；但无法阻止
昨晚垂下来一股力量，
将他们的大陆变成空白。

安静，洁白如一的雪花说，
现在，乌拉尔河和汝拉山
重新与荒远的北极相连。
平原，高山，乡村，城市，
都连成一片，一个容颜，
边界轮廓完全无法分辨。

战旗黯然失色地挂一会儿，
借子夜的冰点假意休战，
枪声与呼喊也全都消停。
然而，待到解冻的时候，
雪水多么红，战鼓多么震耳欲聋！

Snow in Europe

David Gascoyne

Out of their slumber Europeans spun
Dense dreams: appeasements, miracle, glimpsed flash
Of a new golden era; but could not restrain
The vertical white weight that fell last night
And made their continent a blank.

Hush, says the sameness of the snow
The Ural and Jura now rejoin
The furthest Arctic's desolation. All is one;
Sheer monotone: plain, mountain; country, town:
Contours and boundaries no longer show.

The warring flags hang colourless a while;
Now midnight's icy zero feigns a truce
Between the signs and seasons, and fades out
All shots and cries. But when the great thaw comes,
How red shall be the melting snow, how loud the drums!

威廉·悉尼·格雷厄姆（William Sydney Graham，1918—1986）

片纸难言

今早我随时可以
听你用新的语言倾诉。
我几乎找到一种方法，
写下我认为你说的话。

我不能理解的惊人之语
你阐释得非常清楚。

我站在自己的语汇里，
透过细雨的窗口望去，
想把自然发生的事情，
译成欢乐之外的东西。
四月成群的沙锥飞起，
给孤独带去轻盈的讯息。

今早我随时可以听你
倾诉。早春的阵雨
浸透窗户玻璃。我站在
自己的语汇里张望，
看到你的倾诉的脸庞
飞在云端想说些什么。

A Note to the Difficult One

William Sydney Graham

This morning I am ready if you are,
To hear you speaking in your new language.
I think I am beginning to have nearly
A way of writing down what it is I think
You say. You enunciate very clearly
Terrible words always just beyond me.

I stand in my vocabulary looking out
Through my window of fine water ready
To translate natural occurrences
Into something beyond any idea

Of pleasure. The wisps of April fly
With light messages to the lonely.

This morning I am ready if you are
To speak. The early quick rains
Of Spring are drenching the window-glass.
Here in my words looking out
I see your face speaking flying
In a cloud wanting to say something.

丹尼斯·约瑟夫·恩莱特（Dennis Joseph Enright，1920—2002）

叛逆者

每个人都留短发，
叛逆者让头发长长。
每个人都留长发，
叛逆者把头发剪短。
每个人都在课堂上说话，
叛逆者一言不发。
课堂上没人说话时，
叛逆者一言不发。
课堂上没人说话，
叛逆者制造骚乱。
每个人都穿制服，
叛逆者奇异的装束。
每个人都奇装异服，
叛逆者穿得朴素。
伙伴们都爱狗，

叛逆者喜欢猫。
伙伴们都爱猫，
叛逆者说狗好。
每个人都赞美太阳，
叛逆者说得来点雨。
每个人都喜迎降雨，
叛逆懊恼没太阳。
每个人都出去聚会，
叛逆者窝家里看书。
每个人都说：好，请！
叛逆者说：不，谢谢！
每个人都说：不，谢谢！
叛逆者说：好，请！
我们有叛逆者真好，
但叛逆者不见得好做。

The Rebel

Dennis Joseph Enright

When everybody has short hair,
The rebel lets his hair grow long.
When everybody has long hair,
The rebel cuts his hair short.
When everybody talks during the lesson,
The rebel does' n say a word.
When nobody talks during the lesson
The rebel does' n say a word.
When nobody talks during the lesson ,
The rebel creates a disturbance.
When everybody wears a uniform ,
The rebel dresses in fantastic clothes.

When everybody wears fantastic clothes
The rebel dresses soberly.
In the company of dog lovers ,
The rebel expresses a preference for cats.
In the company of cat lovers ,
The rebel puts in a good word for dogs.
When everybody is praising the sun ,
The rebel remarks on the need for rain.
When everybody is greeting the rain ,
The rebel regrets the absence of sun.
When everybody goes to the meeting
The rebel stays at home and reads a book.
When everybody stays at home and reads a book,
The rebel goes to the meeting.
When everybody says , yes please!
The rebel says , No thank you.
When everybody says: No thank you,
The rebel says , yes please!
It is very good that we have rebels
You may not find it very good to be one.

基思·道格拉斯（Keith Douglas，1920—1944）

点射

孩童抛着球长大，
我站在抛物线下，
久久地凝望空中。
那球落入我手里，
在紧握的拳头里发声：

张开手，张开手，
看一件杀人的礼物。

此时，我的瞄准镜里，
出现奄奄一息的战士。
他每一笑，每一动，
姿势习惯，他母亲懂。
十字线已在他脸上，我喊：
射击！死神心领神会，

看，它把血肉之躯
化作尘土。巫术
灵验。诅咒中，我竟
看见爱的中心扩散，
爱的暖流走向空虚。
将人变鬼多么容易。

失重的蚊子触到
墓碑上她弱小的影子，
那么轻，轻得无限。
人与影子相遇，
融合。轻如蚊子的死亡降临，
一个影子就是一个人。

How to Kill

Keith Douglas

Under the parabola of a ball,
A child turning into a man,
I looked into the air too long.
The ball fell in my hand, it sang

In the closed fist: Open Open
Behold a gift designed to kill.

Now in my dial of glass appears
The soldier who is going to die.
He smiles, and moves about in ways
His mother knows, habits of his.
The wires touch his face: I cry
NOW. Death, like a familiar, hears

And look, has made a man of dust
Of a man of flesh. This sorcery
I do. Being damned, I am amused
To see the centre of love diffused
And the wave of love travel into vacancy.
How easy it is to make a ghost.

The weightless mosquito touches
Her tiny shadow on the stone,
And with how like, how infinite
A lightness, man and shadow meet.
They fuse. A shadow is a man
When the mosquito death approaches

蒂莫西·科塞利斯（Timothy Corsellis，1921—1941）

新闻短片：登船

你们去哪里？欢笑的人们？
这是要度假出海？

可爱的大笑或微笑的人们，
为什么不等我来？

我多么爱你们啊，可爱的同胞，
你们微笑着奔赴战场，
你们怎能这样，可爱的同胞，
你们忘记了历史之殇？

笑啊，笑啊，子弟兵
说笑在参战的路上，
你们的母亲不会笑对枪声，
不会笑对肮脏的创伤。

说说笑笑的年轻水手，
不管李四王五，
回来时都笑不出口，
光荣更是乌有。

News Reel of Embarkation

Timothy Corsellis

Where are you going to, laughing men?
For a holiday on the sea?
Laughing, smiling, wonderful men,
Why won't you wait for me?

God, how I love you, men of my race,
As you smile on your way to a war;
How can you do it, wonderful face
Do you not know what's before?

Laugh, laugh, you soldier sons
Joke on your way to the war
For your mothers won't laugh at the sound of the guns
And the tales of the filth and the gore.

Smile and joke young sailor Jack
For it's the self-same story:
There'll be no jokes when you come back
And bloody little glory.

悉尼·凯斯（Sidney Keyes，1921—1943）

战时诗人

我寻找和平，发现
眼里长了刺。
我摸索词句，发现
一只箭在手。
我是建筑工，发现
结实的墙内是流沙。
当我变得恶心疯狂时，
不要嘲笑，不要扼制；
当我伸手抓风时，
不要阻止。
虽然我的脸是烧焦的书，
是荒废的镇子。

War poet

Sidney Keyes

I am the man who looked for peace and found
My own eyes barbed.
I am the man who groped for words and found
An arrow in my hand.
I am the builder whose firm walls surround
A slipping land.
When I grow sick or mad
Mock me not nor chain me;
When I reach for the wind
Cast me not down
Though my face is a burnt book
And a wasted town.

金斯利·艾米斯（Kingsley Amis，1922—1985）

火荒

寒冬的晚上
生不起火来。
全家围着炉子，
阴暗的炉膛内，
浸雨的木柴嘶嘶响，
冒着水泡和蒸汽。
大家各自回屋，
上了冰冷的床，
我也准备起身，
这时，木柴着了，

玫瑰红紫罗兰的火苗
清清亮亮烧着炉子。

孩子们都长大了，
房子，也变了样，
一年四季随时取暖，
为何记忆抓得这么牢？

Wasted

Kingsley Amis

That cold winter evening
The fire would not draw,
And the whole family hung
Over the dismal grate
Where rain-soaked logs
Bubbled, hissed and steamed.
Then, when the others had gone
Up to their chilly beds,
And I was ready to go,
The wood began to flame
In clear rose and violet,
Heating the small hearth.

Why should that memory cling
Now the children are all grown up,
And the house—a different house -
Is warm at any season?

菲利普·拉金（Philip Larkin，1922—1985）

床上聊

床上聊最容易，
同床共枕皆私语，
共现俩人诚意。

日月暗推移，
外面风未息，
云聚云散把天迷。

乌城压天际，
不管我和你，有谁知
咫尺天涯的距离。

哪里去寻觅
真实且善良的言语，
或者不是相反也可以。

Talking in Bed

Philip Larkin

Talking in bed ought to be easiest
Lying together there goes back so far
An emblem of two people being honest.

Yet more and more time passes silently.
Outside the wind's incomplete unrest
Builds and disperses clouds about the sky.

And dark towns heap up on the horizon.
None of this cares for us. Nothing shows why
At this unique distance from isolation

It becomes still more difficult to find
Words at once true and kind
Or not untrue and not unkind.

我已经可以料定

我已经可以料定
“四分之一世纪”
或“三十年中”
我自己的生活。

让我窒息的生活，
起起伏伏
翻着巨大的筋斗
跌下虚空。

接下来的只不过
死法（包括自己的）
死的次序及方式
有待言说。

I Have Started to Say

Philip Larkin

I have started to say
“A quarter of a century”
Or “thirty years back”

About my own life.

It makes me breathless
It's like falling and recovering
In huge gesturing loops
Through an empty sky.

All that's left to happen
Is some deaths(my own included).
Their order, and their manner,
Remain to be learnt.

爱，此时我们得分手

爱，此时我们得分手，
莫等它化成灾难痛苦。
曾经太多的月光哀愁，
如今有太阳中天信步，
心从未如此渴望自由。
来个了断吧，让我们
踢翻世界，抽打丛林，
你我不再将它们拥有；
我们是谷壳看谷粒新用。

有遗憾，遗憾总难免。
但生活得以解放更好。
像两只大船，浸月临风，
激流汇合处分道扬镳，
随浪奔浪涌以至无踪。

Love, We Must Part Now

Philip Larkin

Love, we must part now: do not let it be
Calamitous and bitter. In the past
There has been too much moonlight and self-pity:
Let us have done with it: for now at last
Never has sun more boldly paced the sky,
Never were hearts more eager to be free,
To kick down worlds, lash forests; you and I
No longer hold them; we are husks, that see
The grain going forward to a different use.

There is regret. Always, there is regret.
But it is better that our lives unloose,
As two tall ships, wind-mastered, wet with light,
Break from an estuary with their courses set,
And waving part, and waving drop from sight.

癞蛤蟆

为啥让癞蛤蟆
　在生活里蹲坑？
何不用心编叉，
　赶走这畜生？

一礼拜有六天，
　它都在倒粪。
就为几个钱！
　真真腻歪人。

很多人靠钻营：
　讨座的，鼓舌的，
烂泥扶不上墙的，
　他们都有日子过。

很多人守规矩，
　他们桶里生火，
吃着罐头和落果，
　似乎也还不错。

他们的孩子光脚，
　更别提他们的老婆，
皮包骨头像猎狗，
　可没一个挨饿。

噢，但愿我敢大喊，
　去他妈的那几个钱！
可我知道每一天，
　念想就那么一点点。

像癞蛤蟆的东西，
　在我心头蹲坑。
屁股沉得像霉运，
　雪一样冰冷。

从不许我苟安，
　声名、财气、女人，
都与我无缘，
　只因它提不起臀。

我并不是讲肉身

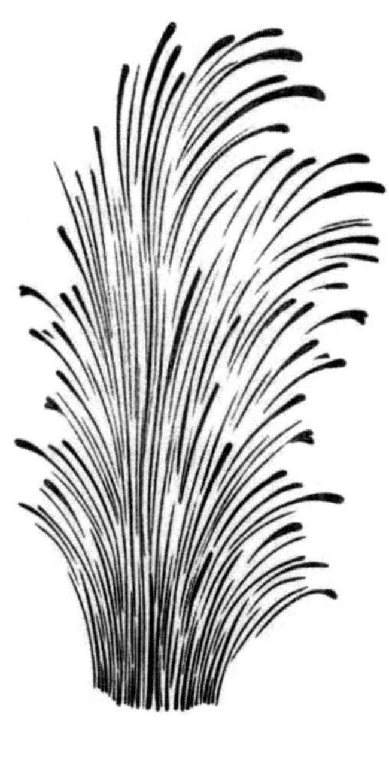

　体现的精神；
我是说二者都难丢，
　因为人有皮有心。

Toads

Philip Larkin

Why should I let the toad work
　Squat on my life?
Can't I use my wit as a pitchfork
　And drive the brute off?

Six days of the week it soils
　With its sickening poison—
Just for paying a few bills!
　That's out of proportion.

Lots of folk live on their wits:
　Lecturers, lispers,
Losels, loblolly-men, louts—
　They don't end as paupers;

Lots of folk live up lanes
　With fires in a bucket,
Eat windfalls and tinned sardines-
　They seem to like it.

Their nippers have got bare feet,
　Their unspeakable wives
Are skinny as whippets - and yet
　No one actually starves.

Ah, were I courageous enough
    To shout Stuff your pension!
But I know, all too well, that's the stuff
    That dreams are made on:

For something sufficiently toad-like
    Squats in me, too;
Its hunkers are heavy as hard luck,
    And cold as snow,

And will never allow me to blarney
    My way of getting
The fame and the girl and the money
    All at one sitting.

I don't say, one bodies the other
    One's spiritual truth;
But I do say it's hard to lose either,
    When you have both.

上教堂

我确定里边没有动静，
就走进去，门戛然关严。
又一教堂：垫子、椅子、圣经，
还有石碑；礼拜的花环——
现已发黄松散；圣像那边
有铜器，小巧的管风琴；
紧绷、腐朽、挥不去的静寂，
不知发酵了多久。我没帽子，

尴尬地摘下裤腿夹表示敬意。

我走上前，手摸着圣水槽。
驻足望去，屋顶几乎崭新
——擦过？修过？必有人知道，
但那人不是我。我上台诵经，
念了几行冗长的诗句，念到
“止于此”时，便抬高嗓门。
一阵窃笑回响。我退回门口，
签了名，捐了六爱尔兰便士，
心想这地方不值得停留。

我还是停下来，像往常一样，
像往常一样，以迷惑告终，
不知在找什么；不知教堂
完全废弃的时候，我们要
把它变成什么，会不会留
几处大教堂做长期展览？
羊皮纸、餐具和圣饼盒会否
锁柜里，其他则雨淋羊踩？
会否像不祥之地令人逃走？

天黑后，会否有狐疑的女子，
让她们的孩子摸某块石板，
采集治愈癌症的灵丹妙剂？
会否在某个被告知的夜晚
来看亡灵行走？某种力量
活在看似随意的游戏、谜语里，
但迷信，和信仰一样，必定告终；
不信[1]也离去时，还有什么遗留？

① 不信（disbelief）：不迷信，或没有信仰。

杂草、荒径、荆棘、断壁、天空，

形象一周比一周难以辨认，
目的越来越模糊。我好奇
谁是最后的一个来探寻
这处所的原貌：敲敲打打、
写写画画、谙熟圣龛的工匠？
沉醉废墟、热衷古董的人？
圣诞迷狂者，巴望闻一闻
教士的袍带、管风琴和药香？
或许那个人是我自己的化身。

厌倦，无知，明知道幽灵余孽
已经散开，却要走郊外踏荆棘，
来祭奠地上的十字，因为它拿捏
只有在分离时才被发现的一切——
婚姻、出生、死亡，及其思想——
特别的壳子为此而建？我不清楚
装备齐全的臭谷仓有什么价值，
却乐于默默地站在此处；

这是庄严大地上肃穆的屋子，
所有压制都在它融合的氛围里
汇集、指认、披上命运的外衣。
不管多少，这一切从来不会废弃，
因为有些人总是会惊奇地发现，
自己永远渴望变得更加肃穆庄严，
并渴望带着它在这里着落，
这里，他听说，适合人变聪明，
只要周围躺着诸多的死者。

Church Going

Philip Larkin

Once I am sure there's nothing going on
I step inside, letting the door thud shut.
Another church: matting, seats, and stone,
And little books; sprawlings of flowers, cut
For Sunday, brownish now; some brass and stuff
Up at the holy end; the small neat organ;
And a tense, musty, unignorable silence,
Brewed God knows how long. Hatless, I take off
My cycle-clips in awkward reverence.

Move forward, run my hand around the font.
From where I stand, the roof looks almost new -
Cleaned, or restored? Someone would know: I don't.
Mounting the lectern, I peruse a few
Hectoring large-scale verses, and pronounce
"Here endeth" much more loudly than I'd meant.
The echoes snigger briefly. Back at the door
I sign the book, donate an Irish sixpence,
Reflect the place was not worth stopping for.

Yet stop I did: in fact I often do,
And always end much at a loss like this,
Wondering what to look for; wondering, too,
When churches will fall completely out of use
What we shall turn them into, if we shall keep
A few cathedrals chronically on show,
Their parchment, plate and pyx in locked cases,
And let the rest rent-free to rain and sheep.

Shall we avoid them as unlucky places?

Or, after dark, will dubious women come
To make their children touch a particular stone;
Pick simples for a cancer; or on some
Advised night see walking a dead one?
Power of some sort will go on
In games, in riddles, seemingly at random;
But superstition, like belief, must die,
And what remains when disbelief has gone?
Grass, weedy pavement, brambles, buttress, sky,

A shape less recognisable each week,
A purpose more obscure. I wonder who
Will be the last, the very last, to seek
This place for what it was; one of the crew
That tap and jot and know what rood-lofts were?
Some ruin-bibber, randy for antique,
Or Christmas-addict, counting on a whiff
Of gown-and-bands and organ-pipes and myrrh?
Or will he be my representative,

Bored, uninformed, knowing the ghostly silt
Dispersed, yet tending to this cross of ground
Through suburb scrub because it held unspilt
So long and equably what since is found
Only in separation - marriage, and birth,
And death, and thoughts of these - for which was built
This special shell? For, though I've no idea
What this accoutred frowsty barn is worth,
It pleases me to stand in silence here;

A serious house on serious earth it is,
In whose blent air all our compulsions meet,
Are recognized, and robed as destinies.
And that much never can be obsolete,
Since someone will forever be surprising
A hunger in himself to be more serious,
And gravitating with it to this ground,
Which, he once heard, was proper to grow wise in,
If only that so many dead lie round.

有诗为证

你父母许是无意，
他们究竟造了你。
传你一身的毛病，
还另外多加几种。
他们也是造来的，
他们父母是蠢货，
穿着旧衣帽逞能，
互扼咽喉要掐死。
困厄一代代相传，
如斜坡滑向深渊。
劝君抽身要赶早，
莫要再把子嗣造。

This Be the Verse

Philip Larkin

They fuck you up, your mum and dad.
They may not mean it, but they do.

They fill you with the faults they had
And add some extra, just for you.

But they were fucked up in their turn.
By fools in old-style hats and coats
Who half the time were soppy-stern
And half at one another's throats.

Man hands on misery to man.
It deepens like a coastal shelf.
Get out as early as you can,
And don't have any kids yourself.

唐纳德·戴维（Donald Davie，1922—1995）

罗德兹[①]

我向北来，面向长毛的墙壁，
敲了敲小客栈的门——像便池上
搭着泛绿的瓦。我走进往里开的门，

来到多石的北方，每条小巷夹道
都那么熟悉，这里或那里，有猫
伸腰钻过墙与路面间的小洞回家。

石头翻过来都熟悉，却没人欢迎，
没人抱着图卢兹红砖墙上的玫瑰，
投来两眼放光的讨好与热情。

那不仅是金箔花带，不仅是面具，

① 罗德兹（Rodez）：法国南部的一个小城，位于图卢兹（Toulouse）东北约150公里处。

我抛却古老夏日永不褪色的花环，
那般决绝，决绝的眼神是难看的

大面积擦伤，我在陡峭的山路上
遭遇褪干颜色的砂岩，那样执拗。
还有教堂，今天是耶稣受难日。

再见了中世纪！虽然有些人
认为我走进了那个时代，那些
僧侣迷信的世纪。现在我离去，

抛弃真正的花环，诚实的面具，
朵朵鲜花抛在教堂门廊和地板上，
任人踩任风耙，今天是受难日。

与所有的世纪告别。那里
没有家的味道，很像曲折的
风情小巷，迷人地欺骗我们。

倒也不全是再见。反而有些
欢迎，我说。一样荒凉的诸多世纪
挤在门廊等着蹂躏，等着加冕。

Rodez

Donald Davie

Northward I came, and knocked in the coated wall
At the door of a low inn scaled like a urinal
With greenish tiles. The door gave, and I came

Home to the stone north, every wynd and snicket

Known to me wherever the flattened cat
Squirmed home to a hole between housewall and paving.

Known! And in the turns of it, no welcome,
No flattery of the beckoned lighted eye
From a Rose of the rose-brick alleys of Toulouse.

Those more than tinsel garlands, more than masks,
Unfading wreaths of ancient summers, I
Sternly cast off. A stern eye is the graceless

Bulk and bruise that at the steep uphill
Confronts me with its drained-of-colour sandstone
Implacably. The Church. It is Good Friday.

Goodbye to the Middle Ages! Although some
Think that I enter them, those centuries
Of monkish superstition, here I leave them

With their true garlands, and their honest masks,
Every fresh flower cast on the porch and trodden,
Raked by the wind at the Church door on this Friday.

Goodbye to all the centuries. There is
No home in them, much as the dip and turn
Of an honest alley charmingly deceive us.

And not yet quite goodbye. Instead almost
Welcome, I said. Bleak equal centuries
Crowded the porch to be deflowered, crowned.

丹尼·阿布斯（Dannie Abse，1923—2014）

老弱诸神

诸神，老如夜晚，不打扰我们。
维纳斯哭得可怜，她阴毛变白，
具有魔力的爱情腰带失去弹力。
海神奇怪，不知三齿鱼叉落哪里。
战神成了疯子——臆想秃鹫展翅。

海王眨眼复活。我的世界，他想，
就是绑架奸淫，就像我的头版
很快被野蛮占据——他有点不爽，
因为被阉割的诸神摇头鼓舌，
吹嘘又无聊地回应一些烂事。

月神逃之夭夭，她怕宇航员。
农神时令在手，一个瞪眼瞎，
也没啥理睬他。忧郁的酒神
说他吐成肝硬化。爱神，这小秃子，
摆弄箭头，想不起心在哪儿。

上了岁数的诸神，个个疲弱，
不过诗人玩偶。要么睡要么癫，
帕纳塞斯[①]的三叶草上没谁游玩。
是，有时夏天光线消失在房间——
只有长胡子的轮廓飘荡在云端。

① 帕纳塞斯（Parnassian）：派生于 Parnassus，阿波罗（太阳神）、狄奥尼索斯（酒神）和缪斯（诗神）女神的圣地。

The Old Gods

Dannie Abse

The gods, old as night, don't trouble us.
Poor weeping Venus! Her pubic hairs are grey,
And her magic love girdle has lost its spring.
Neptune wonders where he put his trident.
Mars is gaga—illusory vultures on the wing.

Pluto exhumed, blinks. My kind of world, he thinks.
Kidnapping and rape, like my Front Page exploits
Adroitly brutal—but he looks out of sorts when
Other unmanned gods shake their heads tut tut,
Respond boastingly, boringly anecdotal.

Diana has done a bunk, fearing astronauts.
Saturn, Time on his hands, stares at nothing and
Nothing stares back. Glum Bacchus talks ad nauseam
Of cirrhosis and small bald Cupid, fiddling
With arrows, can't recall which side the heart is.

All the old gods have become enfeebled,
Mere playthings for poets. Few, doze or daft,
Frolic on Parnassian clover. True, sometimes
Summer light dies in a room - but only
A bearded profile in a cloud floats over.

迈克尔·汉伯格（Michael Hamburger，1924—2007）

又是秋天（选自《游记之四》）

又是秋天。秋雨之间
沉甸热烈。叶子变色，
花还在开，
颠茄、木槿、金银花。
中午时分，
没有林荫的街道上，
太阳回热，
蟋蟀、蚂蚱、飞蛾和蝴蝶，
爬在路上奄奄一息。
它们未染风霜，
生命的结束，
总是起于内部。

如今晨色苍苍，
我随着树枝或砖头上的阳光醒来，
听到鸟儿歌唱，
却听不见鸽子幽暗的呼哨。
无论什么季节，
无论什么天气，
第一缕阳光，虽然斜照，
却总能轻盈
叶子、房顶、露水打湿的草，
还有沉睡的人。

Autumn Again (Excerpt from *Travelling VI*)

Michael Hamburger

Autumn again. Heavy and hot
Between rain. With a flowering still,
Belladonna, hibiscus, honeysuckle
While the leaves turn.
Around noon
From treeless pavements the sun
Hits back. All over them lie
Cicada, locust, moth
And butterfly, dying.
Neither frost nor gale
Hurt them. Their end
Was inside them, always.

But even on grey mornings now
It is birdsong I hear, and the dove's call,
Dark, not heard when I woke
To the slant of rays on to branches
Or brick. In all seasons,
All weathers, the first light,
Though less than the straight, lifts
A weight from foliage, from roofs,
From dew-wet grass, from
Those who slept.

伊丽莎白·詹宁斯（Elizabeth Jennings，1926—2001）

冬恋

让我们冬季孕育爱情，
愿我们心儿悠闲宁静。
只等春光将快乐催生，
或者夏日里，爱情猛醒，
让我们尽欢娱，道离别。
抖落冬衣犹如一片雪。

Winter Love

Elizabeth Jennings

Let us have winter loving that the heart
May be in peace and ready to partake
Of the slow pleasure spring would wish to hurry
Or that in summer harshly would awake,
And let us fall apart, O gladly weary.
The winter skin shaken like a white snowflake.

查尔斯·汤姆林森（Charles Tomlinson，1927—2015）

献给珍妮特的玫瑰

我知道
这玫瑰只是
纸墨玫瑰
但看它怎么长 怎么
长下去

在你的眼里：
花界的玫瑰
（几乎）有它的花期
而我的
立体打印玫瑰
可以任意重来
（你愿意）
无论什么时候
你从头重复
这视觉的盛宴
你都能
学会

A Rose for Janet

Charles Tomlinson

I know
This rose is only
An ink-and-paper rose
But see how it grows and goes
On growing
Beneath your eyes:
A rose in flower
Has had (almost) its vegetable hour
Whilst my
Rose of spaces and typography
Can reappear at will
(You will)
Whenever you repeat
This ceremony of the eye
From the beginning

And thus
Learn how

彼得·波特（Peter Porter，1929—2010）

另一面（节选）

对付罪恶时，
镜子平静，
淤泥中捞出
神圣的面容。

主的关隘
目击败退，
军团出动，
鹰隼落地。

僵化的是
民主之法，
不禁也不可为，
算不得强压。

……

天才的艺术家
打磨虚荣，
人性的臭氧层
冒出的黑洞。

On the Other Hand (Excerpt)

Peter Porter

The calm of a mirror
As it copes with quilt,
The face of a divinity
Brought up from silt.

The Lord of the Passes
Observing the rout,
The grounding of Eagles
As the legions pull out.

The ossification of
Common Law Liberty,
The Not Not-Forbidden
Not quite compulsory.

…

The genius artists
Polishing vanity,
The hole in the ozone
Layer of humanity.

汤姆 · 冈恩（Thom Gunn，1929—2004）

运动，“人，得动”

蓝松鸦在树丛中窸窣的步子，

紧跟着它不为人知的目的；
飞过田野的群鸟，盘桓的燕子，
有它们树上或灌木丛中的窝。
寻着本能、架势，或者二者兼得，
人们的行动有种说不清的暴躁，
或者受困于人云亦云的喧嚣，
或者笼罩于使人疑惑的尘土。

他们骑着摩托，沿路走来：
渺小，漆黑，像热气里的苍蝇，
距离将他们抛近一看，是男孩，
进军的号角挂到大腿小腿。
他们戴着墨镜，裹着冷漠，
油光的夹克上尘土作战利品。
他们系紧困惑——藏得结结实实，
人声鼎沸中似乎听到什么。

他们的顽强，还看不出模样，
然而，从他们骑行的去处，
他们的车辙可以看出方向。
他们惊起鸟儿飞过田野：
很多都自然地向意志服帖。
人们制造机器也制造灵魂，
以他们尚未掌控好的部分，
永远走向挑战未来的道路。

毕竟，这是部分答案。地球上，
个体不一定纷争或者可憎，
他们已半脱兽性，缺少本能。
醒来时发现自己置身运动的
潮流之上，分歧支离，上下沉浮。

没有价值观，人们随波逐流，
抛出别人或被抛出才结束。
总之，人总朝某个方向运动。

加入者只要一分钟的淹留，
自我否定便骑墙于激情意志。
他们四下溃散，所到之处，
既不是鸟巢，也不是圣所，
因为鸟儿和圣徒各有目的。
最次，人得运动；最好是
没能找到一劳永逸的终极，
人总在不断运动中接近目的。

On the Move "Man, You Gotta Go."

Thom Gunn

The blue jay scuffling in the bushes follows
Some hidden purpose, and the gush of birds
That spurts across the field, the wheeling swallows,
Have nested in the trees and undergrowth.
Seeking their instinct, or their pose, or both,
One moves with an uncertain violence
Under the dust thrown by a baffled sense
Or the dull thunder of approximate words.

On motorcycles, up the road, they come:
Small, black, as flies hanging in heat, the Boy,
Until the distance throws them forth, their hum
Bulges to thunder held by calf and thigh.
In goggles, donned impersonality,
In gleaming jackets trophied with the dust,

They strap in doubt—by hiding it, robust—
And almost hear a meaning in their noise.

Exact conclusion of their hardiness
Has no shape yet, but from known whereabouts
They ride, directions where the tires press.
They scare a flight of birds across the field:
Much that is natural, to the will must yield.
Men manufacture both machine and soul,
And use what they imperfectly control
To dare a future from the taken routes.

It is part solution, after all.
One is not necessarily discord
On Earth; or damned because, half animal,
One lacks direct instinct, because one wakes
Afloat on movement that divides and breaks.
One joins the movement in a valueless world,
Crossing it, till, both hurler and the hurled,
One moves as well, always toward, toward.

A minute holds them, who have come to go:
The self-denied, astride the created will.
They burst away; the towns they travel through
Are home for neither birds nor holiness,
For birds and saints complete their purposes.
At worse, one is in motion; and at best,
Reaching no absolute, in which to rest,
One is always nearer by not keeping still.

泰德·休斯（Ted Hughes，1930—1998）

栖鹰

我栖于树端，合着双眼，
勾头勾爪，寂寂然，
没有虚妄的梦幻，
也不会睡眼中演练捕食。

高树予我方便，
气流阳光
都将我偏袒，
大地也仰脸任我检视。

我的爪子锁定糙树皮，
都是我主给予我
利爪和羽翅，
此时我将它抓在脚下。

或者飞起，围着它慢旋，
随心所欲一并杀之，
毋庸置疑，一切为我所有，
我天生就为撕裂头颅。

生死由我，
我直刺活物的骨骼，
不转弯抹角，
也不容他人置喙。

太阳在我身后，
生来就是如此。

我的眼里容不下变化，
我会让事情一直如此。

Hawk Roosting

Ted Hughes

I sit in the top of the wood, my eyes closed.
Inaction, no falsifying dream
Between my hooked head and hooked feet:
Or in sleep rehearse perfect kills and eat.

The convenience of the high trees!
The air's buoyancy and the sun's ray
Are of advantage to me;
And the earth's face upward for my inspection.

My feet are locked upon the rough bark.
It took the whole of Creation
To produce my foot, my each feather:
Now I hold Creation in my foot

Or fly up, and revolve it all slowly -
I kill where I please because it is all mine.
There is no sophistry in my body:
My manners are tearing off heads -

The allotment of death.
For the one path of my flight is direct
Through the bones of the living.
No arguments assert my right:

The sun is behind me.
Nothing has changed since I began.
My eye has permitted no change.
I am going to keep things like this.

情歌

他爱她 她也爱他
他吻出或者试图吻出她的过去和将来
除此之外他没有别的胃口
她咬他啃他嘬他
她要他完完整整进入她
永远妥帖
他们的莺声燕语飞进窗帘

她的眼睛不肯放过任何细节
紧盯着手 腕 胳膊
他紧抱着她
不让生活将她拖走
他想让此刻凝固让未来停止
他想环抱着将她放倒
或者不管怎么都永远如此
她使劲拥抱
把他印进骨头
他的笑是童话中的楼阁
真实世界从不会到来
她的笑是蜘蛛咬
让他一动不动直到她饿了张口
他的话是占领军
她的笑是刺客心
他的目光是复仇的子弹刀锋

她顾盼的眼角里有居心叵测的魔鬼
他的耳语是皮鞭马靴
她的吻是律师的笔迹毫不纷乱
他的爱抚是抛弃之前最后的勾连
她的摩挲是上锁链
他们像动物拖着沉重的套索
粗喘的声音爬过地板
他的许诺是外科医生的口钳
她的许诺是揭他颅顶
给她做胸针
他的誓言是抽她筋
给她打爱情结
在她私密的抽屉后边
他们的尖叫贴上墙根
他们的头分垂着入睡
像剖开的两瓣吊瓜，但爱得难分。

他们沟股交错缠绵而卧，
梦里盘算让对方成人质。

早上各自挂着彼此的脸。

Lovesong

Ted Hughes

He loved her and she loved him
His kisses sucked out her whole past and future or tried to
He had no other appetite
She bit him she gnawed him she sucked
She wanted him complete inside her
Safe and Sure forever and ever

Their little cries fluttered into the curtains

Her eyes wanted nothing to get away
Her looks nailed down his hands his wrists his elbows
He gripped her hard so that life
Should not drag her from that moment
He wanted all future to cease
He wanted to topple with his arms round her
Or everlasting or whatever there was
Her embrace was an immense press
To print him into her bones
His smiles were the garrets of a fairy place
Where the real world would never come
Her smiles were spider bites
So he would lie still till she felt hungry
His word were occupying armies
Her laughs were an assasin's attempts
His looks were bullets daggers of revenge
Her glances were ghosts in the corner with horrible secrets
His whispers were whips and jackboots
Her kisses were lawyers steadily writing
His caresses were the last hooks of a castaway
Her love-tricks were the grinding of locks
And their deep cries crawled over the floors
Like an animal dragging a great trap
His promises were the surgeon's gag
Her promises took the top off his skull
She would get a brooch made of it
His vows pulled out all her sinews
He showed her how to make a love-knot
At the back of her secret drawer

Their screams stuck in the wall
Their heads fell apart into sleep like the two halves
Of a lopped melon, but love is hard to stop

In their entwined sleep they exchanged arms and legs
In their dreams their brains took each other hostage

In the morning they wore each other's face

乔恩·西尔金（Jon Silkin，1930—1997）

蒲公英

鼻涕虫蜗居在
淌着白汁的折茎上。
花儿没有眼睛：夺目的
是尖锐的花瓣，小而粗糙，
像金属碎片。一旦形成，
便不太规整地射出
野性的黄色光芒。
肯定是想
吞噬大地。
成片摇曳时，看着有一英尺高，
落下时，便盖过
各个傲慢的物种。
它者的命是它们的。
在它们与栽培作物之间，
是草。它们就在它贫瘠的地盘上蔓延；
暗中喂肥到处爬行的鼻涕虫。
远看，它们像盘子；

近看，像大自然初成的机件，
铆定她，成功。

Dandelion

Jon Silkin

Slugs nestle where the stem
Broken, bleeds milk.
The flower is eyeless: the sight is compelled
By small, coarse, sharp petals,
Like metle shreds. Formed,
They puncture, irregularly perforate
Their yellow, brutal glare.
And certainly want to
Devour the earth. With an ample movement
They are a foot high, as you look.
And coming back, they take hold
On pert domestic strains.
Others' lives are theirs. Between them
And domesticity,
Grass. They infest its weak land;
Tatten, hide slugs, infestate.
They look like plates; more closely
Like the first tryings, the machines, of nature
Riveted into her, successful.

罗伊·费什尔（Roy Fisher，1930—2017）

消费战争

我见过那花园，我婶子
和她俩孩子以及隔壁的女人，
都死在那，一抔黄土像豆荚鼓起。

夜里，我听到一英里外，
炸弹在拥挤不堪的房子间唱响，
闪着软火，带着敲门的动静；

最后一颗把四人炸进土里，
柴房和叔叔的尸体都被炸飞，
飞到屋顶和房后的街道。

如今花园赤裸发霉，
柴房的铁皮碎成小片
盖在小土堆上，仿佛底下没人。

房子被炸后收拾空。
亲戚们都另起炉灶；
我得堂兄的铅笔用了多年。

堂兄还有一个工作簿归了我，
里边有金色蜡笔画，线条还未细修。
至于他的一生，我所知甚少。

这就是我十岁时留意的事情：
此外，还有我家房子外的四具棺材，
还有巧克力蛋糕，同学们半带震惊的嫉妒。

但我祖父从太平间回家后，
有整整五年跟人讲他头颅里的声音，
然后走出家门躺在荆豆丛中死了。

我父亲从领尸处回家，
让我们提醒他女儿的嘴角长啥样，
我们告诉他。他说：“好像是这样。”

这都是些周边人恰好被我遇上，
那些全家遇难的，其悲痛也不为人知；
人总是记着自家的死难者。

这四个人遇难的血腥片段感触最深，
可供我讲述一个长而又长的故事；
当时无痛苦，此时也无所谓伤痕。

若不是心中升起写小说的念头，
可能在第二天夜里的炮弹轰鸣中，
我对之还有些许感觉，并初识恐惧。

The Entertainment of War

Roy Fisher

I saw the garden where my aunt had died
And her two children and a woman from next door;
It was like a burst pod filled with clay.

A mile away in the night I had heard the bombs
Sing and then burst themselves between cramped houses
With bright soft flashes and sounds like banging doors;

The last of them crushed the four bodies into the ground,
Scattered the shelter, and blasted my uncle's corpse
Over the housetop and into the street beyond.

Now the garden lay stripped and stale; the iron shelter
Spread out its separate petals around a smooth clay saucer.
Small, and so tidy it seemed nobody had ever been there.

When I saw it, the house was blown clean by blast and care.
Relations had already torn out the new fireplaces;
My cousin's pencils lasted me several years.

And in his office notepad that was given me
I found solemn drawings in crayon of blondes without dresses.
In his lifetime I had not known him well.

These were the things I noticed at ten years of age:
Those, and the four hearses outside our house,
The chocolate cakes, and my classmates' half-shocked envy.

But my grandfather went home from the mortuary
And for five years tried to share the noises in his skull,
Then he walked out and lay under a furze-bush to die.

When my father came back from identifying the daughter
He asked us to remind him of her mouth.
We tried. He said 'I think it was the one'.

These were marginal people I had met only rarely
And the end of the whole household meant that no grief was seen;

Never have people seemed so absent from their own deaths.

This bloody episode of four whom I could understand better dead
Gave me something I needed to keep a long story moving;
I had no pain of it; can find no scar even now.

But had my belief in the fiction not been thus buoyed up
I might, in the sigh and strike of the next night's bombs
Have realized a little what they meant, and for the first time been afraid.

艾德里安·亨利（Adrian Henri，1932—2000）

爱情是……

爱情是……
坐在后座凉飕飕
俩人粉丝俱乐部
散步手挽指甲油

爱情是……
冬夜油炸薯条鱼
毛毯里边有奇趣
彻夜不眠灯光徐

爱情是……
圣诞商店的礼物
似在流行之榜首
感觉音乐停止后

爱情是……

白色底裤晾一边
粉色睡衣余温暖
天亮分别在眼前

爱情是……
卿卿我我各入眼
奔放自由也坐监
离我而去自点检

Love Is ...

Adrian Henri

Love is...
Love is feeling cold in the back of vans
Love is a fanclub with only two fans
Love is walking holding paintstained hands

Love is...
Love is fish and chips on winter nights
Love is blankets full of strange delights
Love is when you don't put out the light

Love is...
Love is the presents in Christmas shops
Love is when you're feeling Top of the Pops
Love is what happens when the music stops

Love is...
Love is white panties lying all forlorn
Love is pink nightdresses still slightly warm
Love is when you have to leave at dawn

Love is...

Love is you and love is me

Love is prison and love is free

Love's what's there when you are away from me

彼得·雷德格罗夫（Peter Redgrove，1932—2003）

沉默的男子

我喜欢、适应寒冷，
我的脑子如遇冷石化，
或者很好？心里哇凉，
我喜欢漫步严寒，
好似看到言语从哈气中滚落，
我沿路边走边谈，嘴里
冒着团团白雾。家里
我把妻子关进房间，
把孩子安顿到温暖的地方。
我默不作声，唯恐
让我爱的人着凉。
我仿佛从霉菌里走来，每一口气
都会呼出白雾，都会助长菌毛。
我从不带他们散步，只独自走进寒冷，
等天暖，或是春天来了，再带他们出来。
我小心收藏的，像冷藏的种子，
在干草里，沼泽里，在淤堵的小溪，
在梳子戳不着的小径；
那里浮冰碰撞粘连，
封住泰晤士河任人行走。

A Silent Man

Peter Redgrove

I love the cold; it agrees with me,
I am minded like its petrifaction,
Or do I mean perfection? My heart
I scold and loves to stroll through cold,
And seems to see a better speech
Rolling in fat clouds of breath.
I keep talk for my walks, silent clouds
That flow in ample, mouthing white
Along the paths. At home
Where I've closeted my wife
And instituted children in the warm
I keep my silence, lest
Those I love, regard, catch cold from me
As though i strolled through mould, and breathing.
Puffed white clouds t spore more fur.
I never take them on my long cold walks alone,
I save them for a warmer time, some kind of spring;
Saved up in me like frozen seeds among
Crisp-flaring turf, stiff marsh, gagged stream,
Paths the skidding ferrule will not prick;
Where floes creak and yearn at floes
To fuse and bind the Thames for walking on.

菲利普·霍布斯鲍姆（Philip Hobsbaum，1932—2005）

胖子论性别

拉弗蒂小姐，跟我同级是我公共课同学，巧克力吃得
一天比一天胖，想找男人
却不戒巧克力，我很同情；
吉尼斯[①]把我毁了，胖鼓鼓
牢骚满腹，令我贪杯。
亨利八世[②]咋样？爱德华国王[③]
腆着酒肚子，胡子拉碴，他咋样？
或许，人跟人不一样。
赫伯特·斯宾塞[④]不接纳乔治·艾略特[⑤]
就是嫌她丑：男人想仙女，
轻盈敏捷；女人想金钱、权力、声誉。
而金钱权力名誉随着块头攀升：
亨利王无需魅力，他有斧头、王宫、随从。
也许，最终，这就是为什么
我有希望，而拉弗蒂小姐休想。

---

① 吉尼斯（Guinness）：一种浓烈的黑啤酒。

② 亨利八世（Henry VIII）：身材肥胖的英国国王，于英国文艺复兴开端主政，进行英国宗教改革。

③ 爱德华国王（King Edward）：指爱德华国王七世，身高只有 1.6 米，腰围却足有 1.37 米；胖得有些离谱。

④ 赫伯特·斯宾塞（Herbert Spencer）：英国哲学家和社会学家，将自然选择理论应用于人类社会。

⑤ 乔治·艾略特（George Eliot）：英国小说作家，以对维多利亚社会的现实主义分析为特征。被认为“身体不具有吸引力”，“丑陋得极美”，“长马脸的女学者”。

Stout Person's Meditation on Sex

Philip Hobsbaum

Miss Rafferty, in my General Class, eats chocolates,
Gets fatter every day, longs for a man
But goes on eating chocolates. I sympathize;
Guinness is my ruin, that and misery
Bloating and crumbling, making me want to drink more.
How did Henry VIII get on, or King Edward,
Boozed, bulky, bearded? Perhaps
It's different for men. Herbert Spencer
Decided against George Eliot on the grounds
Of general ugliness: we dream of houris,
Lissom and swift, they dream of bank balances,
Power, prestige. This grows as the bulk grows:
King Henry need no charm, he had an axe,
A palace, followers. Maybe, at last, that's why
There's hope for me but none for Miss Rafferty.

艾德里安·米切尔（Adrian Mitchell，1932—2008）

致国防工作者

军工业，早有预警，
明天你会早早醒，
发现这是光荣的一天，
你的工作都玩儿完。
因为世人要确定，
不再，不再有战争。
现在你该换个饭碗，

与死亡荒芜无关。
别磨蹭，有人丢劝，
国际杀戮这行要内卷。
如今不致残不死伤，
动脑筋发挥一技之长。
和平时代需各种技艺，
造地雷可以改做假肢。
三轮车而非三叉戟，
小提琴而非暴力。
救生船、医药、下水道，
食品、玩具、车辆、公交。
来吧，大量工作等着做，
只要致力和平不再作。

To All in the So-Called Defence Industry

Adrian Mitchell

Arms trade workers, here's an early warning
You might wake up tomorrow morning
And find that this is the glorious day
When all your jobs will just melt away
Because the people of the world are going to make sure
There'll be no more, no more, no more war
So now's the time to switch your occupation
From dealing in death and desolation
Don't hang around now you've been told
The international murder trade's about to fold
You won't have to maim, you won't have to kill,
You can use your brain and use your skill.
Peace needs workers of all kinds—
Make artificial limbs instead of landmines.

Tricycles instead of tridents,
Violins instead of violence,
Lifeboats, hospitals, medicine, drains,
Food and toys and buses and trains—
Come on, there's plenty of work to be done
If we're going to make peace for everyone.

杰弗里·希尔（Geoffrey Hill，1932—）

九月之歌

你或许不招待见，
却并非碰不着。
时候到了，照样忘不了饶不过。

正如所料，你死了。万物前行，
不紧不慢，也到终点。
到处是齐克隆[1]和皮革，
是专属的恐怖，是日常哭喊。

（我为自己
做了首挽歌
一点不假）

九月在藤蔓上育肥。
墙上蹿出火苗。无毒的
烟，飘进我的双眼。

① 齐克隆（Zyklon）：让人联想到齐克隆 B，奥斯威辛集中营（Auschwitz）最令囚犯和犹太人胆战心惊的，号称“死亡工厂”的毒气室和焚尸炉。

这已足够。绰绰有余。

September Song

Geoffrey Hill

Undesirable you may have been, untouchable
You were not. Not forgotten
Or passed over at the proper time.

As estimated, you died. Things marched,
Sufficient, to that end.
Just so much Zyklon and leather, patented
Terror, so many routine cries.

(I have made
An elegy for myself it
Is true)

September fattens on vines. Roses
Flake from the wall. The smoke
Of harmless fires drifts to my eyes.

This is plenty. This is more than enough.

爱德华·卢西-史密斯（Edward Lucie-Smith，1933—）

识得

秃头校长说：“你父亲没了。”

他闪光的头顶和棕色的烟斗
立刻在泪水中模糊。不是悲哀。
只因一种懂得却比悲哀更苦。
我知道悲哀也有用处——父亲死了，
我至少一两周不用再挨拳头；
我为羞愧而哭，然后才是悲哀。

懂得这些时，我十岁零一个月。
我还记得班上的喧闹如何停止，
我悲上心头时我们在开班会，
一些金鱼悄悄动了一下鱼鳍，
倏忽往来在闪光透明的碗里，
碗搁在书架上，像一个监狱。
鱼无动于衷。周围目光转向我。
我心里的某个地方，生出骄傲，
就像金鱼，突然摆了下鱼鳍。

The Lesson

Edward Lucie-Smith

"Your father's gone," my bald headmaster said.
His shiny dome and brown tobacco jar
Splintered at once in tears. It wasn't grief.
I cried for knowledge which was bitterer
Than any grief. For there and then I knew
That grief has its uses—that a father dead
Could bind the bully's fist a week or two;
And then I cried for shame, then for relief.

I was a month past ten when I learnt this:
I still remember how the noise was stilled

In school-assembly when my grief came in
Some goldfish in a bowl quietly sculled
Around their shining prison on its shelf.
They were indifferent. All the other eyes
Were turned towards me. Somewhere in myself
Pride, like a goldfish, flashed a sudden fin.

大卫·韦维尔（David Wevill，1935—）

星（节选）

十一
梦幻：旋转门
永远开合

夜里被梅花鹿的叫声惊醒
似被什么卡住——

无闻却熟悉的
一城陌客
只知姓氏，
他们的意义被禁。

这里有一命案
或失踪——
悬案侦探
搜寻他的影子，

太迟了，通常
只是毫无线索的脚印

通向这儿那儿，

随便选一个。

Asterisks (Excerpt)

David Wevill

XI

Dreams: radical doors
Forever open, closed

Wake at night to the crying of a spotted fawn
Taken by something—

unknown yet familiar
City of strangers
All on first-name terms
Whose meanings are forbidden

Here there has been a death
Or a vanishment—
Self, cold-case detective
In search of his shadow

Too late, as often
Among the clueless footprints
Leading here or there

Choose whichever.

杰瑞米·哈沃德·白兰（Jeremy Halvard Prynne，1936—）

富含维生素 C

她的额下，雪白的羽翅儿
着实惊诧了日子——
它在阳光下滑落，
穿过松动的玻璃，
直冲屋里闪光的勋章，
扫过残缺与信赖。
小黑点儿悄悄滑停，
像苹果籽儿。
波罗的海喜欢沉睡的。

或者像云里绛红，落入
杯中，你任由小鸟
自作聪明地叽喳
洒在水中晃动的
倾斜的日子上。
心思闪过水面，
现出一道圆弧，
我们的确少几分刻意；
水浅了一盏司，

难以容纳太多的
为正义而战。
他从闪光的指缝里
任之蛇形而走，
不过一口烈酒般的炸药，
所谓响动，就是大街上

我们猜不出的白痴念头
被彩灯燃亮。你从同一个门
进来，带着

不自安生的一抹
理性，它不纯的血脉；
我从脉动中听出同样的
不肯溶解的色调。玫瑰
上下渲染过，迎接天上雷霆，
生出人们秉持的和谈效果。
是的，你悄然翻开一页，
那就是你的日子，
在光明中倾斜、暗淡。

Rich in Vitamin C

Jeremy Halvard Prynne

Under her brow the snowy wing-case
Delivers truly the surprise
Of days which slide under sunlight
Past loose glass in the door
Into the reflection of honour spread
Through the incomplete, the trusted. So
Darkly the stain skips as a livery
Of your pause like an apple pip,
The baltic loved one who sleeps.

Or as syrup in a cloud, down below in
The cup, you excuse each folded
Cry of the finch’s wit, this flush
Scattered over our slant of the

Day rocked in water, you say
This much. A waver of attention at
The surface, shews the arch there and
The purpose we really cut;
An ounce down by the water, which

In cross-fire from injustice too large
To hold he lets slither
From starry fingers
Noting the herbal jolt of cordite
And its echo: is this our screen, on some
Street we hardly guessed could mark
An idea bred to idiocy by the clear
Sight-lines ahead. You come in
By the same door, you carry

What cannot be left for its own
Sweet shimmer of reason, its false blood;
The same tint i hear with the pulse it touches
And will not melt. Such shading
Of the rose to its stock tips the bolt
From the sky, rising in its effect of what
Motto we call peace talks. And yes the
Quiet turn of your page is the day
Tilting so, faded in the light.

马丁·贝尔（Martin Bell，1938—）

致多萝茜

确切说，你不漂亮。
大约讲，你还算好。
你在房旁边植桑，
桑边留了一棵草，
草与树默默相依。
夜风起，草拂墙面，
扫去白天让我们入睡。

小孩说的，似真切：
“东西丢了就扯平。”
不对。如果丢了你，
就不会有风吹树长。
会有人拔草，我的花
就不宁静。丢了你，
我得求草坪收我入睡。

To Dorothy

Martin Bell

You are not beautiful, exactly.
You are beautiful, inexactly.
You let a weed grow by the mulberry
And a mulberry grow by the house.
So close, in the personal quiet
Of a windy night, it brushes the wall
And sweeps away the day till we sleep.

A child said it, and it seemed true:
"Things that are lost are all equal."
But it isn't true. If I lost you,
The air wouldn't move, nor the tree grow.
Someone would pull the weed, my flower.
The quiet wouldn't be yours. If I lost you,
I'd have to ask the grass to let me sleep.

汤姆·罗沃斯（Tom Raworth，1938—）

结婚日

戒指窸窣滑上手指

他的确说过那些？
我们走上前，
海雾卷着卵石路上的灯光
冲向崖壁和海面。

我认准一条，探听
替不了直觉，我坐在这儿
打字，冰凉的手指
弹了弹纸边儿。他

从更衣室出来，穿着
礼服，人们
隔着一段楼道没认出他来。
木屋，阳光，我们站成半圆。

相机咔嚓两下

我奇怪她脸色怎么不对，
她说，因为
其实也没什么，我
就填在那余音里。 出了

浴室，那个父亲喝香槟；后来
喝威士忌。我们透过窗户看舰上
放下的橙色救生艇飘向岸边。

我说如果你还是持那种
态度
　　我们坐在车厢里看狗走动

自行车叽里咕噜溜下山

Wedding Day

Tom Raworth

Noise of a ring sliding onto a finger

Supposing he did say that?
We came by the front
Sea fog twisting light above the pebbles
Towards the cliffs towards the sea

I made this pact, intelligence
Shall not replace intuition, sitting here
My hand cold on the typewriter
Flicking the corner ofthe paper. He

Came from the toilet wearing
A suit, people
Didn't recognise him, down the length
Of corridor. The room
Was wooden, sunlight we stood in a half circle

Noise of two cine-cameras

I wonder what's wrong with her
Face, she said, because
There's nothing wrong with it really I
Inhabit a place just to the left of that phrase. From

A bath the father took champagne later
Whiskey. Through the window we watched the frigate's
Orange raft drifting to shore

I mean if you're taking that
Attitude
    We rode in a train watching the dog move

Noise of a bicycle freewheeling downhill

李·哈伍德（Lee Harwood，1939—）

画终

白云飘过大地
大地被海洋包围
天空湛蓝总在白云之上

白云在蓝色中续航——
丝毫不受画布画架的局限——
白云可以画成任何
云彩的形状 或画一撮羊毛
一朵白绒玫瑰
白云将阴影投向地貌 一片灰色
灰与白笼罩着看风景的人
直到他也入画
出房间 过屋门 下楼梯
来到大街上—— 就是一段旅程
云可以拥有房子
看风景的人确信
一串云朵会飘来
他们无以言表
默默地向天空张大嘴巴
毫不神秘——不过是
穿大衣的人群立于山边的轮廓
头上一线云彩
天空湛蓝 白云染灰
其余——下边的地形——
可任由想象
整幅画静静地融入
周围的云彩

The Final Painting

Lee Harwood

The white cloud passed over the land
There is sea always round the land
The sky is blue always above the cloud
The cloud in the blue continues to move

—Nothing is limited by the canvas or frame—
The white cloud can be pictured like any
Other clouds or like a fist of wool
Or a white fur rose
The white cloud passes a shadow across
The landscape and so there is a passing greyness
The grey and the white both envelop
The watcher until he too is drawn into the picture
It is all a journey from a room through a door
Down stairs and out into the street
The cloud could possess the house
The watchers have a mutual confidence
With the approaching string of white clouds
It is beyond spoken words what they are
Silently mouthing to the sky
There was no mystery in this—only the firm
Outline of people in overcoats on a hillside
And the line of clouds above them
The sky is blue The cloud white with touches
Of grey—the rest—the landscape below—
Can be left to the imagination
The whole painting quietly dissolved itself
Into its surrounding clouds

绵白

海像她眼睛一样灰白
这些日子肯定　有绵白的雾
从海上吹来　城镇消融
雾渐浓　只裸露她的肩膀

毫无遮掩地　从海下滚滚而来
冬日的午后——细雨
面朝沙滩　砾石
浪拍海岸　碎白

不可否认
惊讶　惊奇之余
她身上很多细节
要先把握　然后

浸透身心　细雨在外
冬日的午后　她裸露的
双肩　像她眼睛一样白
冲上岸的海水也一样白

整个轮廓称为地理
相会于一系列的色相
唇　肩　胸　腹
城镇消融　性　股　腿

外边　跨越她的赤裸
午后有雨　生出奇迹
她的身体年轻稳健　城镇消融
冬日　像她眼睛一样灰白

Soft White

Lee Harwood

When the sea is as grey as her eyes
On these days for sure　the soft white
Mist blown in from the ocean　the town dissolving

It all adds up   her bare shoulders

Nakedness   rolling in from the sea
On winter afternoons—a fine rain
Looking down on the sand   & shingle
The waves breaking on the shore   & white

It is impossible to deny what
Taken by surprise   then wonder
The many details of her body
To be held first now   then later

In body & mind   the fine rain outside
On winter afternoons   the nakedness
Of her bare shoulders   as grey as her eyes
The sea rushing up the beach as white as

The whole outline called "geography"
Meeting at a set of erotic points
Lips   shoulders   breasts   stomach
The town dissolves   sex   thighs   legs

Outside   then across her nakedness
It rains in the afternoon   then the wonder
Her body so young & firm   dissolves the town
In winter   grey as her eyes

克雷格·雷恩（Craig Raine，1944—）

火星人寄回的明信片

卡克斯顿[①]是多翼的机械鸟，
其中有些带标的备受青睐。

它们能使一双双眼神融化，
它们能使身体无痛而尖叫。

我从没见一个在天上飞行，
但它们偶尔会栖落在手上。

天空厌倦了飞行便起雾，
让那柔性装置地上休息。

世界昏暗带一股书卷气，
就像卫生纸上雕刻图案。

地球就是一台电视机，
不住的雨脚让它暗淡。

T 台是个里边反锁的屋子，
钥匙一转便能解放世界。

红尘滚滚，如此之快，
赶不上可以电影弥补。

但时间捆绑在手腕上，

① 卡克斯顿（Caxtons）：代指明信片一类。卡克斯顿（Caxton）是英国印刷家，出版了第一本英文印刷书。

或藏在盒子里耐心嘀嗒。

千家万户，精灵似的玩意儿睡香，
他们抱起来时还在打呼噜，

如果哭闹，他们就凑近嘴唇，
安抚着香睡。香睡时又故意

用手指抓挠，搔痒一样
把它从酣睡中弄醒。

只许年轻人晒痛苦，
成年人都去惩戒室，

那里只许喝水没有吃食，
他们关上门，独自忍受

喧哗。他们无一例外，
痛苦的气味各不相同。

夜幕降临，色彩逝去，
他们成双成对，暗地里

揣摩着自己——合上眼睛
看五光十色中的自己。

A Martian Sends a Postcard Home

Craig Raine

Caxtons are mechanical birds with many wings
And some are treasured for their markings—

They cause the eyes to melt
Or the body to shriek without pain.

I have never seen one fly, but
Sometimes they perch on the hand.

Mist is when the sky is tired of flight
And rests its soft machine on ground:

Then the world is dim and bookish
Like engravings under tissue paper.

Rain is when the earth is television.
It has the property of making colours darker.

Model T is a room with the lock inside—
A key is turned to free the world

For movement, so quick there is a film
To watch for anything missed.

But time is tied to the wrist
Or kept in a box, ticking with impatience.

In homes, a haunted apparatus sleeps,
That snores when you pick it up.

If the ghost cries, they carry it
To their lips and soothe it to sleep

With sounds. And yet they wake it up
Deliberately, by tickling with a finger.

Only the young are allowed to suffer
Openly. Adults go to a punishment room

With water but nothing to eat.
They lock the door and suffer the noises

Alone. No one is exempt
And everyone's pain has a different smell.

At night when all the colours die,
They hide in pairs

And read about themselves—
In colour, with their eyelids shut.

塞利玛·希尔（Selima Hill，1945—）

晶莹的雪花

他的呼吸总是很差——
是他气管出了毛病——
所以他经常去画棚：
去户外不错，
黑暗中雪花非常亮——
但今晚不是他自己——
一个穿睡衣的女孩儿
从他面前跑进杜鹃花；

他抬头看了看画棚，
正在松树间咔咔作响；
他被老校长瞧见，
校长自然知道是他，
哮喘病人呼吸雪花。
他继续朝画棚走去，
像某些人擦干脚趾——
慢慢地，好像重要的事
总是降临在别人身上，
不久也会降临——你身上。
我觉得他恢复不到正常，
但只要他想画就画得好。

Snowdrops in the Light of the Blaze

Selima Hill

His breathing had always been bad—
there was something wrong with his tubes—
so he often went out to the Art Shed:
it's nice to get out in the air
the snowdrops so white in the darkness—
but tonight he isn't alone—
a girl in a nightie runs past
and into the rhododendrons;
and as he looks up at the building
crackling among the pines
he's seen by the old headmaster
who naturally thinks it was him,
the asthmatic snowdrop collector.
The ride to the station proceeds
like someone drying their toes—

slow, as if something important
were happening to somebody else,
and will soon happen here, and to you.
I don't think he'll ever be normal,
but he draws very well, when he wants to.

温迪·柯普（Wendy Cope，1945—）

十四行诗（有感于《莎士比亚十四行诗》第22首）

戴上镜子不觉得老，
一双老眼还算不赖；
就怕看了照片，人道
青春已过，让人气馁。
每次从椅子上起身，
两个膝盖便会提醒：
到处负重越来越沉。
反抗的还有颈椎病、
关节炎，它们见天地，
从有点儿疼到很疼，
说白了我是堆破烂。
只有一样让我年轻：
我的爱人，之前爱，
如今还爱，还表白。

Sonnet (Inspired by *Sonnet* 22 by Shakespeare)

Wendy Cope

My glass can't quite persuade me I am old—
In that respect my ageing eyes are kind—

But when I see a photograph, I'm told
The dismal truth: I've left my youth behind.
And when I try to get up from a chair
My knees remind me they are past their best.
The burden they have carried everywhere
Is heavier now. No wonder they protest.
Arthritic fingers, problematic neck,
Sometimes causing mild to moderate pain,
Could well persuade me I'm an ancient wreck
But here's what helps me to feel young again:
My love, who fell for me so long ago,
Still loves me just as much, and tells me so.

彼得·瑞丁（Peter Reading，1946—2011）

我们扔了大部分废物

我们扔了大部分废物：
不请自来的烂书，
格子收纳盒，
过时的衣服，
破碎的陶器，
猪宝储钱罐，
莫克姆湾[1]杯，
酒商最后一笔催款，
新近的离婚证，
新近的房契，
猩猩瘪蛋的纪念，

① 莫克姆湾（Morecambe Bay）：英格兰西北部的一个大河口。莫克姆湾杯，指带有莫克姆湾标识的杯子。

世间属于我们的，
一大堆破烂。

剩下干净的桌子，
还有约会时间表。

We Have Ditched Most of the Draff:

Peter Reading

We have ditched most of the draff:
The unbidden spineless books,
The grot-gathering gubbins,
The outvogued vestments,
The cracked crockery,
The pot pig moneybox,
The morecambe bay mug,
The vintner's final demand,
The last-but-one's divorce papers,
The last home's deeds,
The chimp's wizened scrotum souvenir,
World's gear,
The bulk of the whole fucking shitheap.

That which remains is a cleared desk
And a time of appointment.

布莱恩·帕登（Brian Patten，1946—）

你明天醒来时

你明天醒来时我给你一首诗。
一首宁静的诗。
不让你难过。
不让你苦愁。
就是一首诗，
明天醒来给你。

这诗不是我个人所写。
我不能据为己有。
诗句来自你的身体。
你的微笑。
你可认识？

诗就在你枕头下。
在你的衣橱里。
你惊讶地瞪大眼睛，
大喊“它在颤动！
它赤裸惊人，多么新鲜！”

它就在早餐里；
放在爱情燃亮的餐桌上，
为惊喜预留的地方。
明早醒来时，
我们给世界一个大大的吻。

我们把它给房东，阳台上发愁的人；
给那些倚窗做梦的人；

给不知为何挥手的人。
我们的馈赠奇妙而不同寻常，
我们把它献给人类。
明天醒来时，
它在我们心中行走。

When You Wake Tomorrow

Brian Patten

I will give you a poem when you wake tomorrow.
It will be a peaceful poem.
It won't make you sad.
It won't make you miserable.
It will simply be a poem to give you
When you wake tomorrow.

It was not written by myself alone.
I cannot lay claim to it.
I found it in your body.
In your smile I found it.
Will you recognise it?

You will find it under your pillow.
When you open the cupboard it will be there.
You will blink in astonishment,
Shout out, "How it trembles!
Its nakedness is startling! How fresh it tastes!"

We will have it for breakfast;
On a table lit by loving,
At a place reserved for wonder.

We will give the world a kissing open
When we wake tomorrow.

We will offer it to the sad landlord out on the balcony.
To the dreamers at the window.
To the hand waving for no particular reason
We will offer it.
An amazing and most remarkable thing,
We will offer it to the whole human race
Which walks in us
When we wake tomorrow.

利兹·罗茨海德（Liz Lochhead，1947—）

麻烦不在我取什么名字

麻烦不在我取什么名字。
那不代表我是谁。
我也不是为此而生。
麻烦不在我的故土，
虽是比树木扎根还深的地方，
我还要离开（谁不想呢？）

地狱里不会有希望，
孤单无助也不会有希望。
现在你能好好听我说吗？
听我用实际行动来讲？

你说我行之不善，
大体也没错，

我不善，因为没被善待过，
如今我也回报这么多。

心结难解，
但你能帮我。松开
这些疙瘩，认真听着。
我不能直说，如果你愿闻其详，
那么所有的伤害背后，
便是真正的希望。

Trouble is Not My Middle Name

Liz Lochhead

Trouble is not my middle name.
It is not what I am.
I was not born for this.
Trouble is not a place
Though I am in it deeper than the deepest wood
And I'd get out of it (who wouldn't?) if I could.

Hope is what I do not have in hell—
Not without good help, now. Could you
Listen, listen hard and well
To what I cannot say except by what I do?

And when you say I do it for badness
This much is true:
I do it for badness done to me before
Any badness that I do to you.

Hard to unfankle this.

But you can help me. Loosen
All these knots and really listen.
I cannot plainly tell you this, but, if you care,
Then—beyond all harm and hurt—
Real hope is there.

丹妮丝·莱利（Denise Riley，1948—）

不谈情感

这是一个古老而可信的故事

朗朗乾坤，正义昭彰
胳膊插在棉花里

厨房里各种物件
实实在在的避雨窝棚
一切都源自殖民史，主人与奴隶

不愿袖手旁观也不愿秀“肌肉”的胳膊
不愿叠起只想铺开的床上用品
被风重重地吹起的桌子以及上边的珍馐

做不成的母亲，无关肤色
被当成物品勉强不倒的母亲
时而穿过法案疑云望向海湾 默不作声的母亲

一种设计里总有开始承受的一方，非我族类的一方
捆来在厨房里
倘若我 不以你认可的方式深深地忠诚地爱你

牛奶，会像我们一样泼到神秘的大街上

支持，支持

屋子里面有很多小情感
流沙上成人日日讨生活
在爱与生活之间走钢丝
他们连同子女陷于泥沼
像不可拔地而起的云雀

情感支付不起房租

我，无视，房子

Affections Must Not

Denise Riley

This is an old fiction of reliability

Is a weather presence, is a righteousness
Is arms in cotton

This is what stands up in kitchens
Is a true storm shelter
& is taken straight out of colonial history, master and slave

Arms that I will not love folded nor admire for their 'strength'
Linens that I will not love folded but will see flop open
Tables that will rise heavily in the new wind & lift away, bearing their
Precious burdens

Of mothers who never were, nor white nor black
Mothers who were always a set of equipment and a fragile balance
Mothers who looked over a gulf through the cloud of an act & at
Times speechlessly saw it

Inside a designation there are people permanently started to bear it,
The not-me against sociology
Inside the kitchens there is realising of tightropes
Milk, if I do not continue to love you as deeply and truly as you want
And need
That is us in the mythical streets again

Support, support

The houses are murmuring with many small pockets of emotion
On which spongy grounds adults lives are being erected and paid for
Daily
While their feet and their children's feet are tangled around like those
Of fen larks
In the fine steely wires which run to and fro between love and
Economics

Affections must not support the rent

I. neglect. the house

詹姆斯·芬顿（James Fenton，1949—）

那是你的爱？

那是你的爱？
那是你的爱？

精心炮制的谎言——
直击我的双眼。
那是你的爱？

没完没了地扒，
伤人就拿动机说话，
那是你的爱？

种种指责控诉，
说你被如何辜负，
那是你的爱？

像潺水，像深入
责备的深渊，
直到被引入歧途，
原来你有私下的算盘。
小把戏玩儿得不光彩，
那是你的爱？

真可笑，不知不觉
报复怨恨纠结。
可笑的，我想了好久，
想着事情应该不难解决。
最可笑的是，

假装请专业人士建议时，
你想的是摆脱我，
不顾他人，
不惜代价，
对我……

那是你的爱？
那是你的爱？

魅力包裹怨恨，
算计先于关心。
那是你的爱？

善寻蛛丝马迹，
以图最后一击。
那是你的爱？

好事偏往坏处想，
装出受害的模样。
那是你的爱？

你当然值得祝贺，
祝贺你赢了。
就想知道协议条款是什么，
我猜你也讲明了。
那肯定不好挨。
这是你的爱？

求你放过别管我。
请说不再需要我。
账就这么多？

总数可合过？
或是不算完，
还有账要算？

这是你的爱？
这是你的爱？

求你放过别管我。
请说不再需要我。

这是你的爱？

Was That Your Idea of Love?

James Fenton

Was that your idea of love?
Was that your idea of love?

Those brilliantly confected lies—
They hit me straight between the eyes.
Was that your idea of love?

That endless digging for the dirt,
That motive—seeking where it hurt—
Was that your idea of love?

And all those accusations you made
About the subtle ways you'd been betrayed—
Was that your idea of love?

It felt like drowning. It felt like an immersion

In a dark sea of blame
Until I found out that it was all a diversion.
You had a secret game.
You had a game to play and you played rough.
Was that your idea of love?

Funny I never noticed it creeping up on us,
This vengefulness and spite.
Funny how long I went on thinking
There must be a simple way to put things right.
And funniest of all to think of you
Pretending to seek professional advice,
When what you wanted was to be shot of me
At any cost to anyone,
At any price
To me …

Was that your idea of love?
Was that your idea of love?

Resentfulness disguised as charm,
That care in plotting future harm—
Was that your idea of love?

That skilful use of evidence
To batter down each last defence—
Was that your idea of love?

That conjuring of bad from good,
That mimicry of victimhood—
Was that your idea of love?

You certainly deserve congratulation
On an effective campaign.
I'd like to know the terms for outright capitulation
But I suppose you've made it plain
They're going to be tough.
Is this your idea of love?

Be shot of me I beg you. Let me be.
Tell me again you want no more of me.
Was that the reckoning?
Was that the sum?
Or is there more of this—
Is there more of this to come?

Is this your idea of love?
Is this your idea of love?

Be shot of me I beg you. Let me be.
Tell me again you want no more of me.

Is this your idea of love?

布雷克·莫里森（Blake Morrison，1950—）

别减肥

求求你，亲爱的，别减肥啦。
减肥怎么就有尊严？
那些书我都读过。

我看过你跑步蹬车，
甚至跟你掉过几斤肉。
这已足够。朋友间
靠什么？为了半斤秤流汗
不值得。
饼干我吃够了。
也不信那鬼话。
减不减试着从我的角度看。
我想你在我这儿加重而不是变轻。

Against Dieting

Blake Morrison

Please, darling, no more diets.
I've read the books on why it's
Good for one's esteem.
I've watched you jogging lanes and pounding treadmills.
I've even shed some kilos of my own.
But enough. What are love handles
Between friends? For half a stone
It isn't worth the sweat.
I've had it up to here with crispbread.
I doubt the premise, too.
Try to see it from my point of view.
I want not less but more of you.

安德鲁·莫申（Andrew Motion，1952—）

损失

美军在伊拉克死亡人数接近 3800 时，
彼得雷乌斯将军说“事实上人们不习惯接受损失”
有种坏消息就像漏了的船，

时而淘干，时而变满，时而又空，
留下些长篇故事的细枝末节。
其中就有一个士兵，他在大街巡逻时，

来到一个酒吧，他想看棒球，就转了转天线，
却发现白衣人围一圈，怒色难掩，
也许是伊斯兰圣战者，他们在

朗诵诗歌“我的生活”，翻译说“就像一袋面粉
被风抛向赤裸的荆棘。”然后又更正说“不，不，
像风中的尘土，像不可救药的人。”

Losses

Andrew Motion

General Petraeus, when the death-count of American troops
In Iraq was close to 3,800, said “The truth is you never do get
Used to losses.” There is a kind of bad news vessel with holes,

And sometimes it drains, then it fills up, then it empties again’—
Leaving, in this particular case, the residue of a long story
Involving one soldier who, in the course of his street patrol,

Tweaked the antenna on the TV in a bar hoping for baseball,
But found instead the snowy picture of men in a circle talking,
All apparently angry and perhaps Jihadists. They turned out to be

Reciting poetry. "My life", said the interpreter, "is like a bag of flour
Thrown through wind into empty thorn bushes." Then "No, no, he said,
Correcting himself. 'Like dust in the wind. Like a hopeless man."

马提音·克鲁斯菲克斯（Martyn Crucefix，1956—）

舞蹈

附近的巷子里，
我瞥见一辆卡车，
粘着土的水管肋骨一样，
盘在两米高的轴上，
好像玩具消防车。
靠近驾驶舱的位置，
对称又平衡的
一对儿透明的
红褐色的箱体，
不知啥用途。
卡车缓慢地爬行在
剑桥大道上，
箱里似水的东西在打转。
阳光被劈成
一条条一束束，
在水箱上滑动，
随着车子走走停停，
在水面上起舞。

我开的车子与卡车并行，
行驶与刹车交替时，
那箱子里的液体
折射的阳光，
轻快地跳动，
有弓形的，有平直的，
S 形的像极了西瓜的条纹。
面无血色满身尿味儿，
我眼前不是路，
而是垂死的男人，
他已经失明，
我有时陪他坐坐。
大概二十年前了，
我回想那时
我或许可以当他的眼睛，
用语言传达
他看不见的一切，
虽然我的嘴闭上了，
但眼睛一直睁着。

The Little Dances

Martyn Crucefix

I glimpse a strange truck
In the nearside lane
With a soiled ribbed hose
Wound on a two-metre reel
Like a toy fire-engine—
And up close to the cab
Balanced and symmetrical
A pair of translucent

Sepia-coloured tanks
I can't imagine what for
But swirling with what seems
No more than water
As the truck moves and crawls
On the Great Cambridge Road—
The sun's rays crack
And split and sashay
In each tank as the truck
Stop and starts the little dance
Between brake and pedal
Each vehicle performs
And as i draw alongside
The liquid shows the frisk
Of light so fluently
Full of refracting bows
And slabs and S-shapes
Like glittering lemon bars
Anaemic and urinous—
And rather than the road
I see a man who was dying
Who'd lost his sight
Who I sat with sometimes
Maybe twenty years ago
And back then I imagined
How I might be his eyes
Having words to convey
What he would never see
Though my mouth stayed
Shut I kept my eyes open

本杰明 · 泽凡尼（Benjamin Zephaniah，1958—）

《太阳报》

相信黑人皆坏蛋，
左翼疯，
上帝癫，
本届政府最能干，
所以，我读《太阳报》。

相信英国强大，
别国效仿它，
美国友善之帮家，
每天，我读《太阳报》。

我不太追逐外国好，
不介意他国炸弹，
林中兔子击鼓欢，
然而，我读《太阳报》。

嘿，我讨厌俄国探贼，
可国内不能少；
我热衷谤诽，
真心喜欢戴妃，
我赌定她也读《太阳报》。

黑人抢劫，
女人做饭，
诗人都行骗，
人都这么说——不需亲自看，
《太阳报》里好消遣。

嬉皮有虮子，
国人喜奶子，
我喜欢第三版和其他段子，
眼神吸进《太阳报》。

喜欢宾戈[①]游戏，
喜欢猎巫泼脏水，
所有报纸都如此，
读读《太阳报》没啥不可以。

没真相，有八卦，
衣橱里面取骨架；
想正常，
想从众，
《太阳报》蒙眼睛。

The Sun

Benjamin Zephaniah

I believe the Blacks are bad
The Left is loony
God is Mad
This government's the best we've had
So I read *The SUN*.

I believe Britain is great
And other countries imitate
I am friendly with The State,

① 宾戈（bingo）：一种使用打印数字票的游戏。

Daily, I read *The SUN*.

I am not too keen on foreign ones
But I don't mind some foreign bombs
Jungle bunnies play tom-toms,
But, I read *The SUN*.

Man, I don't like Russian spies
But we don't have none
I love lies,
I really do love Prencess Di
I bet she reads *The SUN*.

Black piople rob
Women should cook
And every poet is a crook,
It's easy in *The SUN*.

Every hippie carries nits
And every Englishman love tits
I love Page Three and other bits,
I stare into *The SUN*.

I like playing bingo games
And witch-hunting to shame a name
But aren's newspapers all the same?
So why not read *The SUN*.

Don't give me truth, just give me gossip
And skeletons from people's closets,
I wanna be normal

And millions buy it,
I am blinded by *The SUN*.

格伦·麦氏威尔（Glyn Maxwell，1962—）

梦里听得砰一声门响

梦里听得砰一声门响，
醒来已成过往。朋友
走了，这最后一个离去，
剩下你，风平浪静做个男人。

用这片香皂洗把脸，
一周前还是她的，
现在是你的，一把搓光，
就像你和她，不再是朋友。

要像宴席一样吃到底，
这是上周六她要的面包，
没吃完。你说的
面包渣归你，吃吧。

日历前停了一下，
撕了这页，“今天”
也就泛黄，你不再记得，
那 J 是个什么名堂。

咖啡痛饮，深蓝的杯子
喝它个底儿朝上。
鼻头呼着气，这笨猪活着，

抬起头，还不错。

Dream But a Door Slams Then

Glyn Maxwell

Dream but a door slams then.
Your waking is in the past. The friend
Who left was the last to leave and that
Left you, calm as a man.

Wash in a slip of soap belonging
Only a week ago to a girl but
Yours now and washed to a nothing.
As you and she, friends and not.

Eat to the end as toast,
The loaf she decided on, only last
Saturday last. The crust is what
You said you'd have. So have.
Stop by the calendar, though,
And peel. The colour today
Is yellow, and you will never remember
What that means—"J".

Drink to the deep the coffee, down
To the well of the dark blue cup.
The oaf with the nose of steam is alive
And well again. Look up.

博物馆

一个个周日，像诗节间隙，
或雷鸣般的掌声结束；
出于说不清道不明的目的，
乐天派在此地移步，
孤独得像还魂的死尸，
像恐龙包围的造物主。

Museum

Glyn Maxwell

Sundays, like a stanza break
Or shower's end of all applause,
For some old unexplaining sake
The optimistic tread these shores,
As lonely as the dead awake
Or God among the dinosaurs.

凯瑟琳·詹米（Kathleen Jamie，1962—）

母鹿

走在苏醒的梦里，
我看见十九头鹿，
从山梁冲向谷底平川，
然后依次跳过
新支棱起的
过火的焦黑。
这是母鹿的领地，

她们悠闲自得，
活在长期租赁的土地上，
她们就是这么想的。
她们从大坝的豁口鱼贯而出，
那口子从来堵不上，
鹿群穿过满坡石楠，
来到一片砾石之上，
她们停下来，四处张望，
头鹿女王般的威仪，
好像在说："我们
不是最好的伙伴吗？
跟我来，
你们会幸福，但永远别回家。"

The Hinds

Kathleen Jamie

Walking in a waking dream
I watched nineteen deer
Pour from ridge to glen-floor,
Then each in turn leap,
Leap the new-raised
Peat-dark burn. This
Was the distaff side;
Hinds at their ease, alive
To lands held on long lease
In their animal minds,
And filing through a breach
In a never-mended dyke,
The herd flowed up over
Heather-slopes to scree

Where they stopped, and turned to stare,
The foremost with a queenly air
As though to say: "Aren't we
The bonniest companie?
Come to me,
You'll be happy, but never go home."

唐·帕特森（Don Paterson，1963—）

诗

这个星球的初火，
永远地陷入冰网，
诗是无心的钻石
保持的一点火花。
诗不是恋爱后的温度，
而是寂寥中抽出的爱的原子。
所以，如果爱的火炭闷烧，
诗人会听到迸裂，像酒吧歌手的声音——
自负感情激烈，或者淹没在小提琴中；
如果那火炭均匀地发亮，诗人知道
纯粹的诗意，当他来临时，会像
山泉，无名而宁静。

混沌的蓝天下，泉水
歌而无为，不唱你，也不唱我。

Poetry

Don Paterson

In the same way that the mindless diamond keeps
One spark of the planet's early fires
Trapped forever in its net of ice,
It's not love's later heat that poetry holds,
But the atom of the love that drew it forth
From the silence: so if the bright coal of his love
Begins to smoulder, the poet hears his voice
Suddenly forced, like a bar-room singer's—boastful
With his own huge feeling, or drowned by violins;
But if it yields a steadier light, he knows
The pure verse, when it finally comes, will sound
Like a mountain spring, anonymous and serene.

Beneath the blue oblivious sky, the water
Sings of nothing, not your name, not mine.

那条线

杰米硬着陆，
划一道长沟返回大地。
人们把气如游丝的他
拖出。谁也不知他命悬哪条线。
所以今天要感谢无上的天意
将你、我，还有露丝带到一起，
双引擎巨大的机翼载着我们
冲下基里埃山[①]

① 基里埃山（Kirrie Hill）：以前的砂岩采石场，户外运动场地。

你两岁的呼吸强过
世上任何引擎。
死里逃生的曲折
我整整回想了一周。有一条线
把我们牵在一起：看看我们的小屋，
儿子，你母亲正在挥手的那个白点。

The Thread

Don Paterson

Jamie made his landing in the world
So hard he ploughed straight back into the earth.
They caught him by the thread of his one breath
And pulled him up. They don't know how it held.
And so today I thank what higher will
Brought us to here, to you and me and Russ,
The great twin-engined swaying wingspan of us
Roaring down the back of Kirrie Hill

And your two-year-old lungs somehow out-revving
Every engine in the universe.
All that trouble just to turn up dead
Was all I thought that long week. Now the thread
Is holding all of us: look at our tiny house,
Son, the white dot of your mother waving.

西蒙·阿米特吉（Simon Armitage，1963—）

诗

如果雪下得掩了车道，
他会拿铁锨连铲带抛。
他总在夜里将女儿被盖好，
又晃鞋底儿要她实话实招。
他每周工资花一大半儿，
每周花不掉的他也都攒。
他夸奖妻子的每顿佳馔
哪次嘲笑他就拳头砸脸。

他给母亲雇了私人护士。
每周都打车给她送教堂去。
母亲病重他就痛哭流涕，
却两次顺走母亲十枚金币。

人们回过头来将他衡量，
有时他这样，有时他那样。

Poem

Simon Armitage

And if it snowed and snow covered the drive
He took a spade and tossed it to one side.
And always tucked his daughter up at night
And slippered her the one time that she lied.
And every week he tipped up half his wage.
And what he didn't spend each week he saved.
And praised his wife for every meal she made.

And once, for laughing, punched her in the face.

And for his mum he hired a private nurse.
And every Sunday taxied her to church.
And he blubbed when she went from bad to worse.
And twice he lifted ten quid from her purse.

Here's how they rated him when they looked back:
Sometimes he did this, sometimes he did that.

大卫·莫利（David Morley，1965—）

无形的礼物

约翰·克莱尔[①]用词语做巢，
巢穴上泥点一样点缀着韵脚，
他抓取形体，但还不能听到：
就用动词名词的绒毛结个听宫，
克莱尔将形体放下来孕育声音：
轻快的节拍，在他手上敲击，
直到它软软地孵化出来。
他朝自己的手心下偷看，
看到它的眼睛，听到它
唧唧唧，脑子里一片空白。
他摸一下它摇摇晃晃淡黄
湿润的头冠；让它啄手指，
膀根的肌肉富有弹力。此时，
如饥似渴的人们都来听曲儿。

---

① 约翰·克莱尔（John Clare）：英国浪漫主义诗人，以描写自然、乡村生活和爱情著称。

The Invisible Gift

David Morley

John Clare weaves English words into a nest
And in the cup he stipples rhyme, like mud,
To clutch the shape of something he can hold
But not yet hear; and in the hollow of his hearing,
He feathers a space with a down of verbs
And nouns heads-up. There. Clare lays it down
And nestles over its forming sound: taps and lilts,
The steady knocking of the nib on his hand until
It hatches softly beneath him. And when he peers
Below his palm, he spies its eyes, hears its peeps,
But does not know what to think. He strokes
Its tottering yolk-wet crown; feels a nip against
His thumb, buds of muscle springy at the wing, and all
The hungers of the world to come for this small singing.

备寻[①]

又作陪寻。
把寻或四开面。
是罗马人用过的标记，
用于告诉别人他们的方向。
是树枝搭的格子或者扭结的树叶，
也可以是捆绑的树皮，用于传递信息。
用些约定俗成的形式花样，或者
形式与花样的排列和组合。
也可以称作叶子，

① 备寻（patrin）：连同下文的陪寻（pateran）、把寻（paytrin）、四开面（sikaimasko），皆为音译与意译的混合。

或直白点，
书页。

书页。
或直白点，
也可以称作叶子，
形式与花样的排列和组合。
用些约定俗成的形式花样，或者
也可以是捆绑的树皮，用于传递信息。
是树枝搭的格子或者扭结的树叶，
用于告诉别人他们的方向。
是罗马人用过的标记，
把寻或四开面，
又作陪寻。

Patrìn

David Morley

Or pateran,
Pyatrin, or sikaimasko.
The marker used by Roma
That tells others of their direction,
Often grids of branches or leaf-twists or
Bark-binds. Used for passing on news
Using prearranged forms, patterns
Or permutations of these. Yet
It also means a leaf or,
Simply, a page.

Simply, a page
Yet it also means a leaf

Or permutations of these
Using prearranged forms, patterns.
Bark-binds used for passing on news,
Often grids of branches or leaf-twists
That tell others of their direction.
The marker used by Roma:
Pyatrin, or sikaimasko,
Or pateran.

爱丽丝·奥斯瓦尔德（Alice Oswald，1966—）

满月

天啊！
我昨晚做的什么梦？
我梦见变成月亮。
醒来发现我还睡着。

是这样：我的脸从里到外雾化，
来去自如地穿过小小的窥孔，
没有声音，没有嘴，没法表达我的烦恼。
只有影子沿山坡下倾，还不太平行。

我的月光需要描摹，
近于霜却更柔和，近于余灰却更完整，
几乎由水构成，严格说来却没特征，
不过是一种逆光，称为穿透力。

就像在林子里，他们推挤着带风帽的形状，
彼此抹杀后，头就凝结成一体，

有月亮族，有声音族，比如鹿，比如麋鹿。
经过那里时，他们的目光可以穿透物体。

我是这样：有形无形有形无形，
没什么材质像光一样多变，
我攀爬，倒挂在自己的骨头上，思考：
天啊！我昨晚是谁？

Full Moon

Alice Oswald

Good God!
What did I dream last night?
I dreamt I was the moon.
I woke and found myself still asleep.

It was like this: my face misted up from inside
And I came and went at will through a little peephole.
I had no voice, no mouth, nothing to express my trouble,
Except my shadows leaning downhill, not quite parallel.

Something needs to be said to describe my moonlight.
Almost frost but softer, almost ash but wholer.
Made almost of water, which has strictly speaking
No feature, but a kind of counter-light, call it insight.

Like in woods, when they jostle their hooded shapes,
Their heads congealed together, having murdered each other,
There are moon-beings, sound-beings, such as deer and half-deer
Passing through there, whose eyes can pierce through things.

I was like that: visible invisible visible invisible.
There's no material as variable as moonlight.
I was climbing, clinging to the underneath of my bones, thinking:
Good God! Who have I been last night?

偶合

爱情时时像行船
远航要靠巧扬帆
帆儿张开如燕翅
燕子飞起风兜衣
衣服若归你所有
恐怕它要张大口
大口呼嘘如号角
号角吹起千重调
响来响去非我已
一调一个鬼把戏
把戏如同走钢丝
一步一移靠运气
运气来了如嫁娶
嫁娶如爱一个理

Wedding

Alice Oswald

From time to time our love is like a sail
And when the sail begins to alternate
From tack to tack, it's like a swallowtail
And when the swallow flies it's like a coat;
And if the coat is yours, it has a tear
Like a wide mouth and when the mouth begins

To draw the wind, it's like a trumpeter
And when the trumpet blows, it blows like millions …
And this, my love, when millions come and go
Beyond the need of us, is like a trick;
And when the trick begins, it's like a toe
Tip-toeing on a rope, which is like luck;
And when the luck begins, it's like a wedding,
Which is like love, which is like everything.

朱丽亚·考伯斯（Julia Copus，1969—）

詹金斯老师

最近，越来越冷清，
校门口，街道上，
她醒来便想起从前的呼唤，让她走到如今的呼唤。
在朦胧的，糖纸一样模糊的天光下，
她或者烧水，或者跪地拔草，
多少个黄昏，现在（街灯点亮）
她感觉自己充满活力，再次走进
高窗明亮的教室，
手执粉笔，同事们人见人爱，走进
轻快的节奏，那些工作的日子。
甚至在梦里，她的呼吸都随着学童的脚步起伏，
她的意识，渗透血液，有个对位，
课本一个个拍在书桌上，
准是她要给他们上课。

准是她要给他们上课，
课本一个个拍在小书桌上，

她的意识，渗透血液，有个对位，
甚至在梦里，她的呼吸都随着学童的脚步起伏，
轻快而有节奏，那些工作的日子，
手执粉笔，同事们人见人爱，走进，
高窗明亮的教室，
她感觉自己充满活力；再次走进
多少个黄昏，现在（街灯点亮），
她或者烧水，或者跪地拔草，
在朦胧的，糖纸一样模糊的天光下，
她醒来便想起从前的呼唤，让她走到如今的呼唤，
校门口，街道上，
最近，越来越冷清。

Miss Jenkins

Julia Copus

More and more, lately, when absence thickened the air
at the schoolgates, in the street, first thing on waking,
she'd think of her former calling, the way it had defined her.
In the dim, sugar-paper blur of the light,
while boiling the kettle or kneeling over weeds,
many times at dusk now (the streetlights coming on)
she'd feel herself alive, transported
once again to the bright, tall-windowed classroom,
chalky-fingered, cherished by her peers, and walking—
that brisk and rhythmic pace she adopted, all her working days.
Even in sleep, her breath would rise and fall with
the sharp pat pat of the children's feet approaching and
she'd sense—in her blood—like a counterpoint beneath it,
the slap of books upon each child-size table
wherever she set up class for their arrival.

Whenever she set up class for their arrival
—the slap of books upon each child-size table—
She'd sense in her blood, like a counterpoint beneath it,
the sharp pat pat of the children's feet approaching and
even in sleep her breath would rise and fall with
that brisk and rhythmic pace she adopted, all her working days.
Chalky-fingered, cherished by her peers, and walking
once again to the bright, tall-windowed classroom,
she'd feel herself alive; transported.
Many times at dusk now (the streetlights coming on),
while boiling the kettle or kneeling over weeds,
in the dim, sugar-paper blur of the light,
she'd think of her former calling, the way it had defined her,
at the schoolgates, in the street, first thing on waking—
More and more, lately, when absence thickened the air.

母亲的后车座上

我们走了，来不及
安慰你，告诉你空洞的微明里，
我们几乎碰到手，我想
止住滚烫的泪水细流般在脸上腿上淌，
我的手伸向天空涌进的窗缝，
乙醚一样冰凉，我看见你肥大的鼹鼠手抓着八月的尘霾。
我的脸贴在玻璃上；
我喊你——爸爸！那时车子呼啸着驶向远方，
我的手像截肢一样刺痛。
我仍然记得你在说着什么，
寂寂的话语像尖叫飞扬的和弦在我全身扩散，
像热烈的晚霞倾注西天。

随之而来的沉默是我唯一的破获——
马达轰鸣淹没你的声音，
你我之间隔着冰滑的玻璃。

你我之间隔着冰滑的玻璃。
马达轰鸣淹没你的声音，
随之而来的沉默是我唯一的破获——
像热烈的晚霞倾注西天。
寂寂的话语像尖叫飞扬的和弦在我全身扩散，
我仍然记得你在说着什么，
我的手像截肢一样刺痛。
我喊你——爸爸！那时车子呼啸着驶向远方，
我的脸贴在玻璃上；
乙醚一样冰凉，我看见你肥大的鼹鼠手抓着八月的尘霾。
我的手伸向天空涌进的窗缝，
止住滚烫的泪水细流般在脸上腿上淌，
我们几乎碰到手，我想
安慰你，告诉你空洞的微明里，
我们走了，来不及。

The Back Seat of My Mother's Car

Julia Copus

We left before I had time
To comfort you, to tell you that we nearly touched
Hands in that vacuous half-dark. I wanted
To stem the burning waters running over me like tiny
Rivers down my face and legs, but at the same time I was reaching out
For the slit in the window where the sky streamed in,
Cold as ether, and I could see your fat mole-fingers grasping
The dusty August air. I pressed my face to the glass;

I was calling to you—Daddy!—as we screeched away into
The distance, my own hand tingling like an amputation.
You were mouthing something I still remember, the noiseless words
Percing me like that catgut shriek that flew up, furious as a sunset
Pouring itself out against the sky. The ensuing silence
Was the one clear thing I could decipher-
The roar of the eingine dorwing your voice,
With the cool slick glass between us.

With the cool slick glass between us,
The roar of the engine dorwning, your voice
Was the one clear thing I could decipher—
Pouring itself out against the sky, the ensuing slience
Pericing me like that catgut shriek that flew up, furious as a sunset.
You were mouthing something: I still remeber the noiseless words,
The distance, my own hand tingling like an amputation.
I was calling to you, Daddy, as we screeched away into
The dusty August air. I pressed my face to the glass,
Cold as ether, and I could see your fat mole-fingers grasping
For the slit in the window where the sky streamed in
Rivers down my face and legs, but at the same time I was reaching out
To stem the burning waters running over me like tiny
Hands in that vacuous half-dark. I wanted
To comfort you, to tell you that we nearly touched.
We left before I had time.

雅各伯·波利（Jacob Polley，1975—）

回家

我要床、烤牛肉和雨水，
我想穿淘汰的旧衣装，
想借它们活动下脑子，
定下这颗凡心去思想。

这是我的裤子和腰带，
熨好的衬衣，鞋子有序，
听过、看过、嗅过的都在，
统统都盖上了大报纸。

我喝过热水，去买东西，
结账的时候，我竟发现
卸掉套了许久的头盔，
脖子眼睛上压痕变浅。

橙色的夜晚我站外边，
听城市的嘈杂与喧嚣。
我喜欢和平中的野蛮，
没人问宁静有什么好。

若有人问，我也说不清，
虽然我也并非不知道：
羊与羊毛，牛与牛棚，
蜜蜂与它们金色的巢。

荒漠之中我读过古书，
沙粒横扫塌陷的帐篷，

此情此景，发卡和头梳
有着不同寻常的界定。

像我试图品味的词语，
经尘土洗礼更加美好，
只有接近荒漠的边际，
我才为翻书挑灯高照。

灯光熄灭一片漆黑，
我躺在嘶嘘中无眠，
直到清醒将无眠撕碎，
漫游的梦境散开握拳。

家，经过火爆和偷袭，
以为自己找对了地方，
却一直在战斗中失去
回归的希望。

思想让我以别处为家，
有种陌生感将我袭击，
我把旧衣服拿下衣架，
穿它回归久违的自己。

Homecoming

Jacob Polley

I wanted bed, roast beef and rain,
To wear the clothes I'd left behind
And have them make me think again
Steadily, with a civil mind.

There were my trousers, leather belts,
My ironed shirts and rank of shoes.
Those things I heard and saw and smelt
Were over there, beyond the news.

I had hot water, stuff to buy
And, when I checked, the groove impressed
Around my head and over my eyes
By armour borne so long was less.

On orange nights I stood outside
And listened to the city roar.
I liked the way peace brutalised
Yet no one asked what peace was for.

If they had, I wouldn't have said,
Though not because I didn't know:
Sheep and shearing, cows and sheds,
Honeybees and hives of gold—

On desert time I'd read old books
While sand blew through and sagged the tent.
But back here all those combs and crooks
No longer meant what they had meant,

As if the words I strove to taste
Through dust were sweeter for their age
Only when being bordered waste.
I'd shake my torch for one more page

And when it died into the dark

I'd lie awake inside the hiss
Until my waking came apart
And aimless dreams undid my fists.

Home: I'd thought I'd held the place
Through firestorm and sneak attack
While all the time I'd fought to lose
Any hope of coming back.

My mind made home somewhere else,
And so my strangeness strikes me down
While wearing clothes I'd left on shelves
For some return far from my own.

烟火

过去我父亲生炉子时，
用楼梯板
搭在炉底石上。

一天早上他从冰冷的台阶走下来，
张开双手
在通红的炉壁上烤火。

他把铁炉门打开，
像开银行的保险箱，
发现炉膛里一点不热，只有一堆灰。

他把发白的火炭敲碎，
里边冒出一小簇蓝火，
然后把煤灰从炉条上捅掉。

灰斗一点点装满，
有炉口宽一堆，
他像移炸弹一样将灰从黢黑的炉膛掏出。

他满脸飞着煤烔，
出后门口儿，
把灰倒入垃圾桶，

然后截柴棍儿，
团报纸，
划火柴，

将引火点着。
烟滚，火散，
炉子吞风作响，

他便摇晃煤桶，
将煤块儿填入炉中，
把炉门关上。

这一次
父亲拿本书，将书脊拆开
扔进炉膛；

他的日记
年复一年
一页页烧出响来，

皮革的封皮移位，爆起，
然后脱落。

不久我就来了，

从母亲的心坎上挣脱
长大，看父亲
烟熏火燎中折断烧焦的鸟儿。

我奇怪
是否自己也吊在黑暗中熏烤，
每当母亲唱歌或说话时，
我看见她喉咙咽下火光。

Smoke

Jacob Polley

My father kept a stove
With dogs legs
On a pink hearthstone.

One morning he climbed down the icy stairs
And spread his palms
On the blood-warm metal flanks.

He cranked open the iron doors,
Like a black banks safe
But found no heat and ash heaped in its place.

He cracked grey whittled coals
Released brief blue flames,
And knocked downy soot through the bars of the grate.

The ash-pan, softly loaded

And almost as wide as a doorway,
He carried like dynamite through the dark house,

His bright face blown with smuts.
At the back door
He slid the ash into a tin dustbin,

Then snapped sticks,
Crumpled newspaper,
Struck a match

And dipped it between the kindling.
Smoke unrolled, flames spread,
The rush of the stove eating air started up,

And my father would shake on rocks
From an old coal hod
And swing the doors shut.

But this time
He took a book, broke its spine
And slung that instead:

His diaries
Year by year
Purred as their pages burned,

Their leather boards shifted, popped
And fell apart.
Soon I would arrive,

Pulled from under my mothers heart,
And grow to watch my father
Break the charred crossbeam of a bird from the flue.

Wondering if I too
Had hung in darkness and smoke,
Looking up at the light let down her throat
Whenever my mother sang or spoke.

第五章

其他重要诗人作品

托马斯·莫尔（Thomas Moore，1779—1852）

不要唤他的名字（选自《爱尔兰曲》第一册）

不要唤他名字，让他树下安眠，
那里摆放他的遗物，冰冷寒酸。
悲哀，静默，幽暗，泪水流淌，
像夜里露水落在坟头草叶上，
滚落的夜露，无声无息的哭泣，
会让他安眠的坟茔充满绿意；
我们的泪水虽是悄悄地流淌，
我们对他的记忆常青于心上。

Oh! Breathe Not His Name (Excerpt from *Irish Melodies*, Vol. I)

Thomas Moore

Oh! breathe not his name, let it sleep in the shade,
Where cold and unhonour'd his relics are laid:
Sad, silent, and dark, be the tears that we shed,
As the night-dew that falls on the grass o'er his head.
But the night-dew that falls, though in silence it weeps,
Shall brighten with verdure the grave where he sleeps;
And the tear that we shed, though in secret it rolls,
Shall long keep his memory green in our souls.

奥斯卡·王尔德（Oscar Wilde，1854—1900）

济慈墓

摆脱了世间的不公和他的病痛，
终于在上帝命制的蓝纱下安息。
爱情与生命被剥夺于青葱之季，
最年轻的殉道者就安放于此冢。
塞巴斯蒂[1]般美好而又早遭摧残，
此墓没松柏遮阴也无紫衫守护。
只有那轻柔的紫罗兰点点泣露，
在他的尸骨上编织不谢的花环。
啊，为苦难而破碎的高傲心灵！
啊，米特林岛[2]上最甜美的声音！
啊，以诗描画英伦的拳拳赤子！
你的声名沾水书写，将得永祀，
我们的泪水将对你的记忆滋润，
像伊莎贝拉[3]让她的罗勒树常青。

The Grave of Keats

Oscar Wilde

Rid of the world's injustice, and his pain,

---

① 塞巴斯蒂（Sebastian）：罗马圣徒，卒于公元288年。传说他先被箭射中，然后被打死。

② 米特林岛（Mitylene）：希腊东部的一个岛屿，位于爱琴海东部。在古代，它以抒情诗而闻名。

③ 伊莎贝拉（Isabella）：源于约翰·济慈的一首叙事诗，该诗改编自薄伽丘的《十日谈》中的一个故事。讲述一个年轻女子，她的家人打算把她嫁给“贵族和他的橄榄树”，但她爱上了她兄弟的雇员洛伦佐。当兄弟得知此事后，他们谋杀了洛伦佐并埋葬了他的尸体。他的鬼魂在梦中通知伊莎贝拉。她挖出尸体，把他的头埋在一盆罗勒树（Basil—tree）里，一边苦苦挣扎，一边痴迷地照料着。

He rests at last beneath God's veil of blue:
Taken from life when life and love were new
The youngest of the martyrs here is lain,
Fair as Sebastian, and as early slain.
No cypress shades his grave, no funeral yew,
But gentle violets weeping with the dew
Weave on his bones an ever-blossoming chain.
O proudest heart that broke for misery!
O sweetest lips since those of Mitylene!
O poet-painter of our English Land!
Thy name was writ in water—it shall stand:
And tears like mine will keep thy memory green,
As Isabella did her Basil-tree.

拜谒罗马

一

谷粒由灰变红，
其间我的精神
荡出北方城门，
逃于群山之中。
这里我望向老家，
朝圣路已走完，
走过血阳落山，
开进神圣罗马。
啊，万福之女，
七山由你掌管！
母亲啊，一尘不染，
冠以三重金辉！
罗马啊，罗马啊，
我经长途跋涉，

来至圣街献歌，
伏于你的脚下。

二

然而多么开怀，
我一直向南走，
直至台伯河[1]口，
朝菲耶索里[2]跪拜！
穿过松林交织，
踏过阿诺金涛，
看那晨曦缭绕，
看亚平宁紫气。
走过青藤门庭，
穿过苍榄枝丫，
直到坎帕尼亚[3]
拱起七山宝顶！

三

来自北海的香客，
独寻庙宇神奇，
寻找宝座金匙，
于我何等快乐！
神父枢机主教，
身披紫霞金粉，
生而卓绝超群，
信众高洁向导。
趁我尚在人间，

① 台伯河（Tiber）：意大利中部的一条河流，发源于托斯卡纳亚平宁山脉（Tuscan Apennines），向南流经罗马注入第勒尼安海（Tyrrhenian Sea）。

② 菲耶索里（Fiesole）：意大利中部的一个城镇，在俯瞰阿诺河（Amo River）和佛罗伦萨市（Florence）的小山上有别墅和花园。

③ 坎帕尼亚（Campagna）：意大利罗马周围的低洼平原。

看着我王主定，
在他经过时倾听
银号吹响凯旋！
面对神殿祭坛
高高举起牺牲，
将隐蔽的神灵
呈现世人眼前。

四

岁月往复如梭，
时光带来巨变！
让我心摆脱不安，
然后教我唱歌。
金光波动的田野，
捆成灰色秸秆，
红叶一片片，
像鸟拍翅飞落。
荣耀之旅走完，
我仍手持火把，
寻找圣名的他，
他遮掩的容颜。

Rome Unvisited

Oscar Wilde

I

The corn has turned from grey to red,
Since first my spirit wandered forth
From the drear cities of the north,
And to Italia's mountains fled.
And here I set my face towards home,

For all my pilgrimage is done,
Although, methinks, yon blood-red sun
Marshals the way to Holy Rome.
O Blessed Lady, who dost hold
Upon the seven hills thy reign!
O Mother without blot or stain,
Crowned with bright crowns of triple gold!
O Roma, Roma, at thy feet
I lay this barren gift of song!
For, ah! the way is steep and long
That leads unto thy sacred street.

II

And yet what joy it were for me
To turn my feet unto the south,
And journeying towards the Tiber mouth
To kneel again at Fiesole!
And wandering through the tangled pines
That break the gold of Arno's stream,
To see the purple mist and gleam
Of morning on the Apennines.
By many a vineyard-hidden home,
Orchard, and olive-garden grey,
Till from the drear Campagna's way
The seven hills bear up the dome!

III

A pilgrim from the northern seas—
What joy for me to seek alone
The wondrous Temple, and the throne
Of Him who holds the awful keys!

When, bright with purple and with gold,
Come priest and holy Cardinal,
And borne above the heads of all
The gentle Shepherd of the Fold.
O joy to see before I die
The only God-anointed King,
And hear the silver trumpets ring
A triumph as He passes by!
Or at the altar of the shrine
Holds high the mystic sacrifice,
And shows a God to human eyes
Beneath the veil of bread and wine.

IV

For lo, what changes time can bring!
The cycles of revolving years
May free my heart from all its fears,—
And teach my lips a song to sing.
Before yon field of trembling gold
Is garnered into dusty sheaves,
Or ere the autumn's scarlet leaves
Flutter as birds adown the world,
I may have run the glorious race,
And caught the torch while yet aflame,
And called upon the holy name
Of Him who now doth hide His face.

艾伦·厄普得（Allen Upward，1863—1926）

美人鱼

水手倚靠宝船，用白皙的手指梳理海的碧发，以为自己听到了美人鱼的声音，便将身体投入波涛。

The Mermaid

Allen Upward

The sailor boy who leant over the side of the Junk of Many Pearls,
And combed the green tresses of the sea with his ivory fingers,
Believing that he had heard the voice of a mermaid, cast his body
Down between the waves.

威廉·巴特勒·叶芝（William Butler Yeats，1865—1939）

神矢

盈思寤寐为芳容
刻骨铭心意不平
豆蔻年华人未识
谁家有女初长成
雍容高贵颜如玉
窈窕白皙肤似苹
今忆佳人已迟暮
泣结良善日西征

The Arrow

William Butler Yeats

I thought of your beauty, and this arrow,
Made out of a wild thought, is in my marrow.
There's no man may look upon her, no man,
As when newly grown to be a woman,
Tall and noble but with face and bosom
Delicate in colour as apple blossom.
This beauty's kinder, yet for a reason
I could weep that the old is out of season.

前盟

因你背弃那深重的前盟，
我才把其他人看作知己；
然而，每当我直面死亡，
每当我爬上睡眠的巅峰，
每当我开怀痛饮酣畅淋漓，
我总是突然看见你的脸庞。

A Deep-Sworn Vow

William Butler Yeats

Others because you did not keep
That deep-sworn vow have been friends of mine;
Yet always when I look death in the face,
When I clamber to the heights of sleep,
Or when I grow excited with wine,
Suddenly I meet your face.

饮酒歌

喝醇酒入口，
相爱爱凝眸，
你我晓真意，
不必到白头。
举杯近我口，
相看叹悠悠。

A Drinking Song

William Butler Yeats

Wine comes in at the mouth
And love comes in at the eye;
That's all we shall know for truth
Before we grow old and die.
I lift the glass to my mouth,
I look at you, and I sigh.

格兰德洛[①]的溪水与落日

译一

太阳滑行溪水流，
起止难辨动疏忽。
满心轻松似明媚，
蠢事做成已难收，
心神不定总相违。

忏悔若使心不洁，

① 格兰德洛（Glendalough）：爱尔兰威克洛郡的冰川河谷，因公元 6 世纪建立的中世纪早期修道院而闻名。

韬光养晦当不错，
或可出众又超群，
只怕敢想不敢做，
枉论自己是何人。

太阳溪水或眼皮，
如何动得闪余晖？
余晖如何透肉身。
如何我生亦如此，
自我革命做新人？

译二
溪流落日，
我心欢喜，
愚否痴否，
我志他移。

悔不涤秽，
与我何益！
敢求诸己，
不做俗人？

日转水流，
开目凝眸，
灵光闪过，
吾身洞彻。
何能如此，
赋我新生？

Stream and Sun at Glendalough

William Butler Yeats

Through intricate motions ran
Stream and gliding sun
And all my heart seemed gay:
Some stupid thing that I had done
Made my attention stray.

Repentance keeps my heart impure;
But what am I that dare
Fancy that I can
Better conduct myself or have more
Sense than a common man?

What motion of the sun or stream
Or eyelid shot the gleam
That pierced my body through?
What made me live like these that seem
Self-born，born anew?

一顷草地

唯余图画、书籍，
晨练草地一顷。
空气清新当活动，
人老力已倾。
正子夜，一幢老屋，
寂寂无声只有鼠。

欲望渴求消歇。

生命即将终止，
心思磨平，想象
松垮，支离破碎
正消耗殆尽，
却难去伪存真。

老夫聊发少年狂，
定要重塑自我，
要做泰门[1]李尔[2]，
或威廉·布雷克[3]。
个个敢撞南墙，
直至真理回响。

米开朗琪罗[4]最知：
思想可以穿云，
或乘狂暴而起，
惊动装殓的死人。
否则就被忘掉，
老鹰隼的头脑。

---

① 泰门（Timon）：威廉·莎士比亚在《雅典的泰门》中创作的悲剧性人物。泰门出身贵族，生性豪爽，乐善好施。许多人乘机骗取钱财，导致泰门倾家荡产，最后泰门在绝望中孤独地死去。

② 李尔（Lear）：指威廉·莎士比亚创作的著名悲剧人物李尔王。他将国土分给三个女儿，最后却被大女儿和二女儿抛弃。

③ 威廉（William）：指英国著名诗人和画家威廉·布雷克（William Blake），人称“远离尘世”的疯狂天才。

④ 迈克尔（Michael）：指原文中的 Michael Angelo。疑指米开朗琪罗（Michelangelo），指意大利文艺复兴时期伟大的绘画家、雕塑家、建筑师和诗人。

An Acre of Grass

William Butler Yeats

Picture and book remain,
An acre of green grass
For air and exercise,
Now strength of body goes;
Midnight, an old house
Where nothing stirs but a mouse.

My temptation is quiet.
Here at life's end
Neither loose imagination,
Nor the mill of the mind
Consuming its rag and bone,
Can make the truth known.

Grant me an old man's frenzy,
Myself must I remake
Till I am Timon and Lear
Or that William Blake
Who beat upon the wall
Till Truth obeyed his call;

A mind Michael Angelo knew
That can pierce the clouds,
Or inspired by frenzy
Shake the dead in their shrouds;
Forgotten else by mankind,
An old man's eagle mind.

内战时期的沉思（节选）

一、祖屋

富家开花的草坪上，
枝叶沙沙的山林间，
云行雨施生机盎然，
不费力也沟平谷满，
山之高耸令人目眩，
鬼斧神工全凭自然。
从不屈就人工机巧，
也不屈从他人召唤。

梦想，不过是梦想！
荷马若非超越梦想，
就不会有千古绝唱，
是生活自身喜悦高昂，
流光溢彩。今只像
空贝壳被抛出污江，
备五彩却无泉水滋养，
遮蔽了遗产丰厚辉煌。

不乏狂徒不乏强权，
招来建筑艺术大腕。
一模一样的狂徒强权，
要石头里面觅温婉。
温婉难见谁都期盼。
但主人一死老鼠窜，
或许重孙子把房占，
铜鼎在手是个鼠贪。

何如花园落下孔雀，
步态优雅走上旧阶。
或朱诺在古瓮展现
旁若无人的花仙。
何如草坪小径平坦，
任人穿着拖鞋打禅，
或者儿童可劲游玩，
如今伟大沦陷于野蛮？

何如族徽光耀门庭，
祖屋高起营造威名。
地板抛光四通八达，
房子宽敞连着走廊，
祖先肖像高悬廊上。
何如弘扬祖先荣光，
或者佑于无上光荣，
而今伟大沦于苦痛？

二、我的房子

古桥，更有古塔，
围墙圈起农舍，
一顷贫瘠的土地，
象征性的玫瑰花，
老榆夹杂荆柯，
雨声伴着风吹，
挨着个敲打；
恐慌的水鸡，
再一次涉水，
被过河的牛群惊吓。

旋转楼梯，石拱房屋，
灰白的石头壁炉，火塘敞开，
一支蜡烛，一页稿纸，
柏拉图式的参悟，
恍如高阁，生出影来，
愤怒的魔鬼；
万物忽恍，
留宿的逆旅，
不管上店赶集，
都看见这子夜的烛光。

这里两个先行者。一个大兵
圈着他的马匹度日。
在这不安的地方，
长久的战乱，突发的夜警，
他和他减员的马匹好似被抛弃，
遗忘与被遗忘；
我身后子孙发现，
还有我，颂扬
孤独的思想，
正合做敌对的旌幡。

三、我的桌子

沉重的支架，一块木板，
木板上一把永恒的剑。
剑边有纸有笔，
可论道德伦理。
我的日子如彼的盲目，
像一块儿镶边的桌布，
将装剑木头掩盖，

乔叟[①]不知宽窄。
铸剑之初，佐藤[②]的屋里，
它就像新月，照亮房子，
一卧就五百年。
倘若没有改变，
没有月亮，只有绞痛的心
酝酿着永恒的艺术品。
博学之士指出，
当时铸剑之处，
无论是画卷还是陶片，
都精美绝伦令人生叹，
父子代代相传，
跨越了多少年，
就像那把剑一样永恒。
曾经精魂迷恋多少人，
他人事业刻着
我心灵的颜色。
作为最富有的继承人，
深知都不可越过天门。
既有志于守拙，
内心承受折磨；
他，面对衣冠楚楚，
虽然不过是村言野语，
却理智又清醒，

① 乔叟（Chaucer）：英国中世纪诗人，乔叟之名源于法语单词 chaussier，意思是鞋类制造商鞋匠。

② 佐藤（Sato）：铸剑人的名字。据叶芝书信记述，一个读过他诗歌的日本人来访，给他一把剑做礼物。此剑家传，已有五百年历史，剑柄上有铸剑人的名字。叶芝婉拒不成，便说当送剑人（当时还没有结婚）的第一个孩子出生时，可以把剑奉还。

似朱诺之雀[1]长鸣。

四、我的后人

继承祖辈脑力充沛，
我定要把梦想培植，
身后留下一男半女，
头脑同样充满活力。
可生活很少芳香四溢，
很少光荣染上朝辉。
花瓣飘零满园飞；
平平常常一片绿。

只怕后人心灵衰落，
不知不觉丢了花朵，
时光荏苒世事繁多，
玩物丧志，或嫁蠢货。
汗水铺就台阶高塔，
可会落顶一片瓦，
猫头鹰占了崩塌大厦，
叫苍凉于荒天下？

流转风潮天下传，
猫头鹰跟着连天转。
世间最富当属我，
惯看爱情友谊多。
为结故友择邻处，
儿女动情翻盖屋。

① 朱诺之雀（Juno’s peacock）：见于《伊索寓言》：有一次，一只孔雀向朱诺申请，希望除了其他吸引力，还要有夜莺的声音。朱诺拒绝了他的请求，告诫他满足自己的命运，不事事都想得第一。

无论兴盛与衰微，
这些石头就是丰碑。

五、门前的路

和蔼的福斯塔[1]——
胖墩墩的乐天派，
说着内战的笑话，
好像死在枪口下，
世上才玩得最嗨。

皮肤晒黑的军官
带着邋遢的兵蛋子
站我门前，我冷言
骂冰雹雨的鬼天
风暴中折断雪梨 。

我数着插翅的煤球——
一群雷鸟顺流而去。
抚平心里的嫉妒，
回到卧室，陷入
冰天雪地的梦里。

六、窗边的八哥窝

我家屋墙松动，
蜜蜂在墙缝筑巢，
八哥叼枝虫造王宫。
来吧，来吧，蜜蜂，

① 福斯塔（Falstaffian man）：福斯塔式的人物。源于莎士比亚笔下的人物，外形肥胖　喜狂欢闹饮。

来八哥的空窝筑巢。

我们被禁锢，开门
什么事都说不好，
某人被害，某屋被焚，
真相到底无处寻：
来吧蜜蜂，来空窝筑巢。

石木垒起的关卡，
约十四天内战消耗，
昨天夜里他们开拔，
一路血泊死士如麻：
来吧蜜蜂，来空窝筑巢。

因饱食太多的妄想，
心也变得野蛮强暴，
宿怨日多，爱却渺茫，
来吧，来吧，蜜蜂，
来八哥的空窝筑巢。

Meditations in Time of Civil War (Excerpt)

William Butler Yeats

I. Ancestral Houses

Surely among a rich man's flowering lawns,
Amid the rustle of his planted hills,
Life overflows without ambitious pains;
And rains down life until the basin spills,
And mounts more dizzy high the more it rains
As though to choose whatever shape it wills

And never stoop to a mechanical
Or servile shape, at others' beck and call.

Mere dreams, mere dreams! Yet Homer had not Sung
Had he not found it certain beyond dreams
That out of life's own self-delight had sprung
The abounding glittering jet; though now it seems
As if some marvellous empty sea-shell flung
Out of the obscure dark of the rich streams,
And not a fountain, were the symbol which
Shadows the inherited glory of the rich.

Some violent bitter man, some powerful man
Called architect and artist in, that they,
Bitter and violent men, might rear in stone
The sweetness that all longed for night and day,
The gentleness none there had ever known;
But when the master's buried mice can play.
And maybe the great-grandson of that house,
For all its bronze and marble, 's but a mouse.

O what if gardens where the peacock strays
With delicate feet upon old terraces,
Or else all Juno from an urn displays
Before the indifferent garden deities;
O what if levelled lawns and gravelled ways
Where slippered Contemplation finds his ease
And Childhood a delight for every sense,
But take our greatness with our violence?

What if the glory of escutcheoned doors,

And buildings that a haughtier age designed,
The pacing to and fro on polished floors
Amid great chambers and long galleries, lined
With famous portraits of our ancestors;
What if those things the greatest of mankind
Consider most to magnify, or to bless,
But take our greatness with our bitterness?

II. My House

An ancient bridge, and a more ancient tower,
A farmhouse that is sheltered by its wall,
An acre of stony ground,
Where the symbolic rose can break in flower,
Old ragged elms, old thorns innumerable,
The sound of the rain or sound
Of every wind that blows;
The stilted water-hen
Crossing Stream again
Scared by the splashing of a dozen cows;

A winding stair, a chamber arched with stone,
A grey stone fireplace with an open hearth,
A candle and written page.
Il Penseroso's Platonist toiled on
In some like chamber, shadowing forth
How the daemonic rage
Imagined everything.
Benighted travellers
From markets and from fairs
Have seen his midnight candle glimmering.

Two men have founded here. A man-at-arms
Gathered a score of horse and spent his days
In this tumultuous spot,
Where through long wars and sudden night alarms
His dwinding score and he seemed castaways
Forgetting and forgot;
And I, that after me
My bodily heirs may find,
To exalt a lonely mind,
Befitting emblems of adversity.

III. My Table

Two heavy trestles, and a board
Where Sato's gift, a changeless sword,
By pen and paper lies,
That it may moralise
My days out of their aimlessness.
A bit of an embroidered dress
Covers its wooden sheath.
Chaucer had not drawn breath
When it was forged. In Sato's house,
Curved like new moon, moon-luminous
It lay five hundred years.
Yet if no change appears
No moon; only an aching heart
Conceives a changeless work of art.
Our learned men have urged
That when and where 'twas forged
A marvellous accomplishment,

In painting or in pottery, went
From father unto son
And through the centuries ran
And seemed unchanging like the sword.
Soul's beauty being most adored,
Men and their business took
Me soul's unchanging look;
For the most rich inheritor,
Knowing that none could pass Heaven's door,
That loved inferior art,
Had such an aching heart
That he, although a country's talk
For silken clothes and stately walk.
Had waking wits; it seemed
Juno's peacock screamed.

IV. My Descendants

Having inherited a vigorous mind
From my old fathers, I must nourish dreams
And leave a woman and a man behind
As vigorous of mind, and yet it seems
Life scarce can cast a fragrance on the wind,
Scarce spread a glory to the morning beams,
But the torn petals strew the garden plot;
And there's but common greenness after that.

And what if my descendants lose the flower
Through natural declension of the soul,
Through too much business with the passing hour,
Through too much play, or marriage with a fool?

May this laborious stair and this stark tower
Become a roofless min that the owl
May build in the cracked masonry and cry
Her desolation to the desolate sky.

The Primum Mobile that fashioned us
Has made the very owls in circles move;
And I, that count myself most prosperous,
Seeing that love and friendship are enough,
For an old neighbour's friendship chose the house
And decked and altered it for a girl's love,
And know whatever flourish and decline
These stones remain their monument and mine.

V. The Road at My Door

An affable Irregular,
A heavily-built Falstaffian man,
Comes cracking jokes of civil war
As though to die by gunshot were
The finest play under the sun.

A brown Lieutenant and his men,
Half dressed in national uniform,
Stand at my door, and I complain
Of the foul weather, hail and rain,
A pear-tree broken by the storm.

I count those feathered balls of soot
The moor-hen guides upon the stream.
To silence the envy in my thought;

And turn towards my chamber, caught
In the cold snows of a dream.

VI. The Stare's Nest by My Window

The bees build in the crevices
Of loosening masonry, and there
The mother birds bring grubs and flies.
My wall is loosening; honey-bees,
Come build in the empty house of the state.

We are closed in, and the key is turned
On our uncertainty; somewhere
A man is killed, or a house burned,
Yet no clear fact to be discerned:
Come build in he empty house of the stare.

A barricade of stone or of wood;
Some fourteen days of civil war;
Last night they trundled down the road
That dead young soldier in his blood:
Come build in the empty house of the stare.

We had fed the heart on fantasies,
The heart's grown brutal from the fare;
More Substance in our enmities
Than in our love; O honey-bees,
Come build in the empty house of the stare.

落叶

长叶抚人几度霜，
鼠儿秸下躲秋凉。
高标楸树先移色，
低处草莓也泛黄。
恩爱詹詹时有缺，
激情落寞不堪殇，
自当吻泪从今去，
莫等西风刳断肠。

The Falling of Leaves

William Butler Yeats

Autumn is over the long leaves that love us,
And over the mice in the barley sheaves;
Yellow the leaves of the rowan above us,
And yellow the wet wild-strawberry leaves.
The hour of the waning of love has beset us,
And weary and worn are our sad souls now;
Let us part,ere the season of passion forget us,
With a kiss and a tear on thy drooping brow.

奥达与天鹅[①]

一记突袭——巨大的羽翅
扑住踉跄的女孩，深色脚蹼
抚摸她的大腿，长喙叼住脖子，

① 奥达与天鹅（Leda and the Swan）：根据希腊神话故事改编。神话中，宙斯（Zeus）变成天鹅，强奸奥达（Leda）女神，生下了海伦（Helen）和克莱特涅斯特拉（Clytemnestra ）。

他的胸膛压住她无助的双乳。

惶然的纤指怎能推开羽翼？
荣耀下她只能松开双腿。
天鹅云翳她横陈的娇躯，
无奈何只听到陌生的心律。

一阵下身的战栗引起
颓垣断壁、屋焚、塔毁，

阿伽门农[①]死去。
　　　　如此沦陷，
暴虐、野蛮浸透空气，
他还未松开那冷漠之喙，
她可曾就范于他的强权？

Leda and the Swan

William Butler Yeats

A sudden blow: the great wings beating still
Above the staggering girl, her thighs caressed
By the dark webs, her nape caught in his bill,
He holds her helpless breast upon his breast.

How can those terrified vague fingers push
The feathered glory from her loosening thighs?
And how can body, laid in that white rush,

① 阿伽门农（Agamemnon）：迈锡尼（Mycenae）的国王。阿特柔斯国王（Mycenae）和王后阿罗佩（Queen Aerope）的子孙，墨涅劳斯（Menelaus）的兄弟。墨涅劳斯的妻子海伦（Helen）被帕里斯（Paris）带到特洛伊（Troy）后，阿伽门农在随后的特洛伊战争中指挥希腊联军。

But feel the strange heart beating where it lies?

A shudder in the loins engenders there
The broken wall, the burning roof and tower

And Agamemnon dead.
Being so caught up,
So mastered by the brute blood of the air
Did she put on his knowledge with his power
Before the indifferent beak could let her drop?

梦想衣裳

译一

愿得天堂锦绣，
闪着日月星光，
昼夜般的青皂，
幽暗恰似昏晓。
此锦应须天上寻，
微我只有梦荫荫，
与君清梦铺脚下，
轻轻踩来轻轻踏。

译二（律化）

何当锦绣自天堂
金线银丝日月光
青皂茵茵分昼夜
幽幽明暗晓昏藏
天工可夺披霞帔
庶士无凭梦绮裳
清梦与君铺脚下

轻轻来去任徜徉

He Wishes for the Cloths of Heaven

William Butler Yeats

Had I the heavens'embroidered cloths,
Enwrought with golden and silver light,
The blue and dim and dark cloths
Of night and light and the half-light,
I would spread the cloths under your feet:
But I, being poor, have only my dreams;
I have spread my dreams under your feet;
Tread softly because you tread on my dreams.

仙曲

自注:《迪亚穆伊德与格拉妮娅》[1]仙境中的歌曲，演唱于巨石墓下的新婚之夜。

我们老了，老得快活，
老到
一千年一万年
故事才终了。

给这些不谙世事的孩子
爱抚宁静；
给他们长夜垂露，

① 《迪亚穆伊德与格拉妮娅》(Diarmuid and Grania)：一个爱尔兰民间传说，描述了格拉妮娅与名将芬恩·麦克坎海尔（Finn MacCumhail）结婚之前，跟迪亚穆伊德一起私奔的故事。传说迪亚穆伊德的脸上有一个痦子，人称爱情痣，让格拉妮娅立刻爱上了他。《迪亚穆伊德与格拉妮娅》也是乔治·摩尔（George Moore）和叶芝（W. B.Yeats）合作的一部诗体散文剧，其音乐由英国作曲家爱德华·埃尔加（Edward Elgar4）创作。

天上星星。

给这些不谙世事的孩子
不朽的休憩。
有什么更好，什么更好，
可以比一比。

我们老了，老得快活，
老到
一千年，一万年，
故事才终了。

A Faery Song

William Butler Yeats

Sung by the people of Faery over *Diarmuid and Grania*,
in their bridal sleep under a Cromlech.

We who are old, old and gay,
O so old!
Thousands of years, thousands of years,
If all were told:

Give to these children, new from the world,
Silence and love;
And the long dew-dropping hours of the night,
And the stars above:

Give to these children, new from the world,
Rest far from men.
Is anything better, anything better?

Tell us it then:

Us who are old, old and gay,
O so old!
Thousands of years, thousands of years,
If all were told.

衣裳

歌儿写就做衣裳
神话镶边博古光
谁得一身生异彩
自称只手绣华彰
愚人有意欺天下
才子无心任四方
锦绣荣华装世界
当其裸露见真常

A Coat

William Butler Yeats

I made my song a coat
Covered with embroideries
Out of old mythologies
From heel to throat;
But the fools caught it,
Wore it in the world's eyes
As though they'd wrought it.
Song, let them take it,
For there's more enterprise
In walking naked.

爱的遗憾

说不出的惋惜，
在爱心里浮沉：
贩卖主义之辈，
头顶滚滚乌云，
湿冷的风吹，
昏褐的丛榛，
鼠灰的流水，
都扑向我的爱人。

The Pity of Love

Wiliam Bulter Yeats

A pity beyond all telling
Is hid in the heart of love:
The folk who are buying and selling,
The clouds on their journey above,
The cold wet winds ever blowing.
And the shadowy hazel grove
Where mouse-grey waters are flowing,
Threaten the head that I love.

第二纪元

在不断加宽的漩涡中盘旋，
鹰隼听不到放鹰者的召唤；
事物分崩离析，失去中心；
只有无政府主义放纵于世，
因混血而变暗的潮水蔓延，
到处淹没纯真的盛典；

最杰出的君子没一丝信仰，
最卑鄙的小人则充满激情。

注定某种天启即将到来，
注定世界将跨入第二纪元。
第二纪元！话还没出口，
世界的阴魂便现出巨影，
截断我的视线：某处沙漠
生出狮身人面的形体，
目光冷漠茫然，如同天眼，
它抬起大腿，周围愤怒的
沙漠之鸟投下荫翳的身影。
黑暗再一次降临；但此时
我知道二十个世纪的僵睡
变成噩梦，摇篮里中了蛊，
粗犷的怪兽，它的时辰终于
到来，要爬去伯利恒投生？

The Second Coming

William Butler Yeats

Turning and turning in the widening gyre
The falcon cannot hear the falconer;
Things fall apart; the centre cannot hold;
Mere anarchy is loosed upon the world,
The blood-dimmed tide is loosed, and everywhere
The ceremony of innocence is drowned;
The best lack all convictions, while the worst
Are full of passionate intensity.

Surely some revelation is at hand;

Surely the Second Coming is at hand.
The Second Coming! Hardly are those words out
When a vast image out of Spiritus Mundi
Troubles my sight: somewhere in sands of the desert
A shape with lion body and the head of a man,
A gaze blank and pitiless as the sun,
Is moving its slow thighs, while all about it
Reel shadows of the indignant desert birds.
The darkness drops again; but now I know
That twenty centuries of stony sleep
Were vexed to nightmare by a rocking cradle,
And what rough beast, its hour come round at last,
Slouches towards Bethlehem to be born?

半生无语到今宵

半生无语到今宵
恩爱情仇意已消
剌剌灯光遮阴里
魆魆黑夜隔幕遥
一诗一画堪求索
永世永生揭若昭
风烛残年成智慧
无知年少爱难料

After Long Silence

William Butler Yeats

Speech after long silence; it is right,
All other lovers being estranged or dead,
Unfriendly lamplight hid under its shade,

The curtains drawn upon unfriendly night,
That we descant and yet again descant
Upon the supreme theme of Art and Song:
Bodily decrepitude is wisdom; young
We loved each other and were ignorant.

三大潮流

译一
莎翁之鱼游过大海，远离陆地；
浪漫之鱼游弋网间，落人手里；
那些鱼咋了——全躺在沙滩喘息？

译二
莎翁鱼大海中游，远离岸边不伸头；
浪漫鱼游在网里，一抓便在我手头；
搁浅之鱼张大嘴，谁能解惑说来头。

Three Movements
William Butler Yeats

Shakespearean fish swam the sea, far away from land;
Romantic fish swam in nets coming to the hand;
What are all those fish that lie gasping on the strand?

我心如止水

我心如止水
载物见真容
造化时清烈
缘从寂寂中

We Can Make Our Minds so Like Still Water

William Butler Yeats

We can make our minds so like still water
That beings gather about us to see their own images,
And so live for a moment with a clearer,
Perhaps even with a fiercer life because of our silence.

智慧的诞生

译一
树叶繁多同一根，
青春日损化埃尘，
叶同花落阳光下，
碾作空无妙有真。

译二
叶茂花荣有孽根
乖张时序度青春
此番摇曳晴光里
脱尽繁华归本真

The Coming of Wisdom with Time

William Butler Yeats

Though leaves are many, the root is one;
Through all the lying days of my youth
I swayed my leaves and flowers in the sun;
Now I may wither into the truth.

十九世纪以降

大吕黄钟不复尊
微呈所有奏欢欣
潮来潮去无穷尽
卵石叮咚自此闻

The Nineteenth Century and After

William Butler Yeats

Though the great song return no more
There's keen delight in what we have:
The rattle of pebbles on the shore
Under the receding wave.

爱别离

我交了个娴静的朋友，
乌黑的头发白皙的脸庞，
我梦想：昔日希望全无，
最终会以爱情收场。
一天她望进我的心里，
看到你的身影在那儿；
便泪眼汪汪离我而去。

The Lover Mourns for the Loss of Love

William Butler Yeats

Pale brows, still hands and dim hair,
I had a beautiful friend
And dreamed that the old despair

Would end in love in the end:
She looked in my heart one day
And saw your image was there;
She has gone weeping away.

詹姆斯·乔伊斯（James Joyce，1882—1941）

整日里我听海水

整日里我听海水
悲叹，
像海鸟哀愁独自
向前，
他听见风嚎大海
孤单。

白毛风随处冰冷
打脸。
我听万顷波涛在
深渊。
整日，整夜，听它们
往返。

All Day I Hear the Noise of Waters

James Joyce

All day I hear the noise of waters
Making moan,
Sad as the sea-bird is when, going
Forth alone,

He hears the winds cry to the water's
Monotone.

The grey winds, the cold winds are blowing
Where I go.
I hear the noise of many waters
Far below.
All day, all night, I hear them flowing
To and fro.

詹姆斯·斯蒂芬斯（James Stephens，1882—1950）

深渊

常流常涌
常涌常流
深渊底处
绿翻浪头

泰山压顶
攻不可破
绿意凝结
难消难歇

寒流震震
震震寒流
凉意四起
无声无息

无声无息

The Main-Deep

James Stephens

The long, rolling,
Steady-pouring,
Deep-trenched
Green billow:

The wide-topped,
Unbroken
Green-glacid,
Slow-sliding,

Cold-flushing,
On-on-on-
Chill-rushing,
Hush-hushing,

Hush-hushing

羊肠小道

曲曲折折的小路
沿山丘四处蜿蜒，
石楠中若隐若现，
出没寂寂天光里。
见山羊日月往复，
迷醉于天光寂寂，
时而这儿，时而那儿，
走走停停转转，
一撮撮一簇簇

啃食青草石楠。

更深处的天光里，
无一丝一毫惊动，
万籁无声俱寂。
静静的荆豆丛中，
山羊悄悄卧下来，
凝视流动的云彩。

见人来就拔开脚步，
一边逃一边回头看，
咩着愤怒，走远，
去明媚僻静的地方，
卧在纹丝不动的
静静的荆豆丛中，
面朝俱寂的阳光
继续它们的冥想。

如果我同样开悟，
会寻安静的地方，
穿过石楠中小路
寻着明媚肃穆
去深思去冥想。
有人来我就移步，
怨愤一声，白一眼，
然后转身走远，
到更寂静的地方，
到那纹丝不动
静悄悄的荆豆丛中，
那里弥漫着静谧。

我同样无边的思绪，
穿过天光寂寂，
在隐蔽的小路上，
寻着明媚肃穆，
去深思去冥想，

一直到我能看见
前所未闻之一二
那么的活灵活现
躺在我的心坎儿。

The Goat Paths

James Stephens

The crooked paths go every way
  Upon the hill—they wind about
Through the heather in and out
    Of the quiet sunniness.
And there the goats, day after day,
    Stray in sunny quietness,
Cropping here and cropping there,
    As they pause and turn and pass,
Now a bit of heather spray,
    Now a mouthful of the grass.

In the deeper sunniness,
    In the place where nothing stirs,
Quietly in quietness,
    In the quiet of the furze,
For a time they come and lie
    Staring on the roving sky.

If you approach they run away,
    They leap and stare, away they bound,
With a sudden angry sound,
    To the sunny quietude;
Crouching down where nothing stirs
    In the silence of the furze,
Couching down again to brood
    In the sunny solitude.

If I were as wise as they
    I would stray apart and brood,
I would beat a hidden way
    Through he quiet heather spray
To a sunny solitude;
    And should you come I›d run away,
I would make an angry sound,
    I would stare and turn and bound
To the deeper quietude,
    To the place where nothing stirs
  In the silence of the furze.

In that airy quietness
    I would think as long as they;
Through the quiet sunniness
    I would stray away to brood
By a hidden beaten way
    In a sunny solitude.

I would think until I found
    Something I can never find,

Something lying on the ground,

In the bottom of my mind

托马斯·斯特尔那斯·艾略特（Thomas Stearns Eliot，1888—1965）

抓狂

她一笑，
我就知道自己身陷其中，
直到她的露出几颗训练有素的皓齿。
我被短促地吸进，
时不时透口气，
最终迷失在她黑咕隆咚的喉咙里，
被无形的肌肉痉挛擦破。
老侍者双手颤巍巍将粉白相间的桌布匆忙地铺在
生着绿锈的铁桌上，
说：“这位女士和先生在花园喝茶吧，
这位女士和先生在花园喝茶吧……”
我想如果她的乳房不那么晃来晃去，
下午或许有些断章可以集结起来，
于是我聚精会神小心翼翼地筹谋。

Hysteria

Thomas Stearns Eliot

As she laughed
I was aware of becoming involved in her laughter and being part of it,
Until her teeth were only accidental stars with a talent for squad-drill.
I was drawn in by short gasps,

Inhaled at each momentary recovery,
Lost finally in the dark caverns of her throat,
Bruised by the ripple of unseen muscles.
An elderly waiter with trembling hands was hurriedly spreading a
Pink and white checked cloth over the rusty green iron table,
Saying: "If the lady and gentleman wish to take their tea in the garden,
If the lady and gentleman wish to take their tea in the garden ..."
I decided that if the shaking of her breasts could be stopped,
Some of the fragments of the afternoon might be collected,
And I concentrated my attention with careful subtlety to this end.

清晨的窗外

女仆下厨杯盘作响，
沿着破旧的街道，
她们湿漉漉的灵魂，
去街口发泄着沮丧。

黄色的雾浪卷过街角，
抛来张张扭曲的面庞，
还有短裙溅泥的路人，
被剥下茫然的微笑，
荡悠悠进了屋檐。

Morning at the Window

Thomas Stearns Eliot

They are rattling breakfast plates in basement kitchens,
And along the trampled edges of the street
I am aware of the damp souls of housemaids
Sprouting despondently at area gates.

The brown waves of fog toss up to me
Twisted faces from the bottom of the street,
And tear from a passer-by with muddy skirts
An aimless smile that hovers in the air
And vanishes along the level of the roofs.

南希表妹

南希·埃利科特小姐
她踏过群山，群山开出路来，
她骑过群山，群山开出路来，
越过蛮荒的新英格兰群山，
奔向草场上的
牧犬。

南希·埃利科特小姐
跳各式现代舞还抽烟，
啥感觉，姑婶们也说不好，
但知道很现代。

油漆格架上，
马修和沃尔多守望信仰，
一堆不可更易的律条。

Cousin Nancy

Thomas Stearns Eliot

Miss Nancy Ellicott
Strode across the hills and broke them,
Rode across the hills and broke them—

The barren New England hills—
Riding to hounds
Over the cow-pasture.

Miss Nancy Ellicott smoked
And danced all the modern dances;
And her aunts were not quite sure how they felt about it,
But they knew that it was modern.

Upon the glazen shelves kept watch
Matthew and Waldo, guardians of the faith,
The army of unalterable law.

《波士顿晚报》

《波士顿晚报》的读者
像成熟的谷物在风中摇摆。

傍晚在巷子里悄悄加快脚步，
唤醒一些人生的况味，
把晚报带给另外一些人。
我走上台阶敲响钟声，
疲惫地转身，像点头告别罗什富科[1]，
如果巷子是时光的隧道，他正在巷尾，
我说，“哈里特表妹，《波士顿晚报》到了。”

① 罗什富科（Rochefoucauld）：法国作家，善写格言警句。

The Boston Evening Transcript

Thomas Stearns Eliot

The readers of *the Boston Evening Transcript*
Sway in the wind like a field of ripe corn.

When evening quickens faintly in the street,
Wakening the appetites of life in some
And to others bringing *the Boston Evening Transcript*,
I mount the steps and ring the bell, turning
Wearily, as one would turn to nod good-bye to Rochefoucauld,
If the street were time and he at the end of the street,
And I say, "Cousin Harriet, here is *the Boston Evening Transcript*."

丹妮斯·莱维托芙（Denise Levertov，1923—1997）

与悲伤对话

悲伤啊，我不会待你
如丧家之犬；
我相信你来到后门，
要面包和剔光的骨头，
我不应多想。

我应哄你
进屋，给你
一个角落，
一张躺卧的破垫子，
一只喝水的碟子。

你觉得我不知你一直生活
在我的屋檐下。
你想要个真正的地方
准备过冬。你需要
自己的名字，
你的牵绳和标签。你需要
警告入侵者的权力，
你要把我的家当成你的家，
把我当成你的人，
把你当成
我自己的狗。

Talking to Grief

Denise Levertov

Ah, Grief, I should not treat you
Like a homeless dog
Who comes to the back door
For a crust, for a meatless bone.
I should trust you.

I should coax you
Into the house and give you
Your own corner,
A worn mat to lie on,
Your own water dish.

You think I don't know you've been living
Under my porch.
You long for your real place to be readied
Before winter comes. You need

Your name,
Your collar and tag. You need
The right to warn off intruders,
To consider
My house your own
And me your person
And yourself
My own dog.

谢默斯·希尼（Seamus Heaney，1939—2013）

格兰摩十四行诗第 6 首

他活在不可名状的光里。
看到中午细雨里的金钟，
暮光下接骨木如月方升，
风吹高地，绿野一片银灰。
“我要看清，”他说，“看破
迷雾，弄清模糊的一切。”
像个男人毅然跨上单车，
冲过结了冰的莫约拉河。
绝无仅有的男人。可是
1947 年下雪的那个隆冬，
大地像小屋灯火通明，
东西冻得结晶停滞，
入夜后风雪飘摇的屋顶，
回荡着雪雁飞过的叫声。

Glanmore Sonnets VI

Seamus Heaney

VI

He lived there in the unsayable lights.
He saw the fuchsia in a drizzling noon,
The elderflower at dusk like a risen moon
And green fields greying on the windswept heights.
"I will break through," he said, "what I glazed over
With perfect mist and peaceful absences"—
Sudden and sure as the man who dared the ice
And raced his bike across the Moyola River.
A man we never saw. But in that winter
Of nineteen forty-seven, when the snow
Kept the country bright as a studio,
In a cold where things might crystallize or founder,
His story quickened us, a wild white goose
Heard after dark above the drifted house.

博物学家之死

市中心的绿地里，亚麻常年
在水沆里腐朽；沉沉的绿冠
也在溃烂，压在大块草皮下。
一天天酷热的太阳烘烤着。
小小的气泡冒出来，绿头苍蝇
围着腐烂的气味儿嗡嗡地飞。
还有蜻蜓，还有花斑蝴蝶，
然而，最好玩儿的要数蛙卵，
热乎乎的黏液像凝结的水，
漂浮在坑沿的阴凉处。我每年

春天都把果冻似的小点点
装满果酱瓶带走，摆在家里的
窗台上，摆在学校的书架上，
等候小圆点胀破，变成敏捷的
小青蛙。沃尔老师会告诉我们
青蛙爸爸怎么叫，怎么称为牛蛙，
青蛙妈妈怎么产下几百个蛋，
那就是蛙卵。我们还可以通过蛙
辨认天气——黄蛙晴红蛙雨。

　　直到有一天草里牛粪臭气熏天，
愤怒的青蛙向亚麻塘进军；我钻篱笆
寻到一片从未听过的沙哑的蛙叫。
低密的呱呱声在空中弥漫。
塘埂上大肚皮的青蛙立在草皮上；
肥大的脖子像船帆。一些蛙在蹦：
扑通扑通地个个吓人。还有一些
坐着像泥弹，不方不圆的头在放屁。
我恶心，转身，跑开。大个的黏液王
聚集在一起似要报复，我知道
如果我伸手下去定会被蛙卵粘住。

Death of a Naturalist

Seamus Heaney

All year the flax-dam festered in the heart
Of the townland; green and heavy headed
Flax had rotted there, weighted down by huge sods.
Daily it sweltered in the punishing sun.
Bubbles gargled delicately, bluebottles
Wove a strong gauze of sound around the smell.

There were dragonflies, spotted butterflies,
But best of all was the warm thick slobber
Of frogspawn that grew like clotted water
In the shade of the banks. Here, every spring
I would fill jampotfuls of the jellied
Specks to range on window sills at home,
On shelves at school, and wait and watch until
The fattening dots burst, into nimble
Swimming tadpoles. Miss Walls would tell us how
The daddy frog was called a bullfrog
And how he croaked and how the mammy frog
Laid hundreds of little eggs and this was
Frogspawn. You could tell the weather by frogs too
For they were yellow in the sun and brown
In rain.

Then one hot day when fields were rank
With cowdung in the grass the angry frogs
Invaded the flax-dam; I ducked through hedges
To a coarse croaking that I had not heard
Before. The air was thick with a bass chorus.
Right down the dam gross bellied frogs were cocked
On sods; their loose necks pulsed like sails. Some hopped:
The slap and plop were obscene threats. Some sat
Poised like mud grenades, their blunt heads farting.
I sickened, turned, and ran. The great slime kings
Were gathered there for vengeance and I knew
That if I dipped my hand the spawn would clutch it.

保罗·穆顿（Paul Muldoon，1951—）

蛙

像石子
一样凸起。
眼睛恰似
泡泡浮在心渊里。
我放下锤子凿子，
用抹子把它铲起。

爱尔兰的子孙
都源自留下的那一对儿，
它们整夜立在
三一学院的花园池塘；
《联和法案》[①]之后，
两瓶红酒戳在水里浸凉。

当然，这个故事得有
寓意，与时代相应。
何如把青蛙放在额头，
从中挤出寓意，
就像从橙子或柠檬
挤出新鲜的果汁？

The Frog

Paul Muldoon

Comes to mind as another small upheaval

① 《联合法案》（Act of Union）：于 1801 年 1 月 1 日生效，将爱尔兰并入大不列颠，成立大不列颠及爱尔兰联合王国。

Amongst the rubble.
His eye matches exactly the bubble
In my spirit-level.
I set aside hammer and chisel
And take him on the trowel.

The entire population of Ireland
Springs from a pair left to stand
Overnight in a pond
In the gardens of Trinity College,
Two bottle of wine left there to chill
After the *Act of Union*.

There is, surely, in this story
A moral. A moral for our times.
What if I put him to my head
And squeezed it out of him,
Like the juice of freshly squeezed limes,
Or a lemon sorbet?

观光客

七月里，一个周日的下午，
我和爸妈弟妹还有帕特叔叔，
坐着最亲爱的帕特叔叔的
破福特出发了。

我们不去墓园——那里都是些
死于疱疹、瘟热、骨痨的——
我们直接开到崭新的巴利高利环岛，

阿中[1]第一岛。

帕特叔叔跟我们讲，某夜
特巡[2]在巴利高利附近将他拦截，
砸碎他的自行车，

让他唱萨什[3]骂罗马教皇。
他们用手枪死劲顶住他的额头，
到家时脑门还有个 O 形印记。

The Sightseer

Paul Muldoon

My father and mother, my brother and sister
And I, with uncle Pat, our dour best-loved uncle,
Had set out that Sunday afternoon in July
In his broken-down Ford

Not to visit some graveyard—one died of shingles,
One of fever, another's knees turned to jelly—
But the brand-new roundabout at Ballygawley,
The first in mid-Ulster.

Uncle Pat was telling us how the B-Specials
Had stopped him one night somewhere near Ballygawley
And smashed his bicycle

① 阿中（mid-Ulster）：阿尔斯特中部。

② 特巡（The B Specials）：皇家阿尔斯特警察局下属的一小部分无偿志愿者，通常在夜晚上街道巡逻，并保持自己的指挥等级。他们的目标是对爱尔兰共和军 (Irish Republican Army) 的行动施加压力。详参 https://www.divideddesignireland.com/b-specials

③ 萨什（Sash）：北爱尔兰的传统歌曲，与新教有关。

And made him sing the Sash and curse the Pope of Rome.
They held a pistol so hard against his forehead
There was still the mark of an O when he got home.

刺猬

蜗牛爬行，像个
气垫船，由自带的
胶垫刹车停住，
它将自己的秘密

说给刺猬。刺猬
不分享自己的秘密。
我们说：刺猬，你要走出
自我，我们会爱你。

我们没有恶意。
只是想听听你
会说什么。只想
你对我们有个回答。

刺猬什么也不说，
保持着它的自我。
我们纳闷，刺猬有啥
好隐藏？这么信不过。

我们忘了，上帝
就在它的刺冠之下。
我们忘了，上帝
再也不会相信世界。

Hedgehog

Paul Muldoon

The snail moves like a
Hovercraft, held up by a
Rubber cushion of itself,
Sharing its secret

With the hedgehog. The hedgehog
Shares its secret with no one.
We say, Hedgehog, come out
Of yourself and we will love you.

We mean no harm. We want
Only to listen to what
You have to say. We want
Your answers to our questions.

The hedgehog gives nothing
Away, keeping itself to itself.
We wonder what a hedgehog
Has to hide, why it so distrusts.

We forget the god
Under this crown of thorns.
We forget that never again
Will a god trust in the world.

参考文献

Alvarez A. 1962. The New Poetry: An Anthology. Publisher Penguin Books Ltd.

Carl R. Woodring, James Shapiro. 1995. The Columbia Anthology of British Poetry. Columbia University Press.

Denise Riley. 2000. Selected Poems. Reality Street Editions London.

Donald Davie. 1985. Selected Poems. Carcanet Press, Ltd.

Francis O'Gorman. 2004. Victorian Poetry: An Annotated Anthology: An Annotated Anthology. Wiley-Blackwell.

Frank Kermode, John Hollande. 1973. The Oxford Anthology of English Literature: Volume II: The Literature of Renaissance England. Oxford University Press (USA).

Geoffrey Hill. 1994. New and Collected Poems 1952-1992. Houghton Mifflin Harcourt.

Helen Gardner. 1972. The New Oxford Book of English Verse. Oxford University Press.

John Wain. 2003. The Oxford Anthology of English Poetry: Volume II: Blake to Heaney. Oxford University Press(USA).

Keith Tuma. 2001. Anthology of Twentieth Century British and Irish Poetry. Oxford University Press.USA.

Margaret Ferguson, Mary Jo Salter. 2005. The Norton Anthology of Poetry. Shorter Fifth Edition. W. W. Norton & Company.

Margery Doud. 2007. Father: An Anthology Of Verse. Plaat Press.

Michael Hulse, David Kennedy, David Morley. 1993. The New Poetry. Bloodaxe Books Ltd.

Michael Robert. 1933. New Country. Books for Libraries.

Nalini Jain, John Richardson. 1994. Eighteenth Century English Poetry: The Annotated Anthology. Routledge.

Noyes F. 1956. English Romantic Poetry and Prose: Selected and Edited with Essays and Notes. Oxford University Press(USA).

Robert Conquest. 1956. New Lines: An Anthology. Macmillan.

Seamas Heaney. 1999. Opened Ground: Selected poems 1966-1996. Farrar. Straus and Giroux.

Simon Armitage, Robert Crawford. 1998. The Penguin Book of Poetry from Britain and Ireland Since 1945. Viking Pr.

王佐良 . 1980. 英国诗文选译集 . 外语教学与研究出版社 .

王佐良 . 1997. 英国诗史 . 译林出版社 .

王佐良 . 2012. 英国诗歌选集 . 上海译文出版社 .

https://www.britannica.com/art/English-literature

https://www.poetryfoundation.org/

https://poems.poetrysociety.org.uk/

https://literature.britishcouncil.org/

http://www.literaturepage.com/

https://keytopoetry.com/

https://www.poemhunter.com/

https://www.best-poems.net

https://englishverse.com/

https://warpoets.org

https://poetryarchive.org

https://belfastgroup.digitalscholarship.emory.edu/

https://old.blakemorrison.net/poetry.htm

https://www.best-poems.net/paul_muldoon/poem-13794.html

译后记

相对于散文、小说和戏剧，诗歌有其特殊的形式，把这种形式翻译出来，非常富有挑战。开始诗歌翻译之前，译者曾尝试绝句、律诗及小令的写作，在熟悉汉语诗律的过程中，比较关注英语诗歌的格律。因莎士比亚十四行诗在结构韵律上要求比较严格，第一篇翻译习作便从十四行诗开始。

像十四行诗这种节奏韵式均有严格规定的诗，必须要把形式翻译出来，否则就像把汉语律诗译成长短句或者散文一样，不仅音韵尽失，有时甚至影响到诗的节奏，进而影响诗的情趣。然而，节律不仅仅是凑音步，押韵也不仅仅求尾音同。因为，汉语作为单音节语言，一字对应一个音节，古人作诗又特别讲求形象，所以绝句或律诗里很少有虚字（即语法功能词）。相反，英语诗歌中，语法功能词较多，那么在翻译中就有个转换处理问题，比如，哪些是必须译出的，哪些是要隐含在上下文中的，如果必须译出，是否在重音的位置，这些都须考虑清楚。此外，汉语不仅一字一音节，一音节还有一声调。古汉语中，四个声调分别归入平声和仄声，一般来说平声高昂，仄声沉郁，在选择韵脚时，也要注意情绪色彩。

当然，诗的形式服务于诗的内容。作为翻译，我们首先关注作者说什么，其次才关注怎么说。这就涉及作品的话题、主旨和情绪，需要在细读作品的基础上，作出审慎的定位，然后再进一步验证。所谓话题、主旨和情绪，是否能将作品的每个细节贯穿起来，也就是俗话说的，这首诗是否读得“通”。这里说的是“每个细节”，可以小到一个字或者一个标点。读者共同的经验是，有时不同版本的翻译，貌似大同小异，但差之毫厘，谬以千里。究其根本原因，就是对原作的理解与整体把握不够。

要准确理解原作，除了文本功夫之外，还要有一定的文学常识、背景知识、参考资料等，这是大家普遍认同的，但需要长期的学习与积累。另外跟积累有关的是译者个人的经历。我们不强求达到什么样的境界才能与诗人沟通，但是调动自己的生活常识，检验我们理解出的作品信息，不失为有效的办法。如果觉得悖理，就需进一步阅读，矫正对原作的误解。有时个人理解与境界达不到诗人的高度，那就最好将存疑的作品暂时搁置，而不是硬译或者阉割原作。当然，诗无达诂，即使译者自以为理解了，也未必是原作者的真意。诚恳的做法是，尽量细读原文，读透字面意思和修辞意义，再参考作者其他作品，得出比较顺通的理解，并验之以生活常识。

译事三难信、达、雅，也是符合诗歌翻译实践的。理解已经不易，表达更是问题，要按原作的风格表达，难上加难。对初学者而言，理解原文题旨与逻辑最为重要；能够忠实地用汉语表达出来，是翻译的基本功；能够按作者的写作风格恰如其分地进行翻译，是翻译的较高要求。信、达、雅三位一体，是衡量译文好坏的铁律，是下笔翻译之前的意念，也是翻译完成之后，规整译文的最后一把尺子。当然，诗歌翻译过程中，最实用的做法是朗读译文，通过朗读或默读，译者可以感觉声音与形象是否融合得好，轻重音交替是否合拍，诗的情绪婉转是否准确，诗的题旨是否连贯。

翻译过程，也是激发译者想象力的过程，很多时候译者会得“意”忘“言”，与作者心有灵犀的刹那，有种非母语某个表达不能尽其意的冲动。但毕竟两种语言有其深厚的文化背景和表达习惯，既然是翻译，还是尽量贴近原作。有不“过瘾”的地方，译者可以二次创作，但其作品已经不是严格意义上的翻译了。因此，本书把所谓得“意”忘“言”之译，或者与原作语言风格有较大差别的译文，均作译文二处理。

译者坚持传递原诗韵律的原则，但并非毫无变异。比如，如果原诗是押韵的，译文也尽量按原文押韵格式押韵。若实在没有回旋余地，也可能改为其他押韵格式，但不管哪种韵式，都尽量一以贯之，以便读者能够感受其中韵律。需要说明的是，汉语韵脚位置一般是实词，有关中心意象或情感活动的字落在韵脚上最为理想。所以，之、乎、者、也、兮、着、了、儿（表示儿话音时）等虚词一般不作韵脚。若语法功能或语助需要，译文行尾出现了这些词，那么韵脚落在虚词前面，也就是行尾第二字上。此外，从押韵的角度，应特别注意头韵、中韵的问题。可能译者对头韵、中韵不像对尾韵那么敏感，初译过程中往往多有疏漏，尤其是头韵，即使局部看得出来，未必译得出来。但对典型的、有规律出现的中韵，译者还是尽量传达，如莎士比亚的《一首歌》、雪莱的《云》、霍普金斯的《上帝的荣耀》，基本遵循并最大程度体现头韵、中韵等。

如果原诗是有节律的，译文也尽量符合原文节律。因为英文大体在音步基础上，通过“轻重”或“重轻”交替形成节律，每行音节数一般为 4、6、8、10、12 等偶数，而汉语诗歌节律以五言或七言为多。在翻译过程中，尽量使用四、六、八、十、十二言，传递原文偶数音节为基础的节律，如实在不能回旋，也会采用五、七、九言的节律。需要说明的是，这里的四、六、八、十、十二言，未必完全对应原文 4、6、8、10、12 音节，比如，有可能以六言翻译 8 个音节或者 10 个音节的诗行。但无论如何，译文的节律是贴近原文节律形式和节律变化的。

韵律节律之外，有些诗呈现出鲜明的形式特点，如大卫·莫利（David Morley）的《备寻》、朱丽亚·考伯斯（Julia Copus）的《詹金斯老师》《母亲的后车座上》，颇有汉语回文诗味道，翻译时也充分考虑其形式特点，把原诗译成回文。还有些诗涉及特殊的诗法，比如，爱丽丝·奥斯瓦尔德（Alice Oswald）的《偶合》，此诗铺陈结构，不以意象、主题、或情绪为线索，而是以一种极特殊的触发联动机制行文，译者也着意突显这种结构特征。

译者翻译时偶发冲动，会把一些格律严整的原作译成绝句或七律，如史蒂文森的《山谷蜿蜒生茳木》；叶芝的《智慧的诞生》《十九世纪以降》《落叶》《梦想衣裳》《衣裳》《半生无语到今宵》。有时，会在原文基础上按某一固定词牌节译，如威斯坦·休·奥登（Wystan Hugh Auden）的《街头向晚》。有时，译者会提供两个或两个以上译本，这种情况大多出于形式方面的考虑，也有题旨上很难有定解的情形，这时提供多个版本译文并加题注。

从格律翻译角度，叶芝的诗非常值得关注。这位诗人有些短小精悍的诗歌，音节排布整齐，意象清晰且有对仗特点，尤其是八行诗节，很适合译成汉语律诗。如果对仗不很明显，依然可按节律译成两首有连带的绝句。在中国翻译史上，将合律的英文诗译成律句早有先例。然而，当代翻译实践中，律句并非翻译常式。事实上我国传统诗词对韵律的要求近乎严苛，如何将传统诗词译介出去，一直是个难题。如果对英语诗歌中韵律整齐的诗作仔细研磨，并验之以律句翻译，相信会从中得到某些启发。

以上是翻译过程中的一点体会，或自己努力的方向，不乏想到做不到的地方，希望读者指正交流。